Eric Malpass was bor
bank after leaving so
become a novelist and he wrote in his spare time for many years. His first book, *Morning's at Seven*, was published to wide acclaim. With an intuitive eye for the quirkiness of family life, his novels are full of wry comments and perceptive observations. This exquisite sense of detail has led to the filming of three of his books. His most engaging character is Gaylord Pentecost – a charming seven-year-old who observes the strange adult world with utter incredulity.

Eric Malpass also wrote biographical novels, carefully researched and highly evocative of the period. Among these is *Of Human Frailty*, the moving story of Thomas Cranmer.

With his amusing and lovingly drawn details of life in rural England, Malpass' books typify a certain whimsical Englishness – a fact which undoubtedly contributes to his popularity in Europe. Married with a family, Eric Malpass lived in Long Eaton, near Nottingham, until his death in 1996.

ERIC MALPASS

THE LONG LONG DANCES

HOUSE OF
STRATUS

This edition published in 2001 by House of Stratus, an imprint of
Stratus Books Ltd., 21 Beeching Park, Kelly Bray,
Cornwall, PL17 8QS, UK.
www.houseofstratus.com

Typeset, printed and bound by House of Stratus.

A catalogue record for this book is available from the British Library
and the Library of Congress.

ISBN 0-7551-0195-2

Gaylord, if pressed, would have admitted to knowing that girls existed, just as little green men from Mars existed. But they were not creatures a chap expected to meet. And certainly, if you did come across a girl, you couldn't be expected to acknowledge her socially.

He was trying, not altogether successfully, to dam the River Trent when his grandfather's voice said, 'Oh, and this is my grandson. Gaylord, this is Mr Mackintosh, who is going to look after the farm for me. And this is Miss Mackintosh. And Julia.'

Julia smiled. Gaylord scowled. Miss Mackintosh said, 'The laddie's awful wet.'

And that was how Julia and her father came to stay with the Pentecosts... From then on, life was never quite the same.

'Will they ever come to me, ever again,
The Long Long Dances… ?'
From Euripides: The Bacchae
Translated by Gilbert Murray and
published by George Allen & Unwin Ltd.

Chapter 1

The little girl dances alone in the river meadows.

She is beautiful, and grave, and eight years old.

When Julia dances, her toes are filled with delight. Her black hair hangs down to her waist. Her arms float like weed in a lazy stream, like a mermaid's tresses...

In the house, her father is writing a letter: 'John Pentecost, Esq. Dear Sir, In answer to your advertisement for a farm manager...graduated at Aberdeen University... considerable experience...only fair to tell you that owing to my wife's death, I have the sole care of a young daughter. But this is my problem, and I can assure you that I shall find ways of dealing with it. Yours faithfully, Duncan Mackintosh.'

As they leave the party, Becky Ashe, née Pentecost, says cheerfully to her husband, 'Now listen to me, my lad. I don't know who that redhead was, and I don't suppose you do either. But the way you were carrying on with her you might have known her for years.'

'I have known her for years,' Peter says sulkily. 'She's my secretary.'

The great cruise ship ploughs northward. Behind it lie the sun and colour and warmth of the Mediterranean; before it, the gathering cold of a northern winter. But in the dining room all is brightness. Miss Dorothea Pentecost looks as happy as any maiden lady sipping champagne on the QE2 under the admiring gaze of an elderly but handsome Frenchman ought to look. He says, smiling, 'What are your family going to say?'

She chuckles deliciously into her Dom Ruinart Blanc de Blancs. 'I don't think they're going to be very pleased, dear.'

'Oh!' From deep in his chest comes that exquisitely modulated cry of concern that only a Frenchman can produce. 'Why not?'

She looks puzzled. Then: 'Bea and John don't need reasons, mon cher. They just react, like that stuff we used to have at school.'

'Litmus paper? And you think I shall turn them red?'

She nods gravely.

'Tell me about them,' he says.

She ponders. 'You've not met Bea, have you?'

'My dear Dorothea, I hadn't met you until we'd been at sea for three days.'

'Oh? Oh yes, so you hadn't. Well, she's my sister.'

'So I gathered,' he said drily.

'And Brother John has a farm, and my nephew Jocelyn and his family live with him, and Jocelyn writes books, I keep meaning to read one of them sometime. But I know it won't be like Elizabeth Goudge.'

He says, almost sharply, 'I thought you said your brother was a solicitor?'

'Did I, dear?' She looks at him vaguely. She often looks as though she's waiting for the mist to clear. 'Oh, yes, of course. He was. But then he retired and bought the farm. He always wanted to be a farmer, even as a boy…'

The ship drives on, towards an England where, as always, a million disparate events are taking place. To take a few: Mrs Agnes Thompson, all alone, while her daughter Wendy is off enjoying herself at the Ingerby Writers' Club, Mrs Agnes Thompson suddenly, and without prior warning, breathes her ladylike last. And that, she thinks grimly as she passes over, will teach Wendy to leave me alone while she goes gadding. But Wendy is in a fool's paradise, having just been appointed Speaker-Finder. And Madam Chairman, who thinks it is high time Wendy stopped devoting her whole life to her poor old mother, says, 'Why don't you have a run out to Shepherd's Warning, dear? Fix up with Jocelyn Pentecost the date of his lecture... '

And, in the same town of Ingerby, Derek Bates lives with his parents. Their house has every comfort known to the television commercials. Derek is a lucky lad. But is he happy? No. Because, for Derek, one more thing is necessary to salvation – a motor bike. Given a motor bike, his cup of happiness would be full. Without it, the cup makes him puke. He is on about it now. 'Oh, give over,' says Mrs Bates. 'You're not having one, that's flat.' But Mr Bates will be master in his own house. He makes the decisions. 'Who says he isn't?' he demands, glaring. Master Bates hugs himself, knowing that the battle is won...

The little girl dances alone in the river meadows. Joy flows along her arms, along her outstretched fingers. It flutters away from her finger tips like singing birds, like pretty butterflies – it flutters away into a dangerous and violent world...

CHAPTER 2

May Pentecost was disliking herself. Her father-in-law had told her about the new farm manager and his motherless daughter, clearly hoping she would say, 'Well, they'd better come and live in the house. Then I can help to look after her. Leave it to me, Father-in-law.'

She had stayed silent. Why? she was now asking herself. Because, she thought severely, like everyone else nowadays I don't want to get involved. Every man is an island. Don't bother to send to know for whom the bell tolls. So long as you can hear it tolling, you're all right, Jack.

Non-involvement, that was what she wanted. So that she could go on looking after a big house, an irascible old man, a busy and absorbed husband, a boy of seven and a baby girl, she thought defensively. It was no good. Conscience was a cruel judge; never paid much attention to Counsel for the Defence. Jocelyn her husband would be a kinder judge than conscience. She went into his study. 'I've got problems,' she said miserably.

Jocelyn Pentecost looked up warily. He could do without problems. He'd got enough in his fictional world without having to worry about real-life ones. But May was looking a bit upset. She said, 'Your father's going to ask this Scotsman to manage the farm. And the Scotsman has a young daughter – and he's a widower.'

All the characters who had been working away so

co-operatively in Jocelyn's head put their hats on and went home. He wondered sadly when he would see them again. He said gently, 'And you can see yourself becoming responsible for the child?'

'I am a woman. I can't stand by and watch a man coping on his own.'

'What's the Scotsman like?'

'As reliable as Aberdeen granite, your father says. And about as talkative.'

'And they'll take the cottage, of course?'

'Yes. I think your father was hoping I'd say they could live here. But – I didn't.'

Rather to his surprise Jocelyn heard the Jocelyn-he-would-like-to-be saying, 'Of course not. Leave it to me, May. I'll speak to my father. You've got quite enough to do with Gaylord and Amanda – to say nothing of father and me.'

May gave him a brilliant, grateful smile that blew his ego up to almost bursting point. 'Thank you, darling. I don't want to be selfish, but I would be grateful. There is a lot to do here.' She went; and he fancied he heard a loud hissing noise. It was the air escaping from his ego. For now he had to give effect to his brave words.

He went to see the old man. 'Er, Father, this manager chap. He's got a daughter, I hear.'

John Pentecost glared. 'Well?'

'Well, I think May feels it's a bit of a responsibility for her. As' – he looked even more uncomfortable – 'as it is, of course.'

'Oh a most capable woman, May. She'll cope.' John Pentecost was a great admirer of his daughter-in-law. Only hoped young Jocelyn appreciated what a fine wife he'd got.

'But – ' This was difficult. With a pen in his hand, Jocelyn could do all things. But speaking, and with the old man glaring up at him – 'But she shouldn't have to, Father.'

'Look! I'm not damn well giving up a man with most excellent references just because –' The telephone rang on his desk. He grabbed it. 'Pentecost. Yes? Yes?' He listened. 'I'm very pleased to hear it, Mr Mackintosh. Yes. That sounds most satisfactory.' He put back the receiver, looked up at Jocelyn with one of his rare smiles. 'Glad about that. Didn't like to think of May getting involved. She's got enough on, poor girl, with us lot, without taking on somebody else's child.'

'You mean – ?'

'Mackintosh has persuaded his sister to move in with them and look after the girl. There's plenty of room for her at the cottage.'

'Oh, good. May will be relieved.'

'So am I relieved. So ought you to be, Jocelyn.' He looked at his son sternly. 'Must admit you sometimes take May's good nature too much for granted, you know.'

Jocelyn went into the kitchen. His wife was baking bread. She looked up, smiled. She was always pleased to see Jocelyn, and it took a lot to get him out of his study during working hours. He said, 'I've, er, had a word with Father.'

He looked, she thought, like a small boy who has just scored his first goal. She smiled. He said, 'I told him I didn't want you getting involved with the little girl.'

'Darling, thank you.'

He produced his pièce de résistance. 'So he had a word with Mackintosh on the telephone, and Mackintosh is going to get his sister to live with them in the cottage.' He waited for the cries of delight.

They came. 'Jocelyn, that was clever of you.' She came and kissed him fondly. Yet there was an amusement in her smile that left him uneasy. If he had slightly manoeuvred the telling in his own favour, could she have realized this? He had to admit that he had never yet succeeded in pulling the wool over his wife's eyes.

Gaylord, if pressed, would have admitted to knowing that girls existed, just as little Green Men from Mars existed. But they were not creatures a chap expected to meet. And certainly, if you did come across a girl, you couldn't be expected to acknowledge her socially.

He was trying, not altogether successfully, to dam the River Trent when his grandfather's voice said, 'Oh, and this is my grandson. Gaylord, this is Mr Mackintosh, who is going to look after the farm for me. And this is Miss Mackintosh. And Julia.'

Julia smiled. Gaylord scowled. Miss Mackintosh said, 'The laddie's awful wet.'

Gaylord looked up into the utilitarian features of Elspeth Mackintosh, all carbolic and Calvinism. He was affronted. He expected Momma to go on when he got wet. It was part of the order of things, and he'd feel a bit deprived if she didn't. But if complete strangers started doing it you'd have chaos.

The man, with what seemed something of an effort, said, 'What are you doing, laddie?'

'Damming the Trent,' said Gaylord.

The man looked unimpressed. Grandpa said, 'You'll cause consternation down river in Nottingham.'

'Och – ' began the man. Then it seemed to occur to him that this was maybe an English joke. He still looked unimpressed. Grandpa said, 'Now, Julia, are you going to stay and help Gaylord devastate the Eastern Counties?'

Gaylord could scarcely believe his ears. Grandpa had always been his friend. There had been a close bond between the gruff, cantankerous old man and the sturdy boy. But now – ? He was bitterly disappointed in Grandpa.

'May I?' Julia's voice was soft, and sweet.

'You can if you like,' Gaylord said. No one could call his answer effusive. But no one could accuse him of being impolite. Such subtleties were meat and drink to the lad.

But now Miss Mackintosh was putting her oar in. 'Och, the lassie's not dressed for splashing about in water.'

Splashing about in water, indeed! A major engineering project, splashing about in water! Women! But the girl said, 'Please. I won't get wet, I promise,' and so deeply hurt had Gaylord been by Miss Mackintosh's belittling of his efforts that he said, ' 'Course she won't, Miss Mackintosh,' and he gave Julia a spade and a grudging smile.

'Now come and see the milking parlour,' said Grandpa. The adults moved off. Gaylord said, 'If that lady's your mother, why is she a Miss?'

'She isn't. My mother died last month. Daddy asked Aunt Elspeth to come and look after me.'

Gaylord went on shovelling mud. This needed thinking about. It had never really occurred to him that God could let anyone as a vital to the scheme of things as Momma, die. He couldn't imagine Poppa left to bring up him and Amanda. He liked Poppa very much, but he'd no illusions about his practical abilities. He said, keeping his head down, shovelling hard, 'I'm sorry your mother's dead.' He was, too. He couldn't see Miss Mackintosh filling the bill as a mother substitute.

'Thank you, Gaylord.'

Gaylord said, 'I bet it's awful, having your mother dead.'

'It is a bit.'

He wanted to say something helpful, and was annoyed with himself for being unable to think of anything, not knowing that such words did not exist.

The little girl was looking sad and forlorn. Now she looked anxious as well. 'Shall we really devastate the Eastern Counties?'

'I don't know. Grandpa might be joking. He does sometimes.'

She said, 'That big log. If we used that – '

Gaylord tried not to look impressed, and wondered why he hadn't thought of it. If she hadn't been a girl, he thought, she'd have been quite a useful companion.

Derek Bates straddled the shiny, powerful machine. He twisted the throttle, pulled down his perspex visor, and roared off: a knight on his great stallion, a Cossack mowing down the peasants, a Valkyrie with L plates. His parents watched him go. 'He'll kill somebody,' said Mum.

'So long as it ain't himself,' said Dad philosophically.

Miss Wendy Thompson sat in the Corporation bus and thought wistfully how nice it would be to drive out in the Mini to the Cypresses Farm and ask Mr Pentecost in person when he could speak to the Club. But she knew she never would. Mother would be opposed to the idea. And when Mother was opposed to an idea, Wendy just gave up. Not because she was by nature weak; but because Mother had at her disposal such an array of weapons, from accusations of ingratitude and thoughtlessness to sick headaches and nasty turns, and because Mother was utterly ruthless in using her armoury, while Wendy was good-natured and friendly, and really very fond of Mother.

She let herself into the house. 'Only me,' she called. No reply. Oh, dear. That was always ominous. She glanced at her watch. 9.30. No, she wasn't late. But it sounded as though she was in trouble for something. She went into the living room. Mother sat, as always, in her rocker.

Wendy had expected the chair to be rocking with impatience and irritation. She was relieved to find that it wasn't. But then she looked closer...

Mother was past impatience and irritation. She was past sick headaches and nasty turns. Her weapons of war were perished. She was an old, dead woman, sprawled with sagging jaw and staring eyes. A thing pitiful in the extreme.

And Wendy did a dreadful, shameful, outrageous thing that no man saw and that it is to be hoped the angels who record the follies of men did not see either – she pirouetted expertly three times around the room, and then fell weeping bitterly on to the sofa.

She'd been very fond of Mother. Now she'd lost her. But Mother, departing, had given Wendy two wonderful, lucent gifts – her own thirty-year-old life; and the bright world. No wonder Wendy was a maelstrom of emotions. Her dear companion, gone! Herself, free, looking with fear and misgiving at the open door of her cage. The world her oyster; and, in her mind, the knowledge that opening the shell was something she would never achieve.

There was another emotion. Wendy was of a sweet and forgiving nature. But Mother had once done something for which Wendy could never really forgive her: something that now made a mockery of the belated gift of her life.

The autumn was long, and lovely; yet with winter creeping in like the remorseless tide, slowly swamping the daylight and the warmth. The golden, mellow days mocked Miss Thompson in the bijou residence from which she still dare not fly. Every day she vowed she would write a little note to Mr Pentecost. Every day she decided to wait, and drive over tomorrow. It is not easy, she found, to make decisions when they have always been made for you.

At the farm, John Pentecost found Mackintosh a man after his own heart: capable, down-to-earth, practical, laconic. But Mackintosh terrified Jocelyn, who was always intensely ill-at-ease with practical men, feeling that to them someone as unpractical as he must seem the feeblest thing in nature. (Their first introduction had unnerved him. 'This is my son Jocelyn,' Grandpa had said. 'Do you help with the farm?' Mackintosh had asked politely. 'No,' Grandpa said scornfully. 'He writes books – novels.' Mr Mackintosh was clearly determined to be courteous. 'I read a novel once. Cold Comfort Farm.' He shook his head. 'The author didn't know the first thing about farming. I hope you stick to something you know about,' he had said severely. Clearly, authorship did not impress him.)

To Gaylord's intense indignation, Miss Mackintosh banned the damming of the Trent as being both dangerous and futile. Futile! He marched into the kitchen. 'Momma. What's futile?'

'Useless and ineffectual,' said Momma.

He knew it. How dare she! He said, 'Miss Mackintosh won't let us dam the Trent. And we'd nearly finished, Momma.'

Momma said, 'Well, dear, Julia is a very sweet little girl, not a hydromechanical engineer. I can see Auntie's point.' But to herself she thought: who does she think she is, telling my son what he can and can't do? She lifted her head, like the warhorse who scents a distant battle.

CHAPTER 3

'A month ago I too was puny, ineffectual. Now I am a giant among men.' Such might have been Derek Bates' testimonial to the motor cycle company.

A month ago, he'd been nobody. Just a spotty youth whom dedicated men were still trying to infuse with a love of Shakespeare and Milton (with no more, and no less, success, as they freely admitted, than they would have had with Bessie the Sow); pushed around by his mates, nattered at, night and day, by his mother, cursed by his dad. But now, what a transformation! Booted, encased from head to toe like a deep-sea diver, his dull eyes and his acne hidden by a merciful bowl of perspex, he straddled his bike. A roar, and he was off; Wagnerian, Apocalyptic in noise and speed and power. Young men and maidens, old men and children, scattered from his path. Jags and Mercs treated him with respect; or, anyway, circumspection. He had discovered what had eluded far abler and more ambitious men than he – the secret of Power!

But if all power corrupts, then already it was corrupting Derek. For him, it was no longer enough to send some old woman scuttling for the pavement. He began to yearn for less fleeting and impersonal demonstrations of his authority.

And more and more he demanded attention. Anyone who did not look up when he roared by, earned his enmity. They deserved to be punished. So that when he saw a small girl so absorbed in her dancing that she refused to notice him, even when he pulled up and angrily revved his engine, he decided to teach her a sharp lesson. Especially since she was quite obviously alone…

The October noontide was a distillation of the summer's glory. Golden, high-piled clouds were seen as through a gauze. The sparrows chatted quietly in dusty hedgerows, like people in church. The cattle swished their tails in silent meditation. A late dragonfly quivered and darted in the sunshine, a living rainbow. Julia, seeing his bright, metallic colours, his exquisite stretched form, was entranced. She became a dragonfly. She stood, motionless, on tiptoe, arms outstretched, fingertips a-quiver. She darted, poised, darted again. A faint smile, almost of ecstasy, touched her long lips. She did not hear the distant sound on the noonday's hush. She did not even notice the cacophony as the motor cyclist stopped outside the open field gate. Had she done so, and looked up, she might have been saved. But she didn't. And Derek Bates was furious. He turned his machine into the meadow, gave the throttle a savage twist, and charged at Julia.

The girl screamed. Derek drove to within a yard of her, then turned suddenly and went into a tight circle round and round Julia. Behind his red visor his mouth was stretched tight in angry triumph. She'd noticed him now, by God. And she wouldn't forget him in a hurry.

Nor would she. One moment Julia had been a dragonfly on a slumbering noon. The next she was a little girl being attacked by a faceless monster on a roaring, screaming machine. The shock was too great for so sensitive a child. She collapsed in a sobbing heap on the grass.

This was even better than Derek could have hoped. He did one more circle, near enough to give her a farewell kick en passant, and then with a roar of triumph made for the gate.

But he saw, with a quick stab of fear, that the gate was now shut. What was far worse, a stocky, powerful-looking old gentleman was leaning on the gate. The grimness of his face was complemented by a certain menace in the way he held his double-barrelled shot gun.

It was not a situation for which Derek was prepared. He was one who liked to choose his antagonists. And he would never have chosen this formidable old bastard. He slowed down, stopped, sat with his engine running.

John Pentecost stared at him with loathing. He was a man whose trim, white moustache showed his emotions. It could twist with impatience, pucker itself with irritation, even, on rare occasions, lengthen in what passed for a smile. Now it bristled with rage. 'Switch that noise off,' John suddenly roared.

Derek did as he was told. 'And take that damn stupid pot off your head,' shouted Grandpa.

Derek had probably never felt so hurt. He removed his helmet. Grandpa looked at the small mouth, the scared eyes, the pallid complexion, and winced. Poor, miserable little devil, he thought. 'Oh, put it back, for heaven's sake,' he said wearily.

Derek put it back, and felt a bit safer.

Out of the corner of his eye John Pentecost saw Miss Mackintosh carrying an unconscious Julia back to the cottage. His fury made him feel quite ill. 'Now, young man,' he said grimly. 'You're going to do something.'

'What?' asked Derek belligerently.

'You're going to dump that outrageous bit of ironmongery in the river.'

14

For perhaps ten seconds the noonday silence was absolute. Then: 'You mean the bike?'

'I mean the bike.'

'I bloody won't,' said Derek.

'You most certainly will,' said Grandpa. And slipped the safety catch.

Derek looked at Grandpa. Grandpa looked at Derek. Who said, 'You wouldn't dare?' But he'd seen enough of the old man to make it a question rather than a statement.

'Oh, I've dared far more than that,' John Pentecost said lightly. 'Remind me to show you my Military Cross sometime.' Then, suddenly, he was no longer speaking lightly. 'Come on. And push it. I won't have that row on my land.'

'But. Mister – ?' Derek was near tears.

'Push it! And shove it in. I shall walk behind. And don't imagine I'm not capable of peppering your backside, because frankly I can hardly keep my finger off the trigger.'

It is doubtful whether Abraham, bidden to sacrifice his son, felt quite as bad as Derek. Derek was being made to sacrifice more than a son: his pride, his manhood, his virility, the only thing in the whole world that could possibly make him feel important. He looked at the wicked gun metal. He looked at the face of the old man. When it came to mercy and loving kindness, there wasn't much to choose between them. He began pushing. He stopped, half-turned. 'Please, mate. I didn't mean to frighten the kid.'

John Pentecost prodded him with the gun. 'I'm not your mate, thank God. Now come on. I haven't got all day.'

Derek came on. But on the river bank he turned. 'I can't do it mister.' Almost hysterically he cried, 'Shove it in yourself, if you like, you old bastard. But don't ask me to do it. I can't. I can't.'

'Push!' said Grandpa.

'No.'

'Push!'

It was the first time in his life, either at home or at school, that Derek had heard the true voice of authority. It bewildered him. But he knew instinctively that this time his usual weapons – wheedling, snivelling, bluster, swagger – would avail him nothing. Oh, if only some of his mates would miraculously appear. But the sleepy countryside stayed still and uncaring. With a great cry of rage and despair and horror, he pushed. The lovely, shiny, complicated machine splashed mightily into the ooze. Derek peered down at it, unbelieving. It couldn't have happened. Life couldn't be so cruel. An interested voice said, 'What's that motor bike doing in the river, Grandpa?' Seeing Grandpa talking to what he had at first taken for a Martian, Gaylord had approached at a rate of knots; and found the motor cyclist something of an anti-climax. Still, you don't get a half-submerged motor cycle every day, so he'd better make the most of it.

Grandpa ignored him. He said magnanimously to Derek, 'If you want a garage to come and salvage it, tell them they have my permission to cross my land.'

'You're not from Mars, are you?' Gaylord asked, always hopeful.

'Mars?' said Grandpa. He turned to Derek. 'I suppose you're disturbed, or maladjusted, or whatever the current clap-trap is. But to me you're just a nasty little thug who kicks children. So get off my land.'

Humiliated Derek might be, a Samson whose hair lay in the shallows of the Trent. But he had seen an antagonist more suited to his metal. He looked down at Gaylord. 'I'll get you,' he sobbed. 'Me and my mates'll carve you up.' He turned to

John Pentecost. Talk of his mates had given him courage. 'And you. You don't think you'll get away with this, do you?' He was weeping, trembling with rage, self-pity, sheer misery. But he was not lacking in effrontery. 'And how do I bleeding well get home?' he demanded.

'You bleeding well walk, dear boy,' John Pentecost said suavely.

With her well-known propensity for rubbing salt in wounds, Fate arranged for Derek to meet a mounted posse of his mates as he trudged home. 'Hey, Derek, where's your bike?'

He told them, playing down his humiliation, playing up the comedy and panache of his attack on the girl, and leaving the old bastard writhing in agony on the ground from a well-aimed kick in the crotch. His pals applauded. Derek's ego began to put forth green shoots. But at the same time his pals were responsible citizens. They stood for law and order, and old geezers who took the law into their hands in this way had to be taught that such crime did not pay. This was the verdict of them all. And so the trail of powder, that led ultimately to destruction and death, began its slow burning.

John Pentecost stumped back to the house, disturbed and troubled, ignoring Gaylord's eager questions. He shut himself in his study, dialled a number. 'That you, Mackintosh? How's the girl?'

'Badly frightened. But not physically hurt, I think.'

'The brute kicked her.'

'He did? Och – . Anyway, Elspeth's getting the doctor.'

'Good. Now I want you over here.'

'Right away.'

John put down the receiver. He went to the door. 'May! Jocelyn!'

They came running, alarmed. 'Sit down, both of you,' he said.

Even May daren't question him when he was in this mood. He sat brooding down at his desk, running his thick, spatulate thumbs backwards and forwards along the edge. The silence stretched to breaking point. He said, 'We're waiting for Mackintosh.'

May said, 'What is it, Father-in-law? It – isn't Gaylord?'

'No,' he said. 'It isn't Gaylord.'

May and Jocelyn looked at each other: she impatient, he anxious. He shook his head slightly. May, who sensed a slight sheepishness in the old man, and was prepared to attack, left it. After all, she'd only got lunch and Amanda and some ironing on her slate. So she might just as well spend her time perched anxiously on the edge of a chair in the old man's study.

The door opened briskly. Mackintosh came in, ignored May and Jocelyn, and dragged a chair up underneath him, all in one movement. 'Now,' he said.

John Pentecost said, 'May, Jocelyn. Mr Mackintosh knows something of what has happened. You do not.'

They waited, each with an anxious fluttering in the stomach. John said, 'Julia was playing in the meadows. A young thug drove into the field on his motor bike, terrified her almost into a faint, and then kicked her.'

They both gasped with horror; she thinking immediately: non-involvement! Suppose I'd taken her in, not shrugged her off, would it still – ? He thinking: the Destroyers; shocked, yet eager to use this example of human behaviour and human pain in perfecting a theory he was working on. 'How – is she?' they asked simultaneously.

The old man looked at Mackintosh, who said, 'She'll be all right, Elspeth thinks. We shall know more when the doctor's seen her.'

Jocelyn said, 'You saw it, Father?'

'I did.'

'But what happened? Did he get away?'

'Now that,' said John Pentecost, 'is why I have called you together. I took it upon myself to make the punishment fit the crime. But I am not the Law of England. And what I did – though I would do it again, regardless – may involve me in difficulties and all of us in danger.'

So May had been right. He had looked sheepish. 'Father-in-law, what did you do?'

'I made him chuck his motor bike in the Trent.'

May crowed with delight. This moment was worth some difficulties hereafter. But Jocelyn looked grave. 'How did you persuade him, Father?'

'Stuck an unloaded gun in his ribs.'

Was there even a flicker about the grey granite mouth of Mackintosh? If so, it was but fleeting. The Scotsman said, 'Legally, they can throw the book at you, Mr Pentecost.'

'If they've the wit. And do you think British justice would let that attacker of little girls go free, and mulct me for punishing him?'

'I'm convinced of it.'

'So am I, Mackintosh, so am I,' the old man said blandly. He became serious again. 'No. When I spoke of danger I meant this. The youth went off swearing vengeance on me and – I'm sorry, May – Gaylord.'

May slipped her hand into Jocelyn's, and was silent.

'Now this youth daren't say "boo" to a goose – unless four of his pals were holding it down. But that's the trouble. They have the pack instinct. And I think that for the time being we have all got to be very watchful; and especially as regards Julia, Gaylord, and even Amanda. I can look after myself.'

May's mouth was so dry that she found speaking difficult. She ran her tongue across her lips. 'I think we should tell the police.'

'What exactly can we tell them? That a teenage youth uttered some vague threats? No. I think we should wait – and watch. Anyone approaching the farm has to come along the river road. They're clearly visible.'

May sighed. 'Oh, Father-in-law, you do make life difficult.'

He said gravely, 'What would you have had me do, May?'

She stood up. On her way to the door she put a hand on his shoulder. 'Exactly what you did do, you reprehensible old man.'

He said, 'The question is, do we go for him? I've got his number. And there's plenty to go for. The attack on Julia. Threatening behaviour to Gaylord and me.'

'You'd never make it stick,' said Mackintosh.

'Even if you did,' said Jocelyn, 'they'd finish up sympathizing with him over the loss of the bike.'

The old man looked wistful. 'I'd have liked a go,' he said.

May turned to Mackintosh. 'I am sorry about Julia, Mr Mackintosh. It's – not a good beginning, is it?'

'She has to learn to take the rough with the smooth, Mrs Pentecost.'

She looked at him. Grizzled hair, grey skin taut over a strong bone structure; a hardness, she thought, about the mouth and the grey eyes. Aberdeen granite! He might have been talking about a pony, rather than his own daughter.

Jocelyn Pentecost had been sitting, hunched and silent. Now he said, 'What is it about beauty?'

His father looked at him with impatience, his wife with dry amusement, Mackintosh, who didn't know him, with astonishment, John Pentecost said, 'I was hoping for practical suggestions, not a discussion on aesthetics.'

'Aye,' said Mackintosh. Jocelyn didn't think he liked him very much.

May said, with spirit: 'Well, I haven't heard any practical suggestions from anybody, up to now. So let's hear what Jocelyn has to say.'

Jocelyn said, 'I only meant – some men give their whole lives to its creation. Others must destroy it whenever they see it. I – wondered why.'

There was a silence. 'Very helpful,' said Grandpa.

Mackintosh rose. 'They also destroy public conveniences, and telephone kiosks, Mr Pentecost. How does that fit in with your wee theory?'

May said, very stiffly indeed. 'I do hope your little daughter will soon be better, Mr Mackintosh.'

'So do I,' said Jocelyn sincerely. But the man had been right. Public conveniences. So beauty, that bright star, was not the catalyst.

'Aye. Thanks,' said the Scot. He turned to the old man. 'I'm glad you dealt with it and not me, Mr Pentecost.'

'You are? Why?'

'My gun would have been loaded,' said Mackintosh. May looked at him quickly, hoping to see some emotion. She saw none. There was no shift in the carved granite. Yet she decided he was not perhaps the cold stone she had imagined.

CHAPTER 4

Every morning, at nine o'clock, the Gas Lane complex of schools sucks in children like a vacuum cleaner: neat children, pretty children, untidy children, loutish children; children who come to learn (or anyway to be taught) about poetry and the binary system and the properties of hydrogen and the Counter Reformation and the use of a chisel and a needle and a computer. What all these little sausage skins make of the minced meat that is daily forced into them, God alone knows. What possible bearing it will have on their future life and understanding and happiness, probably no one, least of all themselves, can say. But they come: those who live within a few hundred yards, on foot; the rest, in Dad's car, in Mum's car, in school busses, on bicycles, the furthest flung even in taxis. And some, the élite, on motor cycles. These sweep with noise and arrogance into the playground. No Monsieur le Comte in a French Revolution film ever swept the peasants from the path of his carriage as ruthlessly as these their schoolmates. The Headmaster, who always has great difficulty in getting his car through the throng, refers to them with a touch of envy as the Gas Lane Hussars.

But it is no use looking for Derek Bates among the Gas Lane Hussars, or even at school. He hasn't a bike. His dad isn't putting himself out to take him in the car. The Council unaccountably won't supply a taxi. And he's certainly not walking nearly a mile just to learn about ruddy Shakespeare. So Derek stays at home; and this has singularly little effect on either Derek, or the school, or the great wide world. It just gives him a little more time to brood, to nurture his resentment like a pot plant.

As well as children, the vacuum cleaner also sucks in a large number of staff, most of whom attend daily with a mixture of resignation, distaste, apprehension, and even downright fear. But there are some who still retain some faith in their life's work, and even in children. Some even go on liking children. Such a one is Miss Wendy Thompson.

Since her mother's death, in fact, Wendy had become even more absorbed in her job. It saved her from making decisions. What to do about the house, what to do about Christmas, what to do with her life, even what to do (write or visit?) about arranging with Jocelyn Pentecost the date of his visit to the Writers' Club – these could always be shelved while she thought up new schemes of work, or marked the little dears' creative writing.

So that when the Headmistress of the Primary said, 'We've a new little girl for you, Miss Thompson, I'll leave her with you,' and Wendy saw a slim child clinging anxiously to the hand of a grey, lonely-looking man, she said happily, 'Splendid. And what's your name?'

The child was silent. The man said, 'Julia Mackintosh. We've just moved down here from the Mearns.'

'The – where?'

'The Mearns, Kincardineshire.' Clearly anyone who didn't know the Mearns was scarcely fitted to teach the young.

'I see. And where are you living now, Mr Mackintosh?'

'World's End Cottage, Shepherd's Warning.'

Strange. Mr Pentecost lived at Shepherd's Warning. She would have liked to ask more. But she did not think Mr

Mackintosh welcomed chat. She said to Julia, 'And is Mummy at work?'

The child hung her head. The man said, with rough incongruity, 'Her mother's with the angels.' Then, suddenly soft, 'Is she no, lassie?' The child began to cry.

Wendy said, 'Oh, dear. I am sorry. That was very foolish of me.'

'You weren't to know,' he said casually.

But Wendy was down on her knees, comforting the child. 'Now, Julia, what do you like to do best in all the world?'

The girl was silent. 'Tell me, dear,' Wendy said coaxingly. 'Then we'll see whether we can do it.'

Julia said something through her tears. Wendy said, 'Did you say dancing?'

The child nodded, staring at the floor.

The man said, 'Her mother was a ballet dancer. She sent the child to ballet lessons. But – this is no a world for ballet dancers.'

Wendy Thompson had straightened up. 'What is it a world for, Mr Mackintosh?'

'Och, women policemen, hairdressers, shorthand typists, politicians.'

Wendy was suddenly very sad. 'I hope you're wrong, Mr Mackintosh,' she said quietly. Her hand was on the child's head, stroking the long, sleek hair. She looked at the Scotsman, wondered what fantastic combination of chance and attraction had brought a ballet dancer to the Mearns. She said, 'And you are quite opposed to her attending ballet school? Even if she showed great promise?'

He nodded. 'I'm a practical man, Miss Thompson, a Bachelor of Science. I wouldn't want my daughter earning her bread doing dying swans.'

She laughed. 'There's more to ballet dancing than dying

swans, Mr Mackintosh.'

'Aye. Well, you teach her her three R's, Miss Thompson. That's your job. Goodbye to you. Goodbye, Julia.' He stooped down, kissed the child with sudden tenderness, and was gone. Rude man, thought Miss Thompson. But her mind wasn't really on him. She was remembering another girl who had wanted to be a ballet dancer, who had known she had both the ability and the perseverance, who in dreams had heard the applause for the Prima Ballerina, and seen the stage strewn with flowers for the Assoluta; who would have thought even the chorus very heaven; yet who also had not been allowed to go to ballet school; in her case by a selfish and possessive mother, God rest her soul.

She took Julia into an empty classroom, sat down. 'Did you like ballet lessons?'

'Oh, yes, Miss.' Her eyes shone. 'It was wonderful.'

Poor kid, thought Wendy. To lose her mother, and have to give up ballet lessons, it must have seemed like the end of the world. 'Now, Julia,' she said firmly. 'Dance.'

The child remained still. Yet even in stillness, Wendy thought, she had a natural grace. 'Won't you dance?' she said again.

The child gave a petulant shake of her shoulder. Wendy drew her towards her. Julia stood against her, twisting slightly from left to right. Wendy said, 'I wanted to be a dancer, too.'

At last the child looked at her. Wendy saw the beautifully etched brows, the long sensitive mouth, the proud set of the head. 'Why weren't you?'

'My mother wanted me to be a teacher.'

Julia thought this over. Then she gave Wendy a quick, sudden, friendly smile.

But she would not dance.

CHAPTER 5

Gaylord was watching Momma feed Amanda. It was a process that never failed to fascinate him. He said, 'If you had twins you could do one each side, couldn't you.'

'That's right, dear.'

'Is that why you've got one on each side?'

'I suppose so.'

Gaylord was impressed. He said, 'Isn't God clever, Momma!'

'Why, in this particular instance?'

'Well – ' He remembered a phrase Grandpa had used about his new manager. 'He's got everything so well thought out.'

Then it occurred to him that God, so far as he knew, hadn't made any special arrangements for feeding triplets. But before he could pursue this promising line of enquiry, the door was flung open and Grandpa burst in, letter in hand. 'May, I – Oh, sorry. Didn't realize Amanda was re-fuelling.'

'It's all right, Father-in-law,' said May, cutting off the infant, who thought it was anything but all right, from her source of supply. 'Whatever's happened?'

'It's my sister, Dorothea. She's taken leave of her senses.'

Gaylord was very interested to hear it. To him, his Great Aunts Bea and Dorothea were not two of God's happier ideas. Any virtues they might have were cancelled out by the

26

fact that they were both inveterate and implacable Gaylord-kissers. On their rare visits, he just couldn't call his soul his own. They were after him like a couple of bears after honey.

He was puzzled. He knew what 'taking leave of' meant. But the meaning of the whole phrase eluded him. He conjured up a picture of Aunt Dorothea at the garden gate waving goodbye to – what? Yet if he asked he didn't suppose anyone would bother to tell him, so he waited. And Momma, fortunately, came to his rescue. 'Why, whatever has she done, Father-in-law?'

'It's not what she's done, dammit. It's what she's going to do.' He shook his head mournfully. 'Poor little Dorothea. Clean off her head. Must be.'

'But what is it, Father-in-law?'

The face he turned on her was tragic. His voice was awestruck. 'She's marrying a Frog.'

'Dear me,' said May, trying to look suitably grave.

' "Dear me"? That all you can say?' The old man was taken aback. He wasn't getting the horrified response he'd expected.

She shouldn't tease the old man, she really shouldn't. May said contritely, 'I'm sorry, Father-in-law. Tell me about Aunt Dorothea.'

He looked slightly mollified. He said, in measured terms, 'Not only is he a Frog. She met him on a Mediterranean cruise.' He waited for this to sink in. 'Quite obviously one of these fellows who make a living out of it.'

'Out of what?'

'Making up to rich old ladies on cruises, to get their hands on their money.'

'I don't imagine you've got a lot of proof.'

'Proof? His name's enough.' He glanced at the letter. 'Edouard St Michèle Bouverie. Can you imagine a chap on a Mediterranean cruise with a name like that not being a crook.'

'It could happen,' said May.

Grandpa looked disappointed in her. 'Anyway,' he said gruffly, 'she and Bea want to bring him over to stay for a few days in early December. That's all right with you, I suppose?'

'Of course,' said May, who had been telling herself that this year she would try to take things easy before the Christmas rush really began; and who, unlike Grandpa, visualized Edouard St Michèle Bouverie as an aristocrat of the old school, who would turn his plate upside down and refuse to be served if anything, from the seating arrangements to the temperature of the wine, displeased him.

'Good girl,' said Grandpa. That was what he liked about May. Took things in her stride. No 'I'm too busy,' or 'I don't think I can.' To show his appreciation he said, 'And listen, May. Don't you go wasting your time on Froggie food for the chap. If he can't eat the sort of plain, nourishing stuff you give us, he can damn well go hungry.'

'Very well, Father-in-law,' said May, who spent much of her time and thought producing meals for the family from her Cordon Bleu Cookery Book. 'We'll have roast beef and Yorkshire pud and semolina every day.'

He gave her a wary look. It seemed to him his daughter-in-law was in a funny mood today.

May slid Amanda into her pram. She looked at her drowsy child with a moment's envy – clean, well-fed, lapped in comfort, with not a care or responsibility in the world, with nothing to do or think about until her next feed. 'Would you like to wheel her outside, Gaylord?' she said.

Gaylord was pleased to do so. He liked Amanda; not as much as he liked the dog Schultz, of course. Schultz did things. But he had nevertheless a fondness for her that often surprised him.

Today, however, he had far too much on his mind to put his head inside the pram and pull funny faces to amuse his sister. Great Aunt Dorothea marrying a Frog! Great Aunts Bea and Dorothea coming in December – to say nothing of the Frog!

He was not only intrigued. He was quite uneasy in his mind. He knew Princesses often married Frogs, if only because Frogs could usually be relied upon to turn into Fairy Princes. But Great Aunt Dorothea was no Princess. And the idea of her and Great Aunt Bea turning up with a Mr Jeremy Fisher didn't fit somehow.

Besides, Gaylord had been beginning to fear that fairy tales were one thing and life was another, and that Frog Princes belonged to the fairy tale side. Yet he had just listened to Momma and Grandpa quite seriously discussing Aunt Dorothea's marrying a Frog, and even talking about what to give the Frog to eat. And if anyone ought to know about these things it was Momma and Grandpa (Poppa he would not have been so sure about). Could it be that fairy tales were real? Had he been too hasty in dismissing them? He did hope so. He parked Amanda by the dustbins. He saw Miss Mackintosh and Julia in the distance. Though he was quite pleased when Julia came and played with him, it was wholly against his principles that he should ever approach her. But today he needed to test reactions. He fell in with them. He said, very very casually, dropping the words on the still November air, 'My Great Aunt Dorothea's going to marry a Frog.'

There was a silence. It must, thought Elspeth Mackintosh, be an English joke. 'Och, awa' wi your daffin',' she said sternly.

'What's that mean?' asked Gaylord. It didn't sound as though it meant: ladies only marry frogs in fairy tales, but he had to be certain.

'Ye're a rude wee boy,' said Miss Mackintosh.

'I'm not,' Gaylord said hotly. 'I only asked.'

But now Julia, eyes shining, said, 'Is she really, Gaylord? I bet he's a Fairy Prince, then.'

'Yes,' said Gaylord. 'That's what I thought.' He went and sought out Poppa, who was taking a walk to stop his brain getting overheated, and to try to unravel his current plot, and who was not entirely overjoyed to see his first born. 'Poppa, Great Aunt Dorothea's going to marry a Frog.'

'So I hear,' said Jocelyn.

Gaylord trudged on in silence. 'Poppa?'

'Yes?'

'Why is Great Aunt Dorothea marrying a Frog?'

'I suppose they've fallen in love with each other.' His duty to his son clashed with his duty to his public. He put the plot from his mind long enough to say, 'Actually, old man, I think the Race Relations Board would prefer you to say: a Frenchman. "Frog" could be regarded as chauvinist.'

Questions multiplied in Gaylord's brain like rabbits. He said, 'Grandpa says Frog.'

'Your Grandfather is the Race Relations Board's senior by fifty years. He would regard its strictures as youthful impertinence.'

'What is the Race Relations Board? And what's – show – something?'

Jocelyn told him. Gaylord tried to fit the jigsaw together. He couldn't. There was a piece missing. Then he remembered. He wrinkled his young brow. 'Poppa?'

'Yes?'

'I still don't see where the Frenchman comes in.'

'He's the man your aunt's going to marry.'

Gaylord pondered. 'Not a Frog?'

'No.' He laughed. 'Ladies only marry frogs in fairy stories, old chap.'

Gaylord felt depressed. If only grown-ups would say what they meant! In spite of himself, he had rather been looking forward to meeting a Mr Jeremy Fisher. But no. As usual, life had come down on the side of the humdrum. But then, thought Gaylord sadly, it always did.

There was no doubt about it, now. Winter had won the battle. Days were short, the majestic clouds of autumn became the grey dusters of November skies. For townspeople, the countryside changed from a bright playground to a sodden, surly lump. The Gas Lane Hussars carried out noisy manoeuvres on the river road; so that May brought her children indoors, and watched apprehensively from the window; and John Pentecost strolled bravely and nonchalantly past with his gun; whereupon the cavalry, with jeers and catcalls, and with obvious reluctance, turned tail for home. Wendy Thompson at last saw Julia dance – and told herself that here was a grace, a talent, it would be cruel to hide. She talked to Julia – and found that, to her, life and dancing were one, it was as simple as that. Yet what could she do? Nothing short of ballet school would serve for this girl. Wendy would certainly speak to her father again, even at risk of a rebuff. When she saw him. But how could she see him unless he came to the school?

Dorothea said, 'It's ever so cold at John's farm in December, Edouard. I don't think John quite understands the central heating. Do remember to pack a hot bottle, dear. And if I were you I should take a little something in a flask.'

A yellow van, equipped with lifting gear, let itself into the meadow without a by-your-leave (as the old man had said it could; but manners are manners), hoicked the machine out of the river, and trundled it back to its owner. Derek did not attend the watery exhumation. He wished to spare himself. Besides, he might meet the old man again. And that he did not want to do until he'd got his mates with him.

John Pentecost strolled across to watch the operation. 'Crazy coot,' said one of the men. 'You'd wonder how he managed to run into the river.'

'You would indeed,' said John Pentecost.

'Could have drowned himself,' said the other.

'He certainly could,' said John Pentecost. But as he strolled home he thought: no police action, apparently. No legal action. Well, perhaps he was sorry. Perhaps he would have preferred an enemy he knew, an enemy that fought according to certain rules. He was left with an enemy that knew no rules, that could strike anywhere, and at any time.

May Pentecost, with Jocelyn's slightly grudging help, decorated the guest room. She bought new sheets and pillow cases. She studied her Cordon Bleu Cookery, and actually drew up a series of menus. Whoever might let down Great Aunt Dorothea, Edouard St Michèle and the Entente Cordiale if there was anything left of it, it would not be she.

The garage did what they could with Derek's motor bike. They cleaned it up, and made it serviceable, and gave it him back. 'Here you are, mate,' they said. 'We've got the tiddlers out of the carburettor. It's as good as new.'

But it wasn't as good as new. It could still do a hundred miles an hour, and make as much noise as a ten-ton lorry. But it no longer sparkled in the sunlight, it no longer gleamed like a knight's charger. It looked, in fact, like a motor bike that has spent some time at the bottom of a river. Worse. It had once been the symbol of Derek's pride and manhood. Now it was the reminder of his humiliation – and the call to vengeance. If by any possible stretch of imagination poor Derek could be compared with Hamlet, then the motor bike inevitably became the ghost of Hamlet's father.

Chapter 6

May Pentecost was a serene woman. Superb health, strength of body and suppleness of mind all helped her to run a big house and at the same time handle with equanimity an irascible father-in-law, a sensitive husband, a highly individual son and a baby daughter. But even she had her moments of female bloody-mindedness. And she had one now. She marched into her husband's study. 'The hour is about to strike,' she said.

Jocelyn, too, had an equable temperament. The only thing that could get him into a really nasty mood was a letter from the Inspector of Taxes, whom he regarded with loathing; not for the reason that most men regard the Inspector of Taxes with loathing; but because this man, while speaking the tongue that Shakespeare spake, yet twisted it into such convolutions, tortuosities and coils that, so far as Jocelyn was concerned, he might as well have tried to communicate in Hottentot. And, having had a letter from the fellow this morning, he felt as prickly as a porcupine. 'What hour?' he asked in a flat voice.

'The aunts are arriving with the Frenchman on Friday evening.'

She was watching him closely. He had the feeling that this was one of those occasions when any reaction except the right one would provoke adverse comment. So he hid his dismay and said, 'Did you say both aunts?'

'I said both.'

She perched on the edge of his desk. He said, 'It's like pestilence and famine.'

He knew now he'd chosen the wrong reaction. There was a glint in his wife's loving eye, and an edge to her fond voice: 'Darling, they are your aunts. And I don't suppose you'll be cooking Aunt Bea's Moussaka or lightly steaming Dorothea's fish.'

He said, desperately trying to shift his ground, 'Of course, it will be lovely having the old dears. It's just – '

'Just what?' She was relentless.

He gave up. He said, 'Have you told young Gaylord?'

'Yes.'

'What did he say?'

'I got the impression he was thinking of emigrating.'

'If only they wouldn't keep kissing him. He loathes it.'

'Well, it won't do him any harm.'

'No. No, of course not,' he said hurriedly.

She picked up the Inspector's letter, glanced at it idly. 'What does he mean, "or (e) if the tax was charged on the assessment to which the deferred charge relates or any part of the deferred amount… "?'

'I wish to God I knew,' he said miserably.

She kissed his forehead. 'Poor Jocelyn.' She went. He too glanced at the letter. He sighed. He read the last paragraph of his novel, crossed it out. He sighed again. All this, he thought, and Aunts Bea and Dorothea too. And a bally Frenchman. He dismissed them from his mind. He dismissed the Inspector. He was a writer, wasn't he, with a duty to God and all mankind that cancelled out any duty to ageing aunts or the Inland Revenue. He began to write, struggling desperately to inject some life into his characters. May put her head round the door. 'I forgot. Dorothea snores.'

'So?' he asked warily.

'So Bea won't share a room with her. We shall have to put one of the aunts in Gaylord's room, and move Gaylord in with your father.'

'I can see them both liking that.'

She ignored him; and said, 'So sometime, would you get the spare bed down out of the attic, and put it up in your father's room for Gaylord.'

It was too involved. He was still wrestling with that damn novel. 'Put what where?'

'Jocelyn. Your aunts are coming for the weekend. All I'm asking you to do is get a bed down.'

'Into – Gaylord's room?' he said, feeling his way like a man walking in pitch darkness on the edge of a parapet.

'No! Into your father's room.'

'But you said – '

'Jocelyn! Listen. Edouard in the guest room, Dorothea in the second guest room, Bea in Gaylord's room, Gaylord and your father in your father's room.'

'I see. So the spare bed has to go in – Father's room. You're right, old girl. Just what I was going to suggest.'

She looked at him with fond exasperation. 'Well bully for you, boy,' she said. She departed, realizing that she had inevitably sent any creative thoughts her husband might have, flying. Poor old Jocelyn, she thought. He doesn't get much chance to write an epic, even if he wanted to.

She did, indeed, leave a husband filled with foreboding. There are men to whom getting a spare bed down from the attic is child's play. There are others to whom it appears as fraught as getting a grand piano down a spiral staircase. Jocelyn Pentecost was at the very head of class 2.

Gaylord and Grandpa walked in the farmyard. Their hearts, too, were filled with foreboding. They walked, hands clasped behind backs, heads down against the bitter wind, pensive. Gaylord said, 'Momma says I shall have to tidy my room.'

'You will? Why?'

'She says Aunt Bea won't relish having a marshalling yard under her feet.'

The old man looked at his grandson with compassion. 'Good Lord! Is Bea moving in with you?'

'No. I'm moving in with you.'

Grandpa stopped in his tracks. He stared. His trim white moustache bristled. 'I'm damned if you are,' he said with more feeling than tact.

'I am. Momma says so.' And when it came to immutability the laws of nature, the laws of the Medes and Persians, God Himself, had nothing on the edicts of Momma.

'We'll see about that,' muttered Grandpa. But he thought: I shall have to speak to May. A fine woman, no one I respect more. But I am not being pushed around in my own house.

Gaylord said, thoughtfully, 'Of course, we could have a midnight feast. Doughnuts and things.'

Grandpa made a noise that sounded like 'Ugh!'

'And pop,' said Gaylord, warming to his subject. 'And licorice sticks.'

But he got the impression that Grandpa was not over-enthusiastic. Well, he wasn't surprised. In fact, nothing ever surprised him about grown-ups. So many times he'd tried to brighten their drab lives. And the only response he'd ever got had been apathy and obstruction.

Grandpa stomped on in silence. He was, there was no doubt about it, in the fell clutch of circumstance.

He cursed his own pusillanimity. If only he'd brought up the subject at breakfast time! Then he would have got his own bombshell in first; and would have been able to pour the cold water of disapproval on other people's bombshells.

But he hadn't. He had waited, telling himself he would choose the right moment to break the news to May. And he had left it too late. Fate, in the form of Bea, Dorothea, and Edouard had shoved him to the back of the queue.

Over lunch he said, 'Er, May, terribly sorry, forgot to tell you. Had a letter from Becky this morning.'

May looked at her father-in-law briskly. She wasn't used to seeing the forthright old man on the defensive. She said suspiciously, 'You're not going to tell me she and Peter are also coming for the weekend?'

He looked sheepish. He wiped his mouth with his napkin. 'Well, she did rather – ' He petered out. May said, 'Suppose you read me the letter, Father-in-law.'

He fished it out of his pocket, read: 'Dear Father, That heel Peter's going to get himself seduced by a gorgeous redhead if I don't play my cards right. Can I bring him for the weekend? Then you and Jocelyn can talk to the poor fool like Dutch uncles. Love to all, Becky.'

'Well, I'm blowed,' said May.

'What's seduced?' said Gaylord.

But Jocelyn cried bitterly: 'Open house! Liberty Hall! How,' he demanded, 'how am I supposed to write when half my time is spent in Dutch uncle-ing and the other half in getting beds down from attics?'

May said, 'Of course they must come, Father-in-law. Not,' she added unkindly, 'that I can see Jocelyn doing anything effectual in this instance.'

Jocelyn knew the signs. It was the wrong reaction again. May, splendid woman though she was, thought that if anyone was entitled to feel sorry for themselves at this juncture, it was she.

By now he had thrown discretion to the winds. 'I bet Tolstoy never had these crowds pouring into Yasnaya Polyana,' he grumbled. '"Not this weekend, Sonya Andreevna," I can hear him saying. "Wait till I've finished War and Peace".'

Grandpa, caught on the wrong foot though he undoubtedly was, could never keep out of an argument. 'You're not writing another War and Peace, I should imagine.'

'That is beside the point,' Jocelyn said stiffly.

May said, 'Well, if you can't spare an hour to try to save your young sister's marriage, Jocelyn – '

Damn, thought Jocelyn. Out-manoeuvred as usual. And Grandpa congratulated himself on his cunning in getting May on his side by the simple expedient of giving Jocelyn his head and just a touch of the spur. He said, much more comfortably, 'Thanks, May, you know how I appreciate it. And it won't make a lot. There'll be plenty of people to do the washing up and the bedmaking.'

'Yes.'

'And you can just put Amanda on Dorothea's knee and forget about her for the whole weekend.'

Gaylord, eager to stick in his little oar, said, 'Aunt Dorothea could feed her.'

'She couldn't darling.'

'Why couldn't Aunt Dorothea? I bet she could if she tried. Bessie the sow feeds dozens.'

Grandpa said irritably, 'Will someone explain to that child the difference between a refined lady of sixty and a philoprogenitive Yorkshire White?'

Gaylord looked hopeful. 'What is the difference?'

May sighed. 'Aunt Dorothea can do all sorts of things Bessie can't do.'

'What sort of things?'

'Oh, petit point, and The Times crossword – '

'And cheating at Bridge,' Grandpa said sourly.

'Father! She doesn't.'

'Of course she does. Why, when we were kids she used to cheat at Happy Families.'

May saw her son's eyes fixed on her, seeking knowledge. Any moment now, she thought, we're going to have a question on how one cheats at Happy Families. She said hurriedly, 'So, you see, it's only fair that Bessie should be able to do some things that Aunt Dorothea can't do.'

'Like grubbing acorns?'

'Like grubbing acorns.'

'Or going oick, oick, oick, oick.' He made dreadful pig noises.

'Exactly, dear.'

Gaylord sat back and kicked his legs, well satisfied. He always liked to clinch a hypothetical discussion with a few well chosen concrete examples. 'Or making that sandpapery noise if she scratches her back on the pigsty door.'

'Yes. Now, Jocelyn. I can leave you to see to the bed, can't I.'

'Of course,' he said absently, yearning to get back to his work, to try to get some life into those characters of his. But secretly he hadn't much hope. He had reached the moment that every dedicated writer fears more than he fears death: the moment when the creative well runs dry; when characters click to a halt like run-down clockwork toys; when the honey no longer drips from the pen; when the pen hand still moves, like a beheaded chicken, though what is written has lost all life. The death in life, the dark night of the writer's soul. The End. He was finished.

The fact that he worked himself into this state about every six months or so did nothing to alleviate his sense of doom. For he had searched his heart, and knew that this time it was different. Jocelyn Pentecost had gone through life with one skin fewer than most men. The troubles of others moved him more, as did also the teeming beauty of life: moved him, compelled him, to seize a pen and write about them. And now – he was no longer moved. He could walk in the hills, listen to a Schubert impromptu, watch nightly from his armchair the smashing of bone and flesh that made up so much of the nine o'clock news – and feel nothing. And he knew why. He had acquired another skin. He had, he supposed, grown up, and become as other men. And the mainspring of his writing had gone.

Grandpa, having got himself out of the doghouse, was determined to stay out. He said, 'I've been thinking, May. If it would save any trouble, you could stick Gaylord in my room.' He glared at his grandson, daring him to say, 'But I've already told Grandpa – '

But Gaylord was still mulling over the Dorothea/Bessie question. 'Or even devouring her young,' he now said happily.

Friday afternoon: the winter's dark already turning the river to gunmetal; the tree branches writhing in the winter's wind; the lights of John Pentecost's farmhouse the only cheerful thing in a lithograph-grey scene.

The farm stood on a slight rise, overlooking the river valley. It would have made a good fortress. There was only one approach, and that was from a lane running beside the river. And Gaylord was watching this lane like a hawk. As soon as he saw Great Aunt Bea's Mini coming along the road he would stand by to repel boarders; or, anyway, do his disappearing act. What this place lacked, he felt very strongly, was a moat and a drawbridge. (In fact, he'd suggested it to Grandpa at the beginning of the week; but had met with the usual grown up lack of enthusiasm. 'What on earth for?' Grandpa had asked. 'To keep the Great Aunts out,' Gaylord had said. A wistful gleam had come into Grandpa's eye. But all he had said was, 'Never get planning permission, old chap.')

So here he was in the hayloft, lying on his stomach on a heap of straw, gazing out through a very convenient knot-hole. Fifteen feet below was the stackyard; beyond that the paddock, the meadows, the river; beyond the river again, an unknown land of fields and trees and a church tower, a sort of through-the-looking-glass land, where Gaylord believed, though he had no factual basis for this belief, that the people spoke Chinese.

There were lights coming along the lane, flashing in and out as the car passed behind trees and hedges. Now he could see the Mini. Any time at all now, Great Aunts Bea and Dorothea, those compulsive kissers, would be out of the car and crying, 'Where is the young scamp? Where is my precious?' To Gaylord they were on a par with that alarming giant fee fie fo fumming as he smelt the blood of an Englishman. He crossed to go down the ladder into the big barn.

Carefully and deliberately he put his plan into action. He climbed into the seed box on the big seed distributor, and shut the lid; pulled his iron rations out of his pocket – a Mars Bar, a bag of hundreds and thousands, and a bottle of Coca Cola. He hadn't much hope of staying hidden till the aunts went home – who could have, with a mother like his, hearing all, seeing all, knowing all? – but it was worth trying. After all, if it was left to Poppa he wouldn't be missed till seedtime came round again and they found his pathetic little skeleton in the hopper; a thought that filled him with a most moving melancholy.

From his study, Jocelyn could not see the river road. He could only wait until the house was filled with the clamour of the aunts' arrival.

But once that happened, he could no longer shut himself away. Hushed voices saying, 'The master is not to be disturbed,' were unknown in the Pentecost household. Anyone could, and frequently did, barge into his study. Well, he supposed it was his own fault. Too amiable by half. Other writers just didn't seem to have domestic lives. You couldn't imagine, 'Just give me a hand with the second best bed, Will. Ben Johnson's coming for the weekend,' any more than you could imagine Wordsworth going round Dove Cottage with a duster. No. Most other writers, it seemed to him, divided their time between writing masterpieces and dallying with their mistresses. But he, Jocelyn Pentecost, had clearly started off on the wrong foot. And now it was too late.

Grandpa, snoozing in the drawing room, heard the sound of tyres on gravel. He opened a baleful eye, shut it again, and began breathing deep and steady. For Grandpa was a realist. He knew that, fond though he was of his sisters, that fondness had got to last over at least a weekend. It was going to be touch and go. There was no point in meeting them until it was absolutely necessary.

Besides, he was still mulling over what May had said. 'Now, Father-in-law, I know you're going to assume that this Frenchman is a crook, just because Aunt Dorothea met him on a cruise. And it's most unfair, both to Dorothea and to him. It's up to you to treat him with the courtesy due not only to a guest but to a future brother-in-law.'

He had glared up at her with that aggressive sheepishness that meant she had struck home. 'My dear May, you're not suggesting that I of all people could treat a guest with anything but courtesy?' He was hurt. If there were two things John Pentecost prided himself on above all others they were his courtesy and his tact.

She had given him that amused grin of hers, and gone off without a word. Well, he'd be courteous. But he wasn't letting a French crook think he could pull the wool over his eyes.

May, too, heard the car and braced herself. We're off, she thought. A whole weekend; with everything and everybody, even Father-in-law, under my control: cooking, entertaining, keeping the peace or trying to, electric blankets, glasses for teeth, morning tea; and those wildly disparate characters, Jocelyn, Father-in-law, Gaylord, the Aunts, Becky, brother-in-law Peter; to say nothing of an unknown Frenchman; even little Amanda who, lacking speech and mobility and understanding, could yet create a mayhem peculiarly her own. She felt like a captain whose ship, stealing out of harbour, gets its first vicious slap from the mighty Atlantic. Nevertheless, she put on a bright smile. She went and threw open the front door with a cry of 'Welcome, Aunts!'

It wasn't the aunts. It was a young lady who, at this strange greeting, seemed prepared to leap back into her Mini as the startled fawn leaps back into the brake.

In the end Madam Chairman had made up Wendy's mind for her. 'Now, Wendy dear,' she had cooed like a serpent down the telephone, 'have you confirmed that date with Jocelyn Pentecost?'

'I – I'm afraid I haven't yet, Pamela.'

'Well look dear, you must. Mrs Trumper's so anxious to hear him but wants us to avoid May as Penny's expecting and little Trumper's ETA is scheduled for the very day of our May meeting, so –'

'I'll write today.'

'It's no use writing, dear. You know what authors are, they never answer letters. No, go and see him, dear, and get a firm date. When Doreen first asked him about coming he said it would be quite all right to call but not to telephone as his father usually answers the 'phone and treats any call that isn't about pigs or combine harvesters with contumely.'

'I'll go this afternoon,' said Wendy.

And go she did, having first discovered from The Author's and Writer's Who's Who that Mr Pentecost had been born in 1935 and educated at a minor public school, was married to Elizabeth May Tideswell, and had written six novels; having also given some extra attention to her pretty but unremarkable little face, and enveloped her small self in her one real luxury, a softly caressing fur coat.

As she drove along the river road she braced herself, for meeting strangers was never easy for her. Mrs Pentecost she saw as a dumpy, friendly little creature, all bun and spectacles, beavering away in the background. But Jocelyn she could see only as a great bull of a man, glaring at her over a simmering electric typewriter, stating curtly that his only possible date was May, a man to whom little Trumper, trailing clouds of glory, was beneath consideration. So that by the time she reached the front door she was in a high state of nervousness. Was this bitter afternoon really a sensible time to call? The house looked so big and forbidding. Her courage ran out like water out of a bath. Fancy her, Wendy Thompson, thinking she could hobnob with a real writer! She, whose only claim to fame was coming second in the March, '71, Poetry Competition!

Nor was she reassured when a tall, elegant and beautiful woman flung open the door with the cry of, 'Welcome, Aunts!'

May said, 'I'm terribly sorry. I was expecting – someone else.'

'Oh, dear. If it's inconvenient. But – Mr Jocelyn Pentecost said it would be quite in order to call sometime.'

May was intrigued. Jocelyn had mentioned no young woman. She looked at the visitor more closely. Very feminine, with her small bones, rather fine grey eyes, and cosseting furs. Yes, despite her present anxious and forlorn expression, she had a certain quiet authority. 'Do come in,' said May.

The girl came inside. 'I'm awfully sorry. But Mr Pentecost said it would be all right.'

'I see. Do sit down. I'll tell him. What name shall I say?'

'Wendy Thompson.'

May marched into the study. She found herself looking into the second anxious, forlorn face in two minutes. 'Are they here?' he asked, like one hearing the tramp of feet outside the condemned cell.

'No. But Wendy Thompson is.'

'Who?'

'Wendy Thompson.'

'Who's Wendy Thompson?'

'I don't know. But she seems to know you. Says you told her to drop in any time.'

Quite obviously, May regarded Miss Thompson's visit as both an irritation and a source of innocent merriment. Not for the first time did Jocelyn wish his wife's sense of humour was a little less astringent. He stood up. 'I'd better come and see what she wants.'

'Oh, no you don't laddie. You'll see her here. I can't face the gathering of Clan Pentecost and Miss Wendy Thompson.'

He sat down. 'Right,' he said coldly.

May went back into the hall. 'Do come this way,' she said. But her voice was drowned by the hideous crash of metal on metal, the prolonged tinkle of glass, followed by the awful voice of Great Aunt Bea demanding to know what damn fool had left a car without lights just where she would run into it.

The effect on the household of this clatter was rather like that of a boot on an ant heap. Gaylord, flinging discretion and hundreds and thousands to the winds, was out of the hopper and gleefully running for the house. It was seldom that disaster, or what sounded like disaster, struck. When it did, Gaylord wanted to be in the front row.

Miss Thompson quite literally wrung her hands and cried, 'It must be my car.'

Grandpa had always believed that Bea wasn't fitted to drive a bullock wagon, let alone a motor. ('Gaylord,' he had said more than once, 'one of these days, you mark my words, your great aunt will drive that car of hers slap through my conservatory;' since hearing which Gaylord had always added a rider to his prayers that, when that joyous day came, he might be granted a full view of the proceedings.) So hearing the clatter of glass, Grandpa abandoned all pretence of slumber and waving The Times like a flail he rampaged towards the hall crying, 'What the devil does Bea think she's playing at?'

'Terribly, terribly sorry,' moaned Miss Thompson.

Jocelyn, hearing the commotion, slumped in his chair. 'Mischief, thou art afoot,' he murmured, knowing that when mischief was afoot he, Jocelyn, always got dragged in, however much he tried to do his lurking-in-the-undergrowth act. So he stayed where he was. They would fetch him soon enough. He wasn't one to go and meet trouble halfway.

May said, 'Excuse me,' to Miss Thompson, and hurried outside.

Miss Thompson longed to follow her, but was too overcome. Even Gas Lane Primary had not fitted her for the brisk life of the Pentecosts. Nor had her own mental preparations for the visit. She sank into a chair. a small boy dashed in, bright-eyed. 'Is anyone hurt?' he asked eagerly.

'I – I do hope not.' Miss Thompson half rose from her chair. This fearful possibility had not, until now, occurred to her.

He listened. 'I can't hear any screams. Can you?'

'No.'

'So perhaps whoever it is, isn't.'

'No.' Miss Thompson felt much relieved.

'Unless they're dead,' said Gaylord. 'I'm going to see.'

He rushed out. A fierce-looking old gentleman rushed in. 'Where's May? What's happened? Who are you?'

'So terribly sorry,' said Miss Thompson. 'I – I just never thought.'

'Never thought what?' John Pentecost barked and bristled.

'Leaving my car without lights, where someone would run into it.'

'My dear madam.' Grandpa's sudden access of old-world courtesy was almost as disconcerting as his rudeness. 'My dear madam, don't give it another thought. My sister Bea would have run into it had it been floodlit like Buckingham Palace.'

'Really? You mean – it may not be entirely my fault?'

He glared. 'If, as I gather, your car was stationary and you were sitting here in the hall when the accident happened – how the devil could it be your fault, madam?' demanded Grandpa, suddenly throwing old world courtesy out of the window. Then he remembered the manners on which he so prided himself. 'No, young lady. Your only mistake was to go within half a mile of my sister Bea when she was at the wheel. Always fatal. Let's go and look at your car.'

She seemed to be having difficulty in rising. He looked at her with sudden compassion. She was very pale, and trembling. He felt an emotion he had not felt for years: a strong, male protectiveness, a desire to slip a manly, comforting arm round those frail shoulders, to quiet that beating heart with gentle words. He said, 'No, you stay here. I'll go and find out for you. Oh, forgive me. I'm John Pentecost.'

'How do you do? I'm Wendy Thompson.'

'You're not – ?' he asked sharply, remembering Becky's letter. The gorgeous redhead? He looked at Miss Thompson's hair. Mouse. 'No. Of course not.' He went. Out into the dusk of the drive.

He went up to the cars. They appeared to be locked together, like stags in mortal combat. Bea was shaking them violently to get them apart. John said sweetly, 'Well, Bea? Still carving a trail of devastation, I see.'

'Nonsense, John. I haven't hit a thing since that army tank got in the way last February.'

'Which army tank?'

'The one I clobbered.'

John looked at the Mini. Impossible. Then he looked at Bea, and reserved judgment. Bea was one of those large, formidable women who look capable of dealing with an entire armoured battalion. with Bea beside him on the bridge, thought Grandpa, Horatius wouldn't have needed to worry. He said irritably, 'Watch what you're doing, Bea. You don't want to reduce both cars to a mass of twisted metal.'

'I'm trying to get them apart, dammit.'

From the middle distance a voice said, 'I bet that lady won't half be cross.'

The moment he had spoken, Gaylord realized his mistake. Aunt Bea dropped the pair of Minis, and peered into the dusk. 'Why, it's my little pickle.' She held out her arms. 'Come and give your old auntie a kiss, dear.'

Gaylord, sticking his lower lip out, didn't budge. He even, by some curious sideways evolutions of his feet, edged a little further into the encircling gloom. But it was no use. Great Aunt Bea looking, in her fur coat, like a grizzly after honey, advanced – just as a low sports car swung into the drive with a flash of headlights and the sound of a two-tone horn. 'Auntie Becky!' cried Gaylord, running to meet it. Averse though he was to kissing generally, he made a very definite exception in the case of Auntie Becky. Her kisses were soft and cool, and she smelt gorgeous. Auntie Becky, in fact, kissed like an artist.

Grandpa always said that Peter's sports car was so low on the ground that it would need a fork-lift truck to get one out of it and upright. But Becky fairly leapt out and stood, holding out her arms and laughing. 'Gaylord, darling!'

She crouched down, holding him tight. Looking up, she saw the old man and the two cars. 'Hello, Father. Going in for the scrapmetal business?'

Peter climbed out, wearing gauntlets and a sheepskin coat. 'Good evening, sir.'

The old man grunted. He remembered Becky's letter. 'What's all this about a redhead, dammit?' he enquired tactfully.

Becky abandoned Gaylord and went and took her father's arm. 'Oh, you impossible old man,' she said fondly, leading him towards the house.

'What redhead?' said Peter sulkily. He heaved out the suitcase.

They ignored him. Gaylord, eager as always to be helpful, said, 'Auntie Becky said in her letter you were going to be somethinged by a gorgeous redhead, Uncle Peter. But I can't remember what.'

Peter, humping the suitcase, said nothing.

'Uncle Peter?'

'Yes?'

'What is a gorgeous redhead?' Gaylord had given the matter quite a little thought, and had decided it was probably either a butterfly or a breed of cattle; yet, if he was right, he couldn't for the life of him see where Uncle Peter came in. So now he waited eagerly to learn the truth.

'It's a bird,' said Uncle Peter with a bitterness that got through even to the seven-year-old mind of Gaylord.

More and more puzzling. If only he could remember what it was that Auntie Becky had said the bird was going to do to Uncle Peter. Poppa had once told him about a Greek gentleman who had had his liver pecked out by birds. He hoped it was nothing like that, for he was a kindly child. But though he had few inhibitions when it came to asking questions, he did feel a certain delicacy in asking grown-ups about their livers.

Now they were nearly at the house. And who should be standing in the doorway but that old grizzly waiting for her honeypot! 'Excuse me, Uncle,' whispered Gaylord, politely. He merged into the shadows; and, using every bit of cover, was soon lost in the winter's night.

John Pentecost remembered something. 'Hey, Bea? Where's this chap of Dorothea's?'

'May took him and Dorothea into the house. Come on. I'll introduce you.'

What had May said, something about the courtesy due to a guest and a brother-in-law? Telling him, of all people. And even as he was thinking this Bea said, 'Edouard's English is excellent. But I've told him you'll probably insist on addressing him in Pidgin English.'

It was an idea, he thought; a subtle way of putting this Frog in his place. But no! Courtesy! – at least until the time came to tell the chap his little game was up. 'Never thought you'd let Dorothea fall for a crook,' he said reproachfully.

Bea stopped in her tracks. 'A what?'

'A crook.'

'He's not a crook.'

' 'Course he's a crook.'

She began walking again. 'One thing I admire about you, John. You've never let complete ignorance of a subject stop you being dogmatic, tendentious and self-opinionated about it.'

The old man fumed. Really, Bea couldn't be in the house two minutes before she started on him. And now she was off again. 'I shall expect you to treat Edouard with all the courtesy due not only to a guest but to a brother-in-law.'

'Whose house is this?' he demanded.

'Yours. That's why I'm reminding you of your duty. And I'm not having you spoiling poor Dorothea's chances.'

First May. Then his elder sister. Both lecturing him as though he was some sort of monster, instead of one of the pleasantest-tempered, most reasonable men you could meet in a day's march. Of course he'd be polite.

But he wasn't having any Frog crooks in the family.

They were all in the comfortable, cottagy living room: May with, it seemed to her, any number of coloured ribbons radiating outward from her head: one to the cooker, where what Grandpa would have called Froggie food simmered and hissed and spat; one to Gaylord, where was he? She hadn't forgotten the motor cyclist incident; one to Amanda, was she sleeping in safety? One to Jocelyn, was he sitting at his desk, still pretending he hadn't heard a damn thing? Or had he had the nous to creep from his lair and rescue poor Miss What's-it, whose car was wrecked, who appeared completely demoralized, and who was attached to May's brain by a particularly broad and quivering ribbon? To leave a guest in this way was unpardonable. But Jocelyn must have done something by now. And she had to be here, to welcome her future uncle. Besides, duty apart, she couldn't have torn herself away. She had to witness the meeting between what Grandpa clearly thought of as East and West.

Great Aunt Dorothea was there: frail, her mind and body, both, seeming to sway and drift like gossamer in the breeze; yet smiling with ineffable sweetness in her late-flowering love.

Monsieur Edouard St Michèle Bouverie was there, smiling at his loved one, gazing with frank and unabashed admiration at the statuesque May, and almost quivering with Gallic excitement when the lovely Becky came into the room.

Becky, laughing, ran across to the old lady and kissed her fondly. 'Congratulations, Aunt Dorothea.'

'Thank you, dear. Isn't that nice! Have you met my gentleman friend?'

'No.' Becky, of the full cheeks, the straw-coloured hair, the happy smile, knew how to hold a man's attention. She put out her hand, higher than she would have held it for an Englishman. 'Je suis enchantée, Monsieur.'

'Oh!' Deep in his throat Edouard gave a French growl of appreciation – a cross between the purring of a cat and the satisfied noise of a dog settling down to a really meaty bone. Reverently he took the white hand, bowed low over it, brushed it with his lips. He straightened, gazed into Becky's eyes. 'Enchanté,' he murmured, deeply moved. His timing was perfect.

Becky took a deep breath. She felt as though she had just drunk half a bottle of champagne. 'Peter – that's my husband,' she explained to Edouard – 'is just seeing to the cases.'

'Ah! You have a husband?' He turned to May, shrugged in mock despair. 'Why do all you lovely young girls have husbands?'

Becky giggled. May, too, felt she'd been at the champagne. It was quite some time since anyone had called her a lovely young girl. It was absurd, of course. You'd only got to think of Gaylord and Amanda. Still? She resolutely didn't think of Gaylord and Amanda.

Peter wandered in. Becky said, 'Ah, here's my husband, Monsieur. Peter, this is Aunt Dorothea's fiancé.'

Edouard grasped him by the shoulders. 'So it is you who have stolen this beautiful young woman from the world.' He pressed his right cheek against Peter's right, his left against Peter's left. 'Oh, fortunate young man!'

'Yes, rather, I suppose so,' Peter said somewhat incoherently. He looked at his radiant wife. Yes, dash it, he supposed he was jolly lucky. If only she wouldn't get bees in her bonnet about redheads. As it was, this French chap ought to try living with her for a bit. He'd soon find it wasn't all a bed of roses. But May thought: I wonder what happens if he kisses Father-in-law on both cheeks. She decided that hers would not be the only imagination that would boggle. She looked at Aunt Dorothea, hoping she was not hurt by all this Gallic exuberance. But Dorothea sat beaming happily on one and all, like a proud owner watching her puppy beg for sugar lumps.

The door opened. Here we go, thought May. But it still wasn't the old man. It was, to her relief, Gaylord.

It had been no light decision of Gaylord's to come into this aunt-infested room. But his plan to remain hidden lay in ruins, destroyed largely by his own curiosity. And he did want to see the Frenchman.

Yet, once again, he was disappointed. The only Frenchman he knew at all intimately was the Emperor Napoleon, of whom a picture hung on his classroom wall. And to find that Aunt Dorothea's lover had neither white breeches nor a cocked hat was a sad anti-climax. He had ventured into the lion's den for nothing.

His heart sank even further when Great Aunt Dorothea held out her arms and cried, 'This is my pickle, Edouard. Come and give your auntie a kiss, boy.'

Well, there was no help for it. The only bright spot was the unexpected absence of Aunt Bea. He advanced with a reluctant, crab-like gait, and was enfolded in what felt to him like a spider and fly embrace. but worse was to come. 'Now kiss your Uncle Edouard,' said Dorothea.

He was affronted. Even his real uncles never made any attempt to kiss him, and this Frenchman, he felt vaguely, hadn't acquired real uncle-status yet. But Edouard earned his undying love and devotion by saying, 'Oh, men don't kiss each other in England, Dorothea,' and he shook hands gravely and firmly with Gaylord.

Gaylord, like everyone else, was enchanté. He said chattily, 'Isn't it funny. I thought at first you'd be like Mr Jeremy Fisher.'

'Indeed? And who is Jeremy Fisher?' He wrinkled his brow. 'A politician?'

May said hurriedly, 'He's just a character in one of the Beatrix Potter books, Monsieur.'

'Oh?' He turned back to Gaylord. 'And what kind of a gentleman is Mr Jeremy Fisher? A nice one? Or' – he pulled a dreadful face – 'a horrible one?'

'Very nice,' May said, without much hope.

'Sort of chap who enjoys fishing,' Peter said helpfully. 'Er – do you, Monsieur?'

Dorothea, whose brain worked very slowly, and seldom for long in one direction, said, 'John took me on a fishing holiday once.'

'Really?' cried May, seizing avidly on this fascinating piece of information. 'And did you enjoy it, Aunt Dorothea?'

'No. John wouldn't let me talk. Said the trout could hear every word. But it's my belief,' she said darkly, 'it was just to stop me chattering.'

Edouard smiled, and squeezed her hand.

'After all,' Dorothea demanded of the company at large, 'have you ever seen a fish with ears?'

'He's a frog gentleman,' said Gaylord.

The room was silent. Edouard looked puzzled but resigned, like a Frenchman who knew he would be puzzled by the English anyway. Then suddenly, he saw the light. He shouted with laughter. He drew Gaylord to him, ruffled the black hair. 'Oh, mon brave. Que tu es gentil.' He was still laughing. He pointed to his stout but immaculate shoes. 'You thought I had webbed feet, yes?'

Gaylord thought him the nicest man he'd ever met.

John Pentecost entered with Bea. He wore the grim look of a man who is determined not to let his younger sister marry a crook, yet is equally determined to be polite to the fellow; he also wore the wary look of an Englishman who fears an attempt is about to be made to kiss him on both cheeks.

He went and kissed Dorothea, who wound an arm round his neck and embraced him fondly. Out of the corner of his eye he took in the French chap.

He had two pictures in his mind: one had a greasy complexion, black, down-turning moustaches that reached to his chin, and an air that was flashy and seedy at the same time. The other had a goatee beard, a black velvet jacket and striped trousers, a grey necktie with a diamond pin and, by anyone less shrewd than John Pentecost, might well have been mistaken for a gentleman.

But this chap didn't fit the bill at all. His brown tweeds were as rough as John's own, his complexion looked as though it spent more time in sun and wind than in the salon, he was laughing, and his left arm lay affectionately round Gaylord's shoulders. At this stage John Pentecost was prepared to pay him the greatest compliment he could pay any foreigner: after a couple of whiskies, and with the light behind him, you could almost forget he wasn't English.

Nevertheless, John was no fool. The chap wasn't English. And John wasn't going to forget it.

Dorothea said, 'And now, John. This is such a happy moment for me.' Delicately she dabbed her eye, though she was still smiling. 'I want you to meet – and love – your new brother-in-law, Edouard St Michèle Bouverie.'

John, keeping a safe distance, nodded stiffly and growled, 'How do you do?'

To his surprise the Frog also bowed stiffly and said, 'How do you do?'

Fight against it as he would, John couldn't help feeling mollified. Chaps, it seemed to him, were divided into two types: those who said 'How do you do?' on being introduced, and those who said, 'Pleased to meet you,' or even 'Hi!' And anyone who used any but the warm, sensible, meaningful 'How do you do?' whatever his nationality, was fit only for treasons, stratagems and spoils. He decided to make an effort. 'Comment ça va, hein?' he asked courteously.

'Bien, merci.' The Frenchman smiled.

'Bon.' There was a silence, while it was borne in on Grandpa that he had, linguistically, shot his bolt. 'Bon,' he repeated after some thought.

Edouard came to his rescue. 'Dorothea tells me you fish, sir.'

'A little trout.' The old man dropped into a chair. 'Don't suppose you'd know anything about that, though.'

'Oh, I've fished some of the Scottish lochs. And in Ireland, of course.'

Grandpa drew his chair a little nearer. It had never occurred to him that Frenchmen could fish; or, indeed, do anything but eat, drink and make love. (The inescapable fact that they played Rugby Football always seemed to him one of the most bizarre facts in nature.)

The gathering began to break up. People excused themselves, drifted away. But the two elderly gentlemen remained seated, their chairs now comfortably close. 'I remember, one evening, on Deeside,' the Frenchman was saying...

CHAPTER 7

Miss Wendy Thompson really was demoralized. She blamed
her own rash impulsiveness for bringing her here in the first
place. Yet it had really been, she knew, a first brave step out
of the small world of Ingerby, and above all out of her shy
and lonely self. She was intelligent enough to know that only
courage would set her free. She had not been afraid to show
courage. And look where it had landed her! She hadn't even
seen Mr Pentecost yet. And the most terrible things had
already happened. She had been greeted by a woman whose
beauty and serenity immediately made her feel she was back
in the Lower Fourth. She had heard her car suffering untold
indignities. Then, in order of appearance, she had met a
crazy small boy, and an old man who had frightened the life
out of her; then a tall, mannish woman who had looked her
up and down and said, in the friendliest manner, 'You the
chick who left that car slap in the middle of the drive?
Damn stupid thing to do. Never mind. We all do something
daft once in a while;' she had gone off chortling hugely; then
a young man, struggling with an enormous suitcase. He had
dumped it in the hall. 'Hello.'

'Hello.'

'Are you a relation?' he had asked.

'No. I just called – '

'Thank God for that. Only I'm fairly new to this family,
and they keeping springing relations on me. Makes me a bit

jumpy. That your car out there?'

'Yes. Do you think it's badly – ?'

'Dunno. Let's go and have a look.'

She was trembling less, she found. She went out with him, and the cold winter air made her feel better. He groped inside his sports car, pulled out the sort of motoring torch that might have been designed for felling bullocks. He shone it on Miss Thompson's car.

She gasped with horror. The offside front wheel was wrapped up in the wing like a badly tied parcel, the headlamp was shattered. But Peter said, 'Oh, that's not bad. You'll be out and about again in a week.'

'A week? But I've got to get home tonight.'

'Not in that car you won't. Never mind.'

She wished everyone wouldn't tell her to never mind. She did mind. Her beautiful Mini! And just when it was hers to drive where she would. And all these people advising her, criticizing her, yet not a sign of the one man she'd driven out to see. She said, 'Actually, I wanted to see Mr Jocelyn Pentecost. But – '

'Old Jocelyn? He probably went into hiding as soon as he heard the crash.'

Her heart sank. A war casualty? 'Why should he do that?'

'Oh. Nicest chap you could wish to meet, old Jocelyn. But not practical. And slow thinking. Avoids any crises like the plague.'

'I see.'

So here she was, in a house of strangers, miles from home, with the winter's night now firmly in command, and with the only man who might show the slightest interest in her presumably cowering under his desk. If she walked along the river road she would eventually, she knew, come to a village where there might possibly be a bus to Ingerby. Or a taxi. But the road was dark, and she was no countrywoman, and the river ran close. She knew that most people would just ask for a lift, or for a taxi to be called, or even for a bed. Some, even, would stand up boldly to the old lady who had run into her car and demand full recompense. but not Miss Thompson who, though not lacking courage, was tonight emotionally incapable of drawing attention to herself.

'Cold out here,' Peter said. 'Let's go in.'

They went back into the hall. 'Excuse me,' said Peter. 'Better find my wife.' He wasn't going to risk any more recriminations by chatting up a female who, unless he was much mistaken, wouldn't see thirty again. Besides, this girl had a frail, bird-like quality. A chap might find himself absent-mindedly enfolding her in his strong, protective arms before he realized what was happening. And all from the highest possible motives, of course. But try telling that to the Marines, he thought with a shudder. He went.

It was at this point that Wendy Thompson's hackles began to rise, and her small body to seethe with indignation. It was outrageous. Here she'd been, on a perfectly civil errand, and what had they done? Smashed her car, left her waiting in the hall, forgotten about her. Well, she wouldn't stay another moment. Blow authors who hadn't the courtesy to meet a visitor, blow the Writers' Club, blow Mrs Trumper, and Mrs Trumper's Penny's unborn! She strode to the front door, flung it open, marched out, and slammed it behind her. Metaphorically she shook the dust of the Pentecost household off her feet for ever.

A light had been switched on in the drive. Beyond that, it was now quite dark. Miss Thompson was appalled. A town dweller, she had never considered the fact that there must, in the nature of things, be bits of the world without street lights. Anger casts out fear. But already her anger was beginning to ebb and her fear to return. Had she not slammed the front door behind her, she might have crept back.

She stood, straining her eyes. After a few seconds she made out the road. She set off.

The wind had dropped – menacingly, did she but know it. The silence was all about her. She sensed, rather than saw, a great winged creature fly across the road. She heard a mournful, fluting note. Owls. It had never occurred to her that owls existed outside radio plays. Cold. Silence. Darkness. Owls.

She was afraid. But she set her small jaw, and marched resolutely on, into the darkness, thankful to have left the Pentecost farm behind her. Mr Poyser, the solicitor who was dealing with Mother's estate, would act for her over the car. He and the garage. She need never go back.

There was a harsh, aggressive noise on the windless evening. A motor cycle was coming up the lane. It thundered past her, half blinding and deafening her, then plunging her back into greater darkness. She saw the rider crouched, toad-like and menacing, on his machine.

As soon as he had passed, he slowed down and stopped. She dared not turn round. She kept walking.

The machine began to follow her, slowly. Its headlamp threw her shadow on the road before her.

She wanted, desperately, to run. But who can run from a machine capable of a hundred miles an hour? She made herself walk. On her left, the river glinted in the light. There seemed to be a ploughed field on her right, protected by a wire fence.

Her nerves were near breaking point. She hurried on. The motor cyclist followed, grimly, surely.

She could bear no more. She stopped, turned, eyes blazing. 'What do you want?' she shouted above the noise of the engine.

Without a word the driver accelerated and swept past her. Thank heaven! But twenty yards on he stopped, turned his bike so that the headlamp illuminated her like an aircraft caught in a searchlight, and switched off his engine.

The silence was appalling. She put up a hand to shield her eyes, moved across to the darkness at the side of the road. The light followed her. She crossed to the river side. The light followed her again. She was trapped in a cone of light.

If she climbed the fence, could she lose herself in the darkness of the field? She did not think so. Stumbling across a ploughed field at night would be slow work. If the rider left his machine he would coon catch her. Besides, she was trembling so much she doubted whether her legs would carry her. Certainly, to get back to the farm across country would be quite beyond her powers.

Wendy Thompson was small, and fragile, and certainly not very brave. But now she made a decision that surprised her. She would march boldly up to this youth and tell him to leave her alone.

Resolutely, she walked into the light. The cyclist did not stir. She was almost level with him now, and he made no move. Perhaps, she thought, with just a glimmer of hope, I shall be able to walk past him. Perhaps hell let me go when he sees I'm not some young girl.

She was level now. That was it. He was interested in something a bit younger, someone with a bit more flesh on her bones.

Then he spoke. His voice was harsh, and flat. 'You live at that farm?'

She had to make several attempts to speak, so dry was her mouth. He shouted furiously. 'I asked you. You live at that farm?'

'No. And – you should be ashamed of yourself, frightening people.'

He was silent. 'I bet you do,' he said. 'I'll throw you in the river if you do. I'm going to throw anybody in who lives there. And hold them down.'

'I don't,' she said piteously.

'Well, you've been there.' He had been sitting astride his bike, his feet on the ground. Now he dismounted. 'That's good enough for me.'

He was still in darkness. She was still in the one patch of light in the whole brooding countryside. Her eyes ached with the brightness. And suddenly a gauntleted hand shot out of the blackness and seized her wrist, and began dragging her towards the icy river. She screamed. It was at this moment that she heard a sound in the distance. It could be footsteps, coming from the direction of the farm. It could be.

Clearly the motor cyclist had heard it too. His grip faltered. 'Help!' screamed Miss Thompson. 'Help!' With a swift movement she jerked her arm free, and began to run on unsteady legs back to the farm. And as she ran she heard the most wonderful sound she had ever heard in her life: the engine of the motor cycle starting up and fading into the distance. But had it faded? Or had it stopped again? She could not be sure.

The footsteps were nearer now. Perhaps they'd missed her at the farm, and someone had come out to look for her. How foolish she would look! But she could bear that, after her recent fears.

The footsteps were light, and quick. 'Hello,' said a friendly voice.

It was the boy. 'Hello,' said Wendy, relieved.

'Where are you going?'

'Shepherd's Warning.'

'You're going the wrong way.'

'I heard your footsteps, and waited,' said Wendy.

But Gaylord was agog. 'I heard the White Nun of Shepherd's Warning. "Help, help," she was screaming.' He gave a lifelike imitation. 'Did you hear her?'

'No?'

'Some people don't. Henry Bartlett's Auntie Ethel says you have to be – psych, something.'

'Psychic?'

'Yes.' He was impressed.

Something wonderful happened. All Miss Thompson's fears for herself disappeared in her fears for this boy, who lived at the farm, and was therefore, in the motor cyclist's genial expression, due to be drowned. She must get him back to the farm without frightening him, warn his parents. In the distance she could see a glow among the trees. She was almost certain the motor cyclist was still lurking in the lane.

But she had reckoned without Gaylord, who had decided that this lady sounded a bit frightened, and no wonder, after his tactless references to the White Nun of Shepherd's Warning. Suddenly he felt very big, and grown-up, and protective. A bit like that Sir Galahad Poppa had told him about. It occurred to him that this lady was even nicer than his current ideal of womanhood, the lady in the Co-op butchers. 'If you like, I'll come with you a little way,' he said kindly. 'Some people fall in the river where it comes up to the road, and get swept away.'

'No. Come on. We must get back to the farm.'

He really had frightened her! 'It'll be all right,' he said reassuringly. 'Henry Bartlett's Auntie Ethel says the White Nun never appears to two people.'

'Come along,' she said sharply.

He stood his ground. 'You can hold my hand if you like,' he said, taking a step towards Shepherd's Warning. He felt terribly, terribly grown-up. If only they could meet a ghost; if only this lady would fall in the river so that he could rescue her!

But the lady, fragile and feminine though she might be, clearly had a will of her own. She grabbed his little paw and dragged him back towards the farm. He was outraged. He felt as St George might have done if his lady had insisted on rescuing him from the dragon.

He stuck out his lower lip. 'You wanted to go to Shepherd's Warning.'

'My dear child,' she said crossly, 'I couldn't have let you go back alone on that dark road.'

'Why not?'

'You're only a little boy.'

This was too much. 'I'm eight, next.'

'Then in that case,' she said, 'You can walk faster than this.' She'd heard the motor bike again.

He concentrated on showing her how fast he could walk. 'Goodness,' she panted. 'I can only just keep up.'

He went even faster. She allowed herself to fall slightly behind. And now, having re-established his male superiority, he could afford to let himself be mollified. He said chattily, 'Wasn't someone silly, leaving their motor car where Aunt Bea could run into it?'

'I was. Very silly.'

'Oh, was it you?' He could afford to be even more mollified. He actually waited for her. A warm little hand slipped into hers. 'Grandpa says that if Great Aunt Bea must drive a car, she ought to have men with sticks running in front, clearing the way.'

The lights of the farm were quite near, now. So was the sound of the loitering motor cycle. 'I'll race you home,' said Miss Thompson.

He was off, like an arrow from the bow. She followed. They reached the doorstep almost together, laughing, panting, friendly. The motor cycle droned away in the distance.

Jocelyn Pentecost wondered vaguely what had happened to Wendy Thompson, whoever she might be. Perhaps, if she was an Opinion Poll, or a what-do-you-think-of-television programmes, she'd got latched on to Grandpa; in which case, he thought grimly, she'd get her money's worth. Anyway, May had said he must wait and receive her. So wait he did.

May came in. 'Well blow me!' she said. 'Chaos is come, and there you sit.'

'I'm waiting for Miss Thompson,' he said patiently.

'You'll wait a long time. She's disappeared.'

'Well, that's all right,' he said. 'Probably didn't need to see me. Saw someone else.'

'I don't mean she's gone. Her car's still here, or what's left of it.' She saw his puzzlement. 'Bea biffed it.'

'She didn't!'

'Of course she did. What did you think the uproar was?'

'Oh, Lord. Anyone hurt?'

'No, thank goodness.'

'And what about Miss Thompson?'

'The guilty party, according to Bea? She was safe in the house when the crash occurred.'

'And now she's disappeared?'

'Like the snows of yesteryear. And – Jocelyn, I don't want to be alarmist, but' – her voice was suddenly bleak – 'I don't know where Gaylord is.'

He stared at her in silence. 'You mean – ?'

'He's not in his room. And I've been shouting my head off outside.'

He had a happy thought. 'He's gone to ground to avoid Bea's kisses.'

'That's what I thought. But – he wouldn't not come when he heard me calling. Oh, it must be all right, I suppose.'

He looked at her thoughtfully. 'You're worried, aren't you.'

She shrugged. 'I suppose I am. Especially after that motor cyclist business.'

He said, 'And you've looked everywhere?'

'Barn, outhouses. All his' – her voice was unsteady for a second – 'all his favourite haunts.'

He said, 'And no one's seen him?'

'Not recently. I shouldn't worry so much if they hadn't both disappeared. I don't see how she could be connected with the motor cyclist. Still – '

It all tied in with his thoughts – the violence that more and more weighed upon him. Its shadow was everywhere – even in the heart of the English countryside. He said, 'I shall telephone the Police.'

For once it was May who looked undecided. 'Darling, I don't think you should. Gaylord must be around. And Miss Thompson might have decided to walk home.'

'Without a word to anyone? Besides, where is home?'

'We don't know. We know nothing about her, except her name. That's what's worrying.' She looked at her husband anxiously. 'Jocelyn, think. You can be absent-minded, you know. Are you sure you don't know a Wendy Thompson?'

'What did she look like?'

'Early thirties. Not quite smart, but a good attempt. Pretty, in a petite, fine-boned sort of way. Very, very unsure of herself. But a nice person, I would have said.'

'No.' He gave her a sudden grin. 'She doesn't sound like one of my little lapses.' The grin disappeared. 'Sorry, May.' He reached for the telephone. 'Wait!' said May. They listened. 'Gaylord!' she said. They hurried down to the front door.

Even anyone as serene as May was not likely to be overjoyed to find the two causes of her worries enjoying themselves hugely on her doorstep. 'Gaylord! Where have you been?' she snapped. Miss Thompson she ignored.

Miss Thompson sniffed the east wind. She sobered up quickly. 'I met your little boy down by the river, Mrs Pentecost, and brought him home as quickly as I could. I thought you might be worried.'

'You're dead right, I was worried. But – thank you, Miss Thompson,' she said, a trifle grudgingly. Then she realized how dreadfully she had neglected this uninvited guest. She said, 'Do come inside. Miss Thompson, you – weren't – walking home?'

'Well, I did realize I'd called at a very inconvenient time, and – '

They were in the hall, now. Wendy Thompson's eyes were bright and sparkling from her exertions, her face was still alight from her triumph in having brought the boy back safely. Jocelyn saw a very different Wendy from the frightened creature of May's first meeting. He said, 'I'm afraid I've treated you very badly indeed, Miss Thompson.'

'Of course not, Mr Pentecost. It was ridiculous of me to turn up like that.' She too saw a very different person from the one she had imagined glancing at her over his typewriter. She smiled at him gratefully.

Gaylord had been unnaturally silent; but there were occasions in life, he always felt, where self-effacement paid dividends. And this, he realized instinctively, was one of them. But now, in spite of himself, he couldn't help saying, 'Momma, I heard the White Nun.' He gave his realistic rendering of her cries.

'Gaylord, be quiet. You'll bring out the fire brigade.' And then, in the way that one thing always led to another with Momma, 'And what were you doing down by the river? You know perfectly well – '

'As a matter of fact,' Miss Thompson said quietly, 'he was protecting me.'

'From what?' May asked coldly.

Gaylord said, 'From the White Nun, Momma. And from falling in the river.'

'If I could have a word – ' Miss Thompson said quietly.

'Go and get ready for bed, Gaylord,' said Momma.

This was an outrage. No merchant in an Eastern bazaar ever haggled over the price of a carpet more than Gaylord haggled over bedtime. And this summary dismissal, with a third party present, put him at a considerable tactical disadvantage. 'But Momma – ?'

'Ten minutes, then. But I mean ten minutes. Now, Miss Thompson. Let's go into the small sitting room.'

CHAPTER 8

The black sky brooded over the silent earth. Not a tree stirred, not a blade of grass. But then, there was a quick sigh, another, then a great sighing, a great susurration of breath that rose quickly to a whistle, to a scream. A flake drifted down out of the blackness, feather-light, another, another, suddenly a million others, dancing and whirling and driving and stinging. John Pentecost, as sensitive to weather changes as a barometer, heard the rising wind. But no one heard the snow, wrapping a winding sheet of white about the lonely farmhouse, industriously blotting out the lanes.

Derek Bates rode home through the swirling flakes. He felt frustrated; knowing in his heart that that woman (and he'd recognized her, the bitch. She taught in the Primary. And she lived just down the road) that woman had got the better of him, just by talking posh. Still, if it hadn't been for someone else coming he'd have had her in the river, he swore he would, they'd have been getting the tiddlers out of her carburettor, he thought with unwonted humour. He slammed into the house, divested himself of his gear in the kitchen, left it for his mother to pick up and put away, and went and slumped in front of the telly. 'What's it like out?' said his dad. 'Bloody snowing,' said Derek. But he did not feel like the cut and thrust of conversation. He stared at the screen. Some bloke with a stocking over his face had gone into a room where an old woman was asleep. Any minute now the old woman was going to wake up and see him. Derek couldn't wait to see her face. Here she went! Cor! Mouth open, eyes popping out of her head. Derek rolled about in his chair. Funniest thing he'd seen for ages. And those stockinged features, like some mindless, emotionless travesty of the human face, coming ever nearer. He'd like to do that to that schoolteacher bitch. Later, Derek pinched a stocking out of his mother's drawer, and tried it on. Over his face, of course. Looking at himself in the mirror he sent shivers down even his own spine. His face, which even he realized had shortcomings, had gone. It its place was a mask of power – and terror!

As they came out of the sitting room, May said, 'We really are grateful to you, Miss Thompson. Even though it does confirm our fears.'

'Very grateful,' said Jocelyn. He smiled down at her. Pretty little thing! Thinking of her out there, at the mercy of that youth, made him feel very protective. She was like some waif out of Grimm or Andersen. He said, 'Stay and have dinner, Miss Thompson. Then I'll run you home.'

May might be very grateful to Miss Thompson. But she'd seen Jocelyn looking fond and fatherly. Much as she loved him she didn't trust him not to get even more fond and fatherly alone with Miss Thompson on the Ingerby road. She said, 'That would be delightful.' She searched her mind for a 'But –' and couldn't find one. Then she heard something that sounded very much like manna falling from heaven. Could it be? An answer to prayer when she hadn't even prayed? She listened. A soft, insistent pattering of tiny fingers on the window. It could be. It was. And Gaylord confirmed it by running in and crying, 'Momma! It's snowing. It's snowing bucketfuls.'

She went and wrenched open the door. Snowflakes danced in like medieval revellers. She looked out. She saw the swirling snow. She saw, as always, everything: her husband, still looking protective; Miss Thompson, still looking frail and feminine; she saw the situation, the implications, the required moves. She said, 'Goodness! Another hour of this and the roads will be blocked. You'd better be getting home, Miss Thompson.'

'I'm afraid – my car – '

'Oh, of course. We'll have to put it under cover. But I think you ought to be getting along. Perhaps Peter will run you in.'

'I'll take you,' said the noble Jocelyn. 'Then we can discuss my lecture.'

May said, 'I thought, if Peter went, it would – '

Jocelyn said, 'I don't think Miss Thompson would be very comfortable. These sports cars are so bumpy.'

Miss Thompson gave Mr Pentecost a look of melting gratitude. May said tartly, 'Well, if it's comfort we're after, what about your father's Rover?'

'Oh, I couldn't ask Father to turn out in this,' Jocelyn said cheerfully.

A rapturous voice cried, 'Poppa, can we have a snowball fight.'

Momma said, 'My dear boy, it's only just starting to settle.'

'Besides,' said Jocelyn, 'I have to run Miss Thompson home. And it's almost your bedtime.'

It sounded exciting. They might get stuck in a drift, be marooned for days. Gaylord saw himself plodding desperately through the drifts to bring help to Miss Thompson, frozen halfway between life and death. 'Can I come?' he asked, expecting, as always, the answer 'no'.

'No, I don't think so,' began Poppa. But to Gaylord's utter astonishment Momma said, almost eagerly, 'Of course, dear. I'll just fetch your coat.'

She hurried off. You could have knocked Gaylord down with a feather. Nearly bedtime, and Momma letting him set off on a long and perilous journey! He didn't understand it. Asked, he would have said that Momma was one hundred per cent predictable. Yet he knew that, just very, very occasionally, she would do something completely unexpected. As she had now. He decided, in his wisdom, it must be because she was a woman.

'I've never seen it snow as hard as this, have you, Poppa?' That was Gaylord, bouncing happily up and down on the back seat.

Miss Thompson said, 'I'm afraid Mrs Pentecost will never forgive me, dragging you out on a night like this.'

The car lurched and slithered. The snowflakes attacked it like angry bees. They flung themselves at the windscreen in their thousands. The wiper blades swept them away, but still they came on like the hordes of Tartary. The headlights showed nothing but a whirling whiteness. Jocelyn was no longer a moderately successful author, a kind husband, a loving father. He was an infinitely delicate instrument, whose eyes, ears, fingers, toes, whose whole body had become a part, the guiding mechanism, of a machine coping in elemental surroundings. There was the road, the snow, the car of which he was a part. Nothing else in the whole wide world.

Or, rather, there shouldn't have been. But there were other things of which he was aware: Miss Thompson's pale face, lit so softly by the light from the dashboard; the softness of Miss Thompson's fur coat, an inch from his shoulder; Miss

Thompson's hands, folded demurely in her lap. So frail! A type one didn't often meet in these days of bouncing women's libbers! It was good, exhilarating, to use his skills to bring her safely through the storm. He said gallantly, 'You haven't dragged me out, Miss Thompson. I'm only too pleased to be of use.'

' 'Course we are,' said Gaylord. Not to be outdone in gallantry he added, 'I bet Sir Galahad never let ladies walk home.'

Miss Thompson felt quite touched. And it was at this point that she suddenly realized something very surprising. She was enjoying herself! The evening had been so dreadful, so embarrassing. Yet everyone had been so nice to her: Jocelyn Pentecost, that young man with the sports car, the little boy, even the old gentleman had been nice when he wasn't barking. She had felt uneasy with Mrs Pentecost, and with that old lady whose car she had inadvertently wrecked. But the gentlemen! Miss Thompson wasn't used to gentlemen. They impinged seldom on her private life. She had not realized what nice creatures they were. O brave new world, that has such people in't, just about summed up Miss Thompson's feelings about gentlemen at this moment. She said, almost coyly, 'We haven't discussed your lecture, Mr Pentecost.'

It was not the best of moments. Jocelyn was beginning to realize two very unpleasant facts: that, blinded by snow, he had almost certainly missed the right-hand turn for Shepherd's Warning, and was therefore going due north when he should have been veering round to south-east; and this left him the choices of turning in this narrow lane, or backing an unknown distance, or driving miles across the bleak upland of No Man's Heath before he came to the next right turn. The other even more unpleasant fact was that the engine had begun to sound as though it was choking on a fishbone.

Confirmation came from Cassandra on the back seat. 'Poppa, you've missed the turn. I'm sure we've missed the turn. We're nearly at No Man's Heath.'

Jocelyn drove grimly on. 'It won't half be blowing on the Heath,' said Gaylord with relish. 'I bet it could blow us over. Henry Bartlett's Uncle Fred got blown over.'

'Did he, dear?' said Miss Thompson, though less from an interest in Henry Bartlett's Uncle Fred than from a desire to keep her end up socially.

Gaylord said proudly; 'Poppa, I think your engine's going to stop.'

Jocelyn said nothing. Miss Thompson said, 'I've thought for some little time, it sounded – Oh, Mr Pentecost, and it's all my fault, dragging you out – '

Now it seemed as though all Jocelyn's being was centred in the ball of his right foot – coaxing, wheedling, urging. All to no avail. The engine spluttered and died. The snowflakes, now that he was no longer driving into them, looked as though they were settling down to cover the car from sight as soon as possible.

Gaylord said, 'No one ever comes along this road. We could stay here for days and days and days, if you ask me.'

'All my fault,' said Miss Thompson. 'I'm so sorry.'

Jocelyn was trying the starter. It ground drearily. Not a flicker of life. Gaylord said cosily, 'Miss Thompson, I've been thinking. If they send out a search party they'll never think of coming this way. They'll go to Shepherd's Warning. They'll never find us.'

Whenever the car broke down, May would say, 'Don't you think you ought to look under the bonnet, dear?' Jocelyn would dutifully go through the motions, knowing that he would have learnt just as much, or as little, from the entrails of the Capitol geese. Despite May's absence, he was just about to go and look under the bonnet when Gaylord began chattily, 'Henry Bartlett's Uncle Fred – '

'Oh, blow Henry Bartlett's Uncle Fred,' said Jocelyn.

Miss Thompson turned and gave Gaylord's fingers an understanding squeeze. 'Tell me, dear,' she said quietly.

Gaylord sounded hurt. 'I was only going to say that he broke down once and rang up the A.A. and when they came they found he'd run out of petrol. Henry Bartlett's mother said he didn't half feel silly.'

Jocelyn had already got one leg out of the car. Now he quietly pulled it back, quietly closed the door. He looked at the fuel gauge. 'Aren't you going to look under the bonnet, Poppa?' enquired Gaylord.

'No,' said Jocelyn bleakly, 'I don't need to.'

Meanwhile, back at the farm, May was worrying about Jocelyn and Gaylord, out in the blizzard with a too helpless female; assuring Aunt Dorothea that an electric blanket wouldn't strike her dead; showing Becky and Peter into Becky's old room, where Becky promptly struck a jarring note by clasping her hands and crying, 'Ah! happy room of my maiden years! Oh, May, why didn't I realize when I was well off?' A question that seemed to make Peter sulkier than ever; wondering how long before the legs and wings of the cooking chicken in the oven began to fall off through overcooking; finding the tomato juice for Dorothea, the gin for Bea and Edouard, and the whisky for Grandpa, and the appropriate glass for each. And now here came Grandpa, an empty soda siphon in one hand, a glass of whisky in the other, and a look of disaster on his face. 'May, the siphon's empty. Just get Jocelyn to slip into the village.'

May said, 'Sorry, Father-in-law. He's out.'

'Out? Out where?' Grandpa always liked to know where everybody was, what they were doing, and why.

'Running Miss Thompson home.'

'Who's Miss Thompson?'

'The girl with the Mini.'

Grandpa was put out. 'Dammit, May, he's got a duty to his family. House full of visitors, his wife toiling over a hot stove – '

'His father wanting soda water,' May put in wickedly.

'Exactly. If that woman hadn't left her car in Bea's path, she'd be home by now, and Jocelyn would be on hand to do something useful. Oh, well, have to go myself I suppose,' he finished grumpily.

'You do know it's snowing a blizzard, I suppose?'

He glared. ''Course I didn't know it was snowing. Wish someone would tell me these things.' He spotted his sister coming. 'Bea, here's a mess. The woman whose car you clobbered. That quixotic fool Jocelyn's run her home. And now there's no soda for my whisky. And it's snowing a blizzard.'

'Snowing?' cried Great Aunt Bea. 'My car's out, John, get that young chap of Becky's to help you put it under cover.' At which point Becky's young chap came running downstairs two at a time, went up to Grandpa and cried, 'Mr Pentecost, sir, you can keep your daughter, and much good may she do you. I'm going.'

May said, 'Oh Peter, just help your father-in-law to get Aunt Bea's car under cover before you go. And Miss Thompson's.'

'I'm damned if – ' began Peter. He caught May's unblinking, serene glance. Was this some trick to keep him here? Well, May was a clever woman. But she'd have to be very clever to keep him here tonight, after what Becky had just said to him. Even so, May had given him pause. He said, 'Sorry, May. Wasn't very polite, I'm afraid.'

May gave him a sudden grin. But John Pentecost had not forgotten the snow. He went to the front door, put his hand on the knob, and said, 'Very well, young man. Go, as you say. And do not come back until you are in the mood to apologize to my daughter, my daughter-in-law, and me.'

'Never!' cried Peter. Grandpa flung open the door, to an explosion of snowflakes. 'Good Lord,' said Peter. 'It's snowing.'

'Of course it's snowing, you silly young man,' said Grandpa. 'But that's no concern of mine. Go on. Off you go.'

'But – look at it! It's up to my exhausts already.'

'You're letting the cold in,' said Grandpa, impassive.

'Oh, dash it,' said Peter. 'Look, sir. I suppose I was a bit hasty. I'll go back and see if Becky and I can't – '

'Good man.' Grandpa put an affectionate hand on the young man's shoulder. 'Do that. But you wouldn't like to slip into the village first, would you?' He saw Peter glance at his half-submerged car. 'You can take the Rover,' he said hurriedly. 'It's higher off the ground.'

'Oh, sir.' Peter was quite overcome. No one was allowed to drive the old man's pride and joy. Peter thought that being allowed to drive John Penetecost's Rover was probably a greater honour than being allowed to marry his daughter. He went. 'Get six siphons,' Grandpa called out after him. 'Then if we're snowbound for months – '

'We shall at least have some soda water in the house,' May said drily. She and her father-in-law strolled back through the hall. May, having mentally crossed Peter off the supper list, and then put him back, was wondering when she was likely to see him again, or her husband and son, and how those unhappy birds in the oven were standing up to things.

Upstairs a door slammed. Becky came down bright-eyed and brittle. 'Has anyone,' she asked, 'seen my heel of a husband?'

'Yes,' said Grandpa. 'He went through that door a minute ago.'

Becky seemed to lose a couple of inches. 'You don't mean – he's gone?' She ran towards the door. May said, 'Becky darling, it's hardly a night for silver sandals and a backless dress.'

Becky said piteously, 'I never thought he'd – May, you don't think he's – gone to her, do you?'

'Depends what you said.' Grandpa was at his most sententious. ' "Words once spoke can never be recalled", remember.'

'But I didn't mean – '

'It isn't what we mean. It's what we say.'

'I suppose I did say some pretty horrible things.'

Becky's lovely face was so troubled and contrite that May put her arms round her and said, 'I won't have you teased, Becky. Your father has sent him to buy soda water, against our becoming snowbound.'

'You mean, he's coming back?' Becky's face cleared wonderfully. 'But why snowbound?'

'If you look outside, you'll see.'

Becky went and peered through a window. She came back, faced her father. 'Well, you selfish old man,' she said. 'Sending poor Peter out in this lot to satisfy your sybaritic tastes. You should be ashamed.'

Grandpa said tetchily, 'If it hadn't been for me and my sybaritic tastes, my girl, Peter wouldn't have been going to the village for soda. He'd have been going to his redhead for solace and comfort.'

'How do you know?'

'He told me, in no uncertain terms, that I could keep my daughter.'

Putting an oar in was something none of the Pentecost family seemed able to resist. May said, 'We really did get the impression you'd hurt him deeply, Becky.'

'Oh, the poor lamb. I was only teasing him about that nice Frenchman.' Tell Becky she had hurt someone, and you were home and dry. May thought: that should reduce one of the week-end tensions, anyway. Now she was left with only her wandering boys, the aunts, Edouard, and the apparent impossibility of ever having supper. Bea reappeared. 'When are we eating, May? Dorothea can't survive for more than five hours without food. Like sparrows.'

'Eat?' said Grandpa. 'We can't eat yet, woman. Not had my whisky and soda.'

'Nonsense, John. Do you good. Soda's a depressant.'

'Well, whisky isn't, by God. It's all very well for you, Bea. You've been soaking up gin like a sponge from the moment you arrived.'

'As a matter of fact, John,' said Bea, carefully weighing her words, 'it wouldn't hurt you to miss your whisky and your supper.' She looked him up and down critically. 'You've been overeating.'

'I enjoy overeating, dammit.'

May slipped her arm into Becky's and led her away. 'Isn't it touching, the old world courtesy of a generation that is passing.' She sighed. 'Only this morning your father was complaining about the decay of manners in the young.'

Jocelyn said, 'Miss Thompson, I have done something utterly foolish. I scarcely know how to tell you.'

She said, with feeling, 'To anyone who can write as well as you, Mr Pentecost, a great deal can be allowed. What have you done?'

Oh, understanding woman. 'I've run out of petrol,' he said.

She actually put a gloved hand on his. 'It happens to everyone, sooner or later, believe me.' But Gaylord struck a less soothing note. 'I bet Momma won't half pull your leg, Poppa. If we ever see her again, that is.' Frankly, he thought it extremely unlikely, in their circumstances.

Jocelyn's heart sank even further, if possible. He said, 'I believe a bus comes along this road at about nine o'clock.' He had a sick feeling that it didn't run every evening, but forbore to point out this depressing fact.

Gaylord gave it as his opinion that, in these conditions, the road would be impassable by nine o'clock, even for buses.

They ignored him. Jocelyn said, 'I do appreciate the way you've taken this, Miss Thompson.'

'Mr Pentecost, what other way could I have taken it?'

'It won't surprise me,' said Gaylord ecstatically, 'if there are wolves.'

Frankly, it wouldn't have surprised Miss Thompson either. Her cosy little world was collapsing so rapidly that anything seemed possible. But Jocelyn said, 'This is Shepherd's Warning Lane End, remember. Not the frozen steppe.'

'What frozen step? Anyway, teacher says hunger can drive them down from the hills they live in. Or they could have escaped from that circus we went to.'

'Gaylord, do try not to end all your sentences with a preposition.'

'What's a preposition?' But he didn't really care. Weren't grown-ups hopeless! Even a gorgeous adventure like this had to be ruined. Mention something really exciting, like wolves, and before you could begin to savour its rich possibilities you found yourself switched on to prepositions.

But he wasn't one to give in easily. Pressing his nose against the window he peered out into the snowy waste. 'I think I can see an Abominable Snowman,' he said hopefully.

Miss Thompson looked at the small, eager face. She was already beginning to know her Gaylord. Yesterday she would probably have tried to reassure the child, pointing out that the existence of Abominable Snowmen even in Nepal was open to question, let alone at Shepherd's Warning Lane End. Now she said, 'Just behind that bush. Look. I saw him move.'

Gaylord found this absolutely delightful. He hadn't been feeling at all certain that he had seen an Abominable Snowman. In fact it could almost, he had to admit, be put down to wishful thinking. But if a grown-up had seen it too? He peered intently. 'It's just scratched its head, Miss Thompson.'

'And its left knee.'

She and Gaylord looked at each other and chuckled happily. All right for some, thought Jocelyn, weighed down by responsibility, guilt and remorse. If only he'd checked the petrol! He said, 'I still haven't discussed the date of this lecture, Miss Thompson.' Not that he cared. He was still trying to remember whether the bus that travelled this lonely road on some evenings was FO (Fridays only) or FX (not on Fridays). It made a difference. But since he and his aunt between them had landed her in this cheerless situation, he ought to show some interest in her affairs.

She said, 'I do realize now that it was very wrong of me to barge in on you, like this, Mr Pentecost. I should have written.'

'Not at all. I'm so glad you came in person. I'm only sorry I've made such a hash of getting you home.'

Well, isn't it incredible, thought Gaylord, that two adults, caught in a fascinating life and death situation, could give their minds to a conversation of such unparalleled dullness. He peered out of the window. 'There are two of them now,' he said. 'They keep looking this way. I think they're wondering whether to devour us.' But neither of his companions took any notice, of course. Not even nice Miss Thompson, who'd been so interested a minute ago. Typical. Butterfly minds, the lot of them.

Yes. Miss Thompson's mind was clean off yetis. 'Mr Pentecost, please don't apologize. I ought not to have come. Only – it was a temptation because I admire your books so much and because – well, I think your work's terribly significant.'

'Significant of what?' To Jocelyn, flattery was a sweet-smelling savour. But a man who has just run out of petrol in a snowstorm needs great gulps of the stuff.

'Well, of – LIFE,' said Miss Thompson.

Jocelyn said, 'One tries to reflect life, of course. But – good Lord, something's coming.' He jumped out of the car.

Gaylord was bitterly disappointed. This promising adventure, it seemed, was coming to an end. Unless, of course, the approaching car refused to stop. But already he could see the Land Rover slowing down, and drawing up beside them.

Mr Duncan Mackintosh jumped down, and came across, unsmiling. 'I thought it was yourself, Mr Pentecost. You'll be in some kind of trouble, maybe?'

If Jocelyn had been given a list of the fifty million people in the British Isles, and had been told to choose the one he would least like to be rescued by, there is no doubt that Mr Duncan Mackintosh would have been the very first man on his list. Now he thought bitterly: fifty million of them! And it has to be this capable, practical, humourless Scot! The man who, above all others, makes me feel like a feeble-minded child. He said, sulkily, 'I've run out of petrol.'

'You're sure that's the trouble? Petrol gauge showing empty, is it?' He peered round at the dashboard. He jabbed a finger at the petrol gauge. 'That's the one.'

'Oh, I thought that was the speedometer,' said Jocelyn. It was a measure of his irritation that for once he was prepared to stoop to cheap sarcasm.

'No.' He pointed. 'That's the speedometer.' Then he tapped the fuel gauge. 'Aye, it's empty all right. You'd better transfer to the Land Rover. Just switch off your lights and make sure all the windows are shut.'

They abandoned the car, Miss Thompson thinking: the man I've been wanting to meet, to tackle about his daughter; Jocelyn thinking, why didn't I let him see I not only knew which was the fuel gauge, I actually knew when it showed empty? Gaylord looking back enviously at the little car already half submerged in snow, the setting for a life and death adventure ruined by this interfering Scotsman.

Jocelyn said, 'Miss Thompson, this is Mr Mackintosh.'

Mackintosh said, 'Miss Thompson teaches my lassie.'

'Well, what a strange coincidence,' said Jocelyn.

'Aye,' said Mackintosh, unimpressed. He drove in silence. Jocelyn said, 'One feels so silly, running out of petrol.'

'I never let my tank get below a quarter full. Stick to that simple rule, Mr Pentecost, and you can't go far wrong.'

How absolutely right he was. And how impossible! But now a determined voice said, 'I think everybody ought to run out of petrol at least once in their lives. Stop them getting priggish.'

Clearly the bolt had shot home. Mackintosh drove a little way in silence. Then he said, 'I'd rather be priggish than daft, Miss Thompson.'

Anger, this time on behalf of Jocelyn Pentecost, again drove out fear. She said, 'When are you going to let your daughter do what she wants with her life, Mr Mackintosh?'

He did not reply. Only a sudden increase of speed showed that he had heard, and resented, the question.

She said, 'I asked you a question, Mr Mackintosh.'

'I heard ye. But may I remind ye, Mistress Thompson, that I'm her father and ye're just the person paid to teach her to read and write.' Only the relapse into his Scottish accent revealed his anger.

Jocelyn said, 'That's a very uncalled for remark, Mr Mackintosh.'

'If ye've any complaints about my behaviour, Mr Pentecost, I'll be glad if ye'll refer them to my employer, Mr Pentecost senior.'

Wendy Thompson said gratefully, 'You don't need to protect me, Mr Pentecost. I'm only interested in Julia's being allowed to dance. Suppose – suppose your parents had refused to let you be a writer, Mr Pentecost.'

Gaylord had been silent too long. 'Momma says that if Poppa hadn't been a writer he'd have been a blacksmith.'

'I doubt ye'd have had the handiness, Mr Pentecost,' said the Scotsman.

'Oh, for heaven's sake, man,' cried Jocelyn. 'It was just my wife's way of saying I'm no good with my hands.'

'Aye. I've often noticed, when the English want to say something they say the exact opposite. And then, when they've got you fair flummoxed' – he was beginning to sound bitter – 'they tell you it was just a wee joke.'

'Why won't you let Julia go to ballet school, Mr Mackintosh?'

'Och, awa',' he muttered. 'Because she'd be tired of it in a week.'

'She wouldn't.'

'And because I don't want any daughter of mine daffin' half naked in front of gawping fools.'

'We're discussing ballet, Mr Mackintosh. Not strip tease. Anyway, presumably you were content that your wife should –'

She had gone too far, stepped over the invisible line which shows what may, and what may not, be said. She knew it, and regretted it. He looked round furiously. 'Ye'll leave my dead wife out of this, Mistress Thompson.'

'Yes. I'm sorry. I shouldn't have said that. But I still think to stop Julia dancing will be to kill a part of the world's small store of joy.'

'Havers!' he said rudely.

'It will be like caging a skylark, Mr Mackintosh.'

He was silent. They were nearly at the farm. Then he sighed, and said, 'Ye're a rare fighting cock, Miss Thompson, for all your size. And I admire spirit. But ye're not to fill my Julia's head with your fancy ideas.'

'Her head doesn't need filling. It's full of them already.'

'Aye. So. Well, there you are, Mr Pentecost. And you remember. Whenever you're down to a quarter, fill up. Then maybe you won't find yourself in this kind of pickle. Goodnight to ye.' He drove away. His rear lights disappeared among the dancing snowflakes. 'Rude man! But he's not finished with me yet,' said little Miss Thompson. Then she looked at Jocelyn with alarm. 'Oh, dear, I'd meant to ask Mr Mackintosh whether he could possibly run me into Shepherd's Warning. But – I got so cross, I forgot.'

'My dear Miss Thompson, you'd never have got to Ingerby, anyway. No, my wife will fit you in somewhere. Then we'll get you home in the morning.'

'Oh, do stay, Miss Thompson,' cried Gaylord, who was still feeling very protective. He was beginning to wonder whether he might not marry Miss Thompson when he grew up, now that Auntie Becky was another's, and the lady in the Co-op butcher's had taken a step down in the charts.

Spend a night, with this alarming family? True, they were no longer quite as alarming as they had been. Mr Jocelyn Pentecost was most courteous and charming, and as for the little boy – On the other hand she still felt very wary of Mrs Pentecost. And, to someone who had almost all her meals alone, nowadays, the thought of supper and breakfast with a large family was frightening. Besides, they might want her to share a room with the old lady whose car she'd wrecked. Miss Thompson was given to describing herself as a lone wolf, though perhaps a lone lamb would be a more apt description; and the thought of her cosy bijou residence, with the doors shut and the curtains drawn, almost brought tears to her eyes. But her cosy bijou residence was separated from her by miles of snowy waste. She had not, it seemed to her, much choice in the matter.

May, finding Miss Wendy Thompson on the doorstep for the third time in one evening, had a not unsurprising sense of déjà vu.

She said, 'Oh, you're back, Jocelyn, I gather you weren't able to get through. Well, I'm not surprised. Now, Gaylord, straight up to bed. Poppa will bring you some supper.' Slight pause. 'Hello, Miss Thompson.'

Jocelyn said, 'I've told Miss Thompson you'll find her a bed, May.' He said it with a light laugh that rang as hollow as a cracked bell.

May, without looking at anybody, said, 'Of course, Miss Thompson, we shall be delighted to have you.'

'I'm afraid I'm being the most frightful nuisance,' said Miss Thompson.

'Not in the least.'

Gaylord, wishing to divert Momma's attention from what he knew, from bitter experience, would prove an idée fixe about his going straight up to bed, said, 'Momma, I saw an Abominable Snowman when we were broken down.'

'Did you, dear?' said May absently. A bell rang in her brain. 'Jocelyn, did you break down?'

It occurred to Gaylord that he had, unwittingly, sold Poppa down the river. He was sorry. United, he and Poppa had some slight chance of standing. Divided, Momma would make mincemeat of both of them. He said hurriedly, 'It wasn't Poppa's fault that we ran out of petrol, Momma. There must have been a hole in the tank.'

May said, 'Jocelyn, darling, you didn't? On a night like this?'

'It was all my fault,' said Miss Thompson.

May said, 'Nonsense, Miss Thompson. Of course it wasn't your fault.'

Jocelyn said, 'The fault was entirely mine.'

To his relief May gave her sudden, joyous laugh and said, 'What on earth does it matter, whose fault? You're all safe.

Except poor Miss Thompson, who's adrift in a house of strangers.' She gave Wendy a smile that made the poor girl her slave for life. 'Never mind, Miss Thompson. You'll find us friendly, when you get to know us. Even my father-in-law doesn't actually bite.'

'Oh, good,' said Wendy Thompson, beaming all over her face, knowing she sounded fatuous but being unable to think of anything else to say to this charming, beautiful and noble woman.

'And there were wolves, Momma,' said Gaylord in a last desperate fling to take his mother's mind off bed.

But the moment he had spoken, he realized his error. Normally, the moment his mother gave any sign that Gaylord's bedtime was on her mind, he became silent and self-effacing. But tonight, he realized, he must have been carried away by his adventure. Momma said, 'Off you go, Gaylord.'

And to her astonishment he went. She hoped he wasn't sickening. But then she saw what Gaylord had seen a second before her, and she understood his sudden submission: Great Aunt Bea, just coming out of the living room.

Bea was followed by Dorothea, Edouard, and John Pentecost.

Edouard carried a gin and tonic, John a whisky. John had an arm about the Frenchman's shoulder, and was talking to him earnestly about the Common Market, an institution which, he firmly believed, would mean an end of both Gilbert and Sullivan and County Cricket. May said, 'Monsieur, you have not met my husband, Jocelyn. Jocelyn, this is Monsieur Edouard St Michèle Bouverie.'

'How do you do?' formed on Jocelyn's lips. But the Frenchman said, 'Ah, Monsieur, you are a man above all others to be envied.'

'Really?' said Jocelyn. Yes, he supposed he was lucky, doing a job that fascinated him, no real money worries, two delightful children –

'Married to this – this "lass unparallel'd".' He made a tulip bud of his fingers, pressed it to his lips, and then with a flamboyant gesture flung the opening bud towards May.

Jocelyn was impressed. 'I see you know your Shakespeare,' he said appreciatively. It always pleased him when foreign devils quoted the Bard.

May said tartly, 'I don't think you know everybody, Miss Thompson.' She made vague introductions. 'Miss Thompson is staying the night with us,' she announced.

The Frenchman gave the impression that this was all he needed to make his cup of happiness full. Dorothea said sternly, 'I hope you'll drive more carefully in future, young lady.' May said, 'Well now, shall we say supper in half an hour?' Just time, she thought to change her frock, lay the table, slap a bit of powder on her nose, and catch the chickens before they finally disintegrated.

'That all right for you, old man?' Grandpa demanded earnestly of his dear friend Edouard.

'Splendid. Just nice time to change.'

'Oh, no need for that, old chap.' He took his arm from his companion's shoulder long enough to slap him on the back. 'Don't you go expecting anything grand. Just pot luck.' He grinned at his daughter-in-law. 'That's right, isn't it, May old girl.'

'That's right,' she said. She turned to the Frenchman. 'Actually, I've done a Coq au Vin with Pommes Anna and aubergines, followed by profiterolles. And I did wonder – ?'

'And you'll have a glass of good English beer to wash it down, eh,' said Grandpa.

'That would be delightful,' said Edouard, who thought English beer flat, warm, and quite undrinkable.

May said, 'Actually, Monsieur, I have cooled two bottles of Meursault Clos de Bouches Chères – the 1971. But' – for a moment she looked, much to Jocelyn's surprise, the helpless female – 'I know so little about wines, and if you would prefer beer – ?'

Edouard turned to John Pentecost. 'My old friend, you will forgive me. For no other wine would I refuse your beer. But for the Meursault – ' He kissed his hand to May. 'It is what the gods drink on Olympus, my charming niece-to-be.'

Jocelyn, drifting into sleep, suddenly lifted his head from the pillow and demanded: 'Where's Miss Thompson?'

May said shortly, 'She's in with Bea. Why, do you want her?'

'Lord, no. Just wondered.'

May sighed, and went back to sleep. Jocelyn said, 'Nice girl, isn't she. By Jove, she stood up to old Mackintosh.'

May was silent. 'Apparently his daughter wants to be a ballet dancer, and he won't have it. But I gather Miss Thompson intends to make a fight for it.'

'Bully for Wendy,' mumbled May.

'What? Oh, sorry, old girl. Sleepy, aren't you?'

Gaylord, too, lay awake a good five minutes thinking about Miss Thompson, devising for her fates worse than death from which he could rescue her (actually he found fates worse than death difficult to devise; but he thought up a few. Being roped to the line while the 3.14 out of Shepherd's Warning thundered ever nearer, was the most horrific); devising situations in which he, Gaylord, needed comfort, and found it in the tender voice, the soft and gentle face, of Wendy Thompson. He drifted into sleep, happy in the knowledge that he had solved one problem about his future, anyway.

Miss Thompson, quite unaware that she had been nominated the future Mrs Gaylord Pentecost, slept less easily. She had been put in with Aunt Bea who, just as Wendy was dropping off, had switched on her light, jerked up in her bed and said, 'Who are you, Miss – er? I always like to know whom I'm sleeping with.'

'I'm Wendy Thompson. I came to see Mr Pentecost about a lecture.' She too sat up. Courtesy, she felt, demanded it.

Bea hugged her knees cosily and said, 'I never get to sleep before four. Do you?'

'Well, yes, I – I sleep pretty well, actually.'

'Really? Then you should count yourself fortunate. But I do hope you don't snore. Do you?' she demanded, suddenly aggressive.

The rude forefathers of the hamlet, each in his narrow cell for ever laid, were not more solitary in their slumbers than poor Miss Thompson; so she was the only person who could possibly know whether she snored, and she was always asleep at the time. So she said, 'I – I don't think so.'

'Dorothea snores. Disgusting habit. Most unladylike.'

Miss Thompson said, 'If I do snore, you must wake me.'

'I shall, don't you worry.'

Aunt Bea still sat clasping her knees, but lapsed into silence. Miss Thompson didn't know whether the audience was over or not, but she was very tired; so she lay down, and soon images and thoughts began to merge and flicker, fantastical as firelight flickering on a wall. Her eyelids closed, her breathing deepened. 'You're getting ready to snore,' warned Bea suddenly.

'I – I'm terribly sorry.' Miss Thompson was wide awake and sitting up in a moment. 'Was I really?'

'Yes. Have you ever studied the Rococo?'

'I'm afraid I – '

'It would be a very silly thing to study,' said Aunt Bea firmly. She sat for some time in silent meditation. 'Gew-gaws,' she said at last. 'Fal-de-lals.'

'Really?' said Miss Thompson.

'One might almost,' pronounced Bea, 'say bric-à-brac.'

'I see.'

The old lady sat staring in front of her. She was silent; but Wendy felt that if she relaxed for a moment, Bea would strike. She was as unnerving as one of those cuckoo clocks in which, ten minutes before the hour, the bird begins to edge malevolently out of his house, filling a whole roomful of people with nervousness and unease.

'I always have cocoa at home,' said Bea.

Wendy, with a touch of spirit, thought: I can't sit here till four in the morning saying 'Really?' and 'I see'. So she said, 'I do think you ought to lie down and try to get some sleep.'

'It would be futile, quite futile.' After a time she said, 'Don't let me keep you awake, Miss Thompson.' She sounded grudging.

Wendy lay down. 'I am quite tired. Goodnight.'

'Goodnight.'

Oh, it was wonderful. Soft pillow, soft bed, tired body. Sleep stealing over her like an incoming tide. Bea said, 'Not afraid of mice, are you?'

'I – I don't like them,' said Wendy, bolt upright once more, and uttering the understatement of the year. She felt about mice as Gaylord's Greek gentleman must have felt about ravens.

Bea said, 'Well, you'd better learn to. There's a whole family of 'em playing catch-as-catch-can in that tallboy, if you ask me.'

CHAPTER 9

By next morning the English climate had turned one of those somersaults for which it is justly famous. The sun edged up into a flawless dome of icy blue steel. The world was a feather bed of snow. In that clean and empty scene there was no spot, no hint of the chaos that was about to descend from a clear sky.

Despite Aunt Bea and the mice Wendy had eventually slept, as she would have put it, like a top.

When we sleepers awake to a new day, we promptly set to work on a jigsaw puzzle of hopes and fears, of duties and cares and delights. Very soon we know we are facing a good day or a bad day, or a perfectly horrid day. But sometimes there is one piece of the jigsaw that is so bright and shining, or so black and huge, that it dominates all the rest.

So it was with Wendy Thompson. Whatever happened today, she was almost certain to spend some time with Mr Pentecost – Mr Pentecost, who was tall, and quietly spoken, and whose eyes lit so quickly into a kindly smile. This piece of the jigsaw shone with such radiance that she scarcely noticed the other pieces.

Even so, she rose to a day of unanswered questions. Never before had she breakfasted with a crowd of strangers. The last thing any of them seemed concerned about was the fact that Miss Thompson was stranded; and she was far too shy to bring up the subject herself.

Mrs Pentecost was kind, of course. 'Now, Miss Thompson, my father-in-law's unvarying breakfast is porridge, fried eggs, bacon, sausage, toast, marmalade and coffee. Jocelyn's is a piece of dry toast, and two cups of weak tea. You are welcome to either, or anything in between.'

Miss Thompson's favourite breakfast was toast fingers to dunk in a boiled egg, but she was far too well-bred to consider doing such a thing in public. Besides, Mrs Pentecost hadn't mentioned boiled eggs. So she said weakly, 'Do you think I might have a little toast and butter?'

It is difficult to think of a more innocuous remark. Yet it brought thunderbolts about her head: 'Toast and butter?' cried John Pentecost. 'You're as bad as Jocelyn there. What you want on a morning like this, young lady, is a good lining to your stomach. Eggs, bacon, porridge.' He rustled The Times indignantly. Enough irritation in the papers these days, without having some pale, mewling creature spoiling his breakfast.

'Well, hark who's talking,' said Aunt Bea. 'Believe me, John, you could cut out breakfast altogether, and lunch probably, and live on your fat for the next six months. Do you the world of good.'

Becky said, 'Nearly all men eat too much. They're only interested in their appetites.' She gave her husband a brilliant, brittle smile.

May, with the kindness and understanding that had already made Wendy her slave for life, said, 'Miss Thompson, ignore them. Here is the toast. Here is the butter. And the marmalade. If you took the dietary advice of this family you'd die of either starvation or surfeit.'

Gaylord said, 'Henry Bartlett's Auntie Mabel's sheep got surfeit in a clover field. And they lay on their backs, all blown up, with their legs in the air.'

May, imagining that her son was about to picture Miss Thompson in just such an unhappy predicament, stepped in hurriedly. 'That will do, Gaylord.'

But for once she had failed to read her son's thoughts correctly. Sir Lancelot never imagined his Guinevere so. And neither did Gaylord his Wendy. He said, 'Henry Bartlett's Uncle George had to puncture them with a sharp stick. Henry said it sounded like when he got a nail in his bicycle tyre.' He made realistic hissing noises.

Jocelyn began, 'You can't say, "It sounded like when – " ' but he was brushed aside by Grandpa who said, with icy precision, 'Two minutes ago, I suggested that Miss Thompson should guard herself against the winter's chill. This kindly and constructive suggestion was immediately seized upon, turned inside out, used as a stick with which to beat not only me but my sex generally, and finally used to introduce a graphic word picture of rustic goings-on worthy of Thomas Hardy.'

Gaylord looked hurt. 'I only said – '

'Well don't,' said Grandpa rudely. He tugged angrily at his napkin.

Miss Thompson felt very uncomfortable, and sat nibbling her toast with downcast eyes, wondering how and when she could get back to her bijou residence. (Oh, the peace of her solitary room, the world forgetting, by the world forgot! And yet – the silence of the grave!) May Pentecost watched her, and thought: poor little mouse, with the superficial detached kindness of a good hostess. But that was where the kindness stopped. Miss Thompson was a woman of thirty, not unattractive: and, as such, made the tigress that sleeps in every woman stir uneasily.

But Jocelyn watched her and thought: how vulnerable she looks, how she must hate being thrown among strangers at this the bleakest hour of the day. He said, 'I wondered whether you'd like to see my study after breakfast, Miss Thompson. Not much to see I'm afraid, but – '

She looked up at her name, flushed with pleasure. 'Oh, Mr Pentecost, I'd love to.'

The tigress in May gave her the tigerish equivalent of a nudge and muttered the tigerish equivalent of 'Hey! Watch it.' May said, 'Oh, don't expect too much, Miss Thompson. It's only one of the small bedrooms, tarted up with a desk and a dictionary or two.'

Miss Thompson said blissfully, 'But that's not what matters. It's a – it's a sort of power house.'

'Good God,' said Grandpa, who thought he'd never heard such damn nonsense in his life. But May was silent, thoughtful. It had never occurred to her to think of her husband's workroom as a powerhouse. And yet – ? Things were created there, just as much as in that vast, simmering power station across the valley. She felt a belated pride – and kicked herself for having left it to another woman to open her eyes.

But now breakfast was drawing to a close. The old man was on his third, and therefore last, piece of toast. (There had been one memorable day when he'd had only two pieces. And, sure enough, by lunch time he'd been down with 'flu. And on the day of Princess Anne's wedding he had, in a burst of patriotic fervour, eaten four. All the other days of his life, it had been three.)

May was just thinking: Well, that's another meal over without anyone being too rude to anyone else, when she suddenly caught sight of Gaylord's face, and realized from its look of delight that his fruit-machine of a brain had come up with the jackpot. She made to rise. But she was too late. 'Uncle Peter. You know Auntie Becky said you were going to be somethinged by a gorgeous redhead but I couldn't remember what?'

'Well, if everyone's finished – ' said May hopefully. No one took the slightest notice of her. Most of them were too agog. Jocelyn, who wanted to get Miss Thompson over so that he could do some work, shifted restlessly. Grandpa was deep in The Times leader. But the two great aunts looked at Peter, and then at Becky, and it is doubtful whether wild horses could have dragged them from the table. Becky watched her husband with a joyous eagerness to see his reactions. Edouard looked at Peter with interest and a dawning respect.

Peter went very red, and said nothing.

Gaylord said triumphantly, 'I've remembered what it was. It was seduced. What does seduced mean, Poppa?'

Jocelyn said, 'It can mean a number of things. It's from the Latin ducere, to lead, and – '

Becky said, 'Oh, Jocelyn, don't be so feeble.' She gave Gaylord the brilliant, intimate smile that had the effect of an undipped headlight on all men from seven to seventy. 'Darling, it means Uncle Peter's being led by the nose like a performing bear.'

It was all very difficult. 'But Uncle Peter said it was a bird.'

'So it is, my pet. A bird of gorgeous plumage.'

Gaylord mulled this over. Birds, performing bears? He gave up. 'Can I go and play now, Momma?'

The tension broke like a fiddle string. May rose. But she looked at Gaylord with some misgiving. She hoped he wasn't losing his grip. It wasn't like him to leave the orange of embarrassment only half sucked.

Everyone rose. Peter surreptitiously mopped his brow. His wife came and took his arm. Smiling up into his face, she led him into the living room. The others followed. 'That young chap going off the rails a bit, is he?' boomed Aunt Bea. 'Had the same trouble with Ben at that age. With an assistant librarian, forsooth.'

Everyone was so astonished at this amazing disclosure about the deceased Great Uncle Ben that complete silence fell. 'Wouldn't have minded so much if she'd been an opera singer,' mused Bea.

'Or even a chorus girl,' said Dorothea.

They pondered. 'And she was a Methodist,' said Bea.

'Name of Myrtle,' said Dorothea. She sighed. They both sighed.

After this there really seemed nothing to say, so they all strolled across to the french windows, drawn by the brilliance of the morning.

The old, white-painted windows opened on to a white lawn, which fell away to meadows and the black snake of river. They stood in the pleasant warmth, separated by a frame of wood and glass from a winter world, from snow and ice and pinching cold. They gazed out.

The only moving thing in that world of brilliant blue and white was a tiny figure trudging along the river road, pulling a sledge.

The party in the living room watched with the fascination the human eye always shows in a moving object. 'Looks like a page who's lost his Good King Wenceslas,' said Grandpa, lighting his dear friend Edouard's first cigar for him.

Gaylord didn't think that sounded very likely, though one could never be sure, of course. He looked more closely. 'It's Henry Bartlett,' he said. Grandpa, his own cigar now going nicely, held out the match. Gaylord blew. 'I knew it wasn't a page,' he said scornfully. 'Momma, can I go and meet Henry? And take Schultz?'

'Yes. Wrap up. It's icy out there.'

He set off. The snow was crisp, dry, sparkling; the most wonderful and extravagant gift a benevolent heaven could give a small boy.

But Schultz wasn't so sure. To a puppy whose body was the size of a small calf, but whose intelligence would sit on a pin head, the discovery that, while he slept, someone had given the whole green world three coats of some sort of whitewash was disconcerting to say the least. And when, after barking at this whitewash, growling at it, backing away from it, charging at it, he found it not only didn't go away, but froze his paws and even tried to swallow him, the effect could almost be described as traumatic. And where were his playmates? Schultz regarded the whole animal kingdom as his playmates, from the birds and bees and butterflies to Heathcliff the bull. But this morning – not a bee in sight, not a butterfly to chase with snapping jaws. Schultz felt he deserved some sort of explanation.

Goodness, it was deep. What with the brilliance of the morning, and the way the snow fluffed up in front of his wellies, and the braggadocio antics of Schultz, and the crisp air, and the thought of snowballs and snowmen and sledging, and the knowledge that he was on his way to meet his dear friend Henry Bartlett – all this made Gaylord so happy that he almost felt like bursting. He had to express his happiness in some way, so he whistled gaily. Or rather, since whistling is a difficult art, and Gaylord had not yet mastered the ability to produce a tune, he went along sizzling happily like a kettle that is just off the boil, kicking at the snow, and watching the round, smooth, pink, bespectacled face of his dear friend Henry approaching like another little sun in that white waste.

They met. 'You know my Uncle Peter?' said Gaylord.

'No,' said Henry.

'He's going to be seduced,' said Gaylord.

Henry Bartlett looked impressed.

'And we nearly perished in the snow last night.'

Henry Bartlett looked even more impressed.

'If Mr Mackintosh hadn't rescued us we should have done.'

Henry Bartlett cogitated. 'I nearly fell in the river,' he said, in a half-hearted attempt to keep up. But it was no use. It didn't ring true. Not like perishing in the snow.

'I bet you'd have frozen to death straight off if you had,' Gaylord said kindly.

Henry Bartlett nodded. They concentrated their thought, ingenuity, and energy on pulling a tangled brier clear of the snow. Schultz, panting, chin almost on the ground, never took his eyes from the brier, and gave it an occasional warning growl lest it have any thoughts of attacking the young master. 'Sledges,' said Henry.

Gaylord waited. Henry said, 'You can't ride and pull at the same time.'

It was a good point. Gaylord could see no flaw in it. Henry said, 'You'd think someone would invent something.'

Gaylord thought so too.

The brier, with a flurry of snow, came clear. They looked at it in mild surprise. Now they had got it loose they didn't quite know what to do with it. Schultz went and sniffed at it hopefully. But it wasn't a playmate. Life was full of disappointments this morning.

Henry said, 'I don't think there's much point in a sledge when you're on your own.' This feeling had been growing on him all the way from Shepherd's Warning.

'No,' said Gaylord. An idea struck him. 'You could pull me,' he said. 'Then,' he added a little less enthusiastically, 'I could pull you.'

It was a brilliant solution. Gaylord sat on the sledge and Henry pulled. And the runners hissed and rang, and Schultz cavorted beside them barking for very joy. And Henry thought how wonderful it was to have a brilliant, clear-minded friend like Gaylord Pentecost.

'Yellow the Leaves,' said Miss Thompson, looking at the shelves in Jocelyn's study. 'It's a lovely title, for a lovely book.'

'Thank you,' he said. He was pleased. He could never not be pleased by flattery. Yet it was, in a way, Dead Sea Fruit. It only served to underline the difference between the Jocelyn Pentecost who had written that book at such joyous speed, and the present dried-up incumbent.

She looked round the room. Her lips were parted, her eyes shone. He had seen the same wonder on faces in the Birthplace at Stratford. 'So this is where it's all done,' she said.

'Actually,' he said, 'I'm afraid it isn't at present. I just don't seem to feel things any more. I've become – anaesthetized.'

'You mean – you're not writing?'

'I'm trying to. Oh, I can still put words together. But – my new novel just won't grow.'

She looked horrified. 'But it must. The world's waiting for it.'

He gave a hollow laugh. 'If I never wrote another line, the world wouldn't even notice.'

She crossed to the window. Outside, two small boys and a dog, in a timeless Brueghel landscape. After a moment she turned and looked up at Jocelyn. An anxious face, she thought, lean and long, yet with laughter lines about the eyes, and a mouth that easily smiled. She said, 'Mr Pentecost, do you mind if I speak plainly?'

He was taken aback. He was used to the family speaking plainly, very plainly. But he wouldn't expect that sort of thing from a comparative stranger. Still, he'd heard Miss Thompson in action against Mackintosh. So he braced himself. 'Of course not,' he said.

She took a deep breath. 'Mr Pentecost, you're not fair to yourself. You can write books, wonderful books. Yet you say dreadful things like "the world wouldn't even notice".'

'It's just the truth,' he said, smiling.

'It isn't. A lot of people are waiting for your next book. You've got to write it.'

'So what do you recommend?' he asked. He was still smiling. Nevertheless, he was already beginning to see himself in a new, and more impressive, light.

'Why, that you take yourself more seriously.' The vague, fluttering Miss Thompson of yesterday was growing in stature as quickly as Jocelyn's mental image of himself. 'That you stop being at everybody's beck and call.'

An iron door clanged. He said coldly, 'My family life is my concern, Miss Thompson.'

When the pleasant, easy-going Jocelyn did speak coldly, he created a surprising chill. Miss Thompson went straight back to being the nervous, unsure creature of the previous evening. She swallowed twice, went very red, and said, 'I'm sorry. That must have sounded very impertinent.' She glanced helplessly round the room. 'I think I should go home now.'

He was immediately contrite. Poor little soul! He never believed that he could frighten anyone. Yet clearly he'd frightened the life out of her. He said, very gently, 'I'm sorry, Miss Thompson.'

She was looking out of the window again. She said, 'Would you believe me if I said that I had only myself and my club in mind when I said "everybody's beck and call"? After all, what do I know of your family life, sir?'

Sir? That word shifted the balance of their relationship. He felt as though he had demeaned her.

She said, 'Asking you to waste your time on us. Me foisting myself on you last night. Me letting you try to run me home. Me, talking to you now when all the time you should be writing. Writing, Mr Pentecost, writing. That's what you were sent into the world for.'

He said, 'I do not regard addressing your club as a waste of my time. And I should get nowhere if I tried to write. Something's happened' – he gave his chest an irritated blow with his fist – 'here.' He too was gazing out of the window, now, at the timeless game of boys and dog and snow. 'And, as for this morning' – he turned and gave her a grave, searching look – 'it has been a great pleasure, Miss Thompson.'

'For me, too,' she said quietly.

They went on staring out of the window. He said, 'Do you know your Hardy? "Yet this will go onward the same Though Dynasties pass"?'

'Yes,' she said. ' "Only a man harrowing clods – " And the thin smoke without flame. And the lovers. He could have added, "And the children at play".'

'Yes,' he said. They were silent. Then, to his astonishment he heard himself say, 'Let's go and join them.'

'Who? Your son, and the other boy?'

'Yes.' He wasn't often boyish. But he was now.

'But Mr Pentecost, I must be getting back. I – '

'See you in the hall in five minutes,' he said. 'Booted and spurred.'

She stared at him. Then she gave him a quick, bewildered grin, and went. He stayed, looking grave. He strolled across to his desk, looked for a moment at his open manuscript.

Then he shut it, with a movement almost of contempt; he went downstairs, and put on coat, scarf, gloves and wellingtons.

Schultz had already forgotten that there had been a time when the earth was green. The snow had become his natural element. He tossed it, burrowed in it, rolled in it, worried it, ate it. One would have said his cup of happiness was full. Yet evidently there was room for a drop or two more. For when he spotted two more playmates coming across the lawn he went quite delirious with joy and cavorted off to meet them. With Miss Thompson he went straight into what May called his window-cleaner act, propping himself against her chest and licking her face with intemperate delight. Since the only other dog Miss Thompson had known socially had been a detestable little poodle of her mother's which spent its entire waking life yapping in hysterical rage, she found the warmth of this welcome indescribably touching.

The boys too seemed pleased to see them. Jocelyn said, 'This is Henry, Miss Thompson.'

Henry went pink; or to be more accurate, pinker. Miss Thompson said, 'How do you do, Henry?' Gaylord thought he ought to tell Miss Thompson about his intention to marry her, but decided this wasn't quite the moment. Jocelyn thought how very much he would like to make a snowman, but didn't like to suggest it. He knew how good-natured the other three were. He didn't want them all toiling away and getting chilblains just to please him. Nevertheless he said, 'I don't suppose anyone would like to make a snowman?'

Gaylord looked eager, then doubtful. 'Do you think Momma would let us?'

It was not the sort of remark Jocelyn would have chosen for Miss Thompson to hear, in view of the undertones of their recent conversation. But he said, smiling, 'Don't worry, Gaylord. I'll take full responsibility.'

Gaylord went on looking doubtful. He always felt very responsible for Poppa. Still, so long as they stood together. 'I'll get some shovels and things,' he said, and turning into a snowcat he disappeared towards the farm buildings in a flurry of snow.

Grandpa, glancing out of the window, said unkindly, 'Good Lord, Jocelyn doing a bit of manual work! And he was out with Peter before breakfast, retrieving that car of his.' He opened the window, called, 'Jocelyn! You'll be knocking yourself up.'

Jocelyn grinned and waved. His father's belief that writing books was the world's most effete way of earning a living sometimes amused, sometimes irritated. Today, so rare was the morning, so pleasant was it to have an admiring companion, he was amused.

Becky said, 'That's what you ought to be doing, Peter.' She grinned. 'Sublimation through toil.'

Aunt Bea cried, 'That's not the way to make a snowman. They're not organized. They're just playing at it.'

'It certainly does look nice out there,' said aunt Dorothea wistfully. 'Let us take a stroll, Edouard.'

Edouard hid his dismay. Snow was very pretty, but one didn't go out in it. Nevertheless, when in Rome – He rose courteously, and gave his arm to his beloved.

John Pentecost, muffled to the eyebrows, and with snow on his boots, marched into the kitchen where May was toiling over a hot stove. 'Hello, my dear.'

It was, she realized, the gruff, affectionate, yet slightly sheepish greeting the old man used when he wanted something. 'Hello, Father-in-law,' she said non-committally, concentrating more on raising an oven shelf than on him. 'Come to lend a hand?'

'Well, actually,' he said, 'I've come to ask a favour. We're all out on the lawn making a snowman. And I wondered' – he paused – 'a bowl of hot punch would go down awfully well, May.'

She straightened up, looked at him in silence, unsmiling. Then: 'Give me twenty minutes,' she said.

'Good girl,' he said, touching her shoulder. He went. That was what he liked about May. She made everything so easy. An extra little job or two meant nothing to her.

Jocelyn was wishing the snowman in Hanover. What had begun as a jeu d'esprit inspired by a brilliant morning had developed into a major construction job with five labourers and a whole army of advisors, critics, foremen and overseers. Why, they'd only just started when Duncan and Elspeth Mackintosh had appeared with Julia. Julia had flung herself shyly but happily into the fray, despite the astonishing presence of her schoolteacher. But Mackintosh and Elspeth had watched with dour disapproval until Mackintosh went and found a shovel and, with a look of martyrdom, began clearing the drive; and, after a few minutes, Miss Mackintosh had called to Julia to 'go and help Daddy with something useful.'

The child looked forlorn. 'Mr Pentecost wants me to help with the snowman, Aunt,' she pleaded.

'Ye heard what I said, Julia,' said Elspeth primly.

Julia looked at Jocelyn for guidance.

Jocelyn was one of those people who have the misfortune to see the other fellow's side in every argument. Of course the drive needed clearing. Of course Mackintosh was right to tackle it. Of course Jocelyn ought to be using his energy on the drive instead of on a snowman. In fact, he would probably have felt shamed into going and helping Mackintosh, had he not been convinced that Mackintosh would tell him he wasn't doing it right.

But others did not suffer from the same disability. Gaylord, seeing the longing in the eyes that had recently been so happy, said out of the side of his mouth, 'You stay here, Julia. This is ever so useful.'

But Miss Mackintosh knew insubordination when she saw it. 'What did ye say, laddie?'

Gaylord gave her a dirty look. 'Och, awa', woman,' he said. He didn't know what it meant, but he sensed that it just about summed up his feelings.

Miss Mackintosh went and planted herself in front of Jocelyn. 'Did ye hear what your son said to me, Mr Pentecost?'

'No?'

'He's a rude wee laddie.'

Jocelyn said sternly, 'Were you rude to Miss Mackintosh, Gaylord?'

'Aye. I was that,' said Gaylord, in what was undoubtedly an embryo Scottish accent.

Jocelyn was horrified. 'When you mean yes, say yes. Not that dreadful Aye sound.'

'And what's wrang wi' the dreadful Aye sound?' demanded the affronted Miss Mackintosh.

Jocelyn had had enough. 'It is either archaic, nautical, or Scots, madam,' he said coldly. Good Lord, he thought, hearing himself. I sounded just like my father.

'And what's wrang wi' Scots?' demanded Elspeth.

'Nothing, in its place,' he said blandly.

Miss Mackintosh bridled; but seemed stumped for an answer. So she called to her brother. 'Duncan, get Julia to help you.'

'Come and give me a hand, Julia,' he called.

Ill temper, on this bright morning, seemed to be infectious. Miss Thompson strode over to the drive. She glared at the Scotsman. 'Can't you see how she's enjoying it with the other children?' she demanded. 'Can't you let her enjoy herself, just for once?'

For a long moment they stared furiously at each other. Then he slammed his shovel into a foot of snow. 'Pentecost can clear his own drive,' he muttered. And working himself into his leather coat he joined his sister and watched the snowman-building party.

That, however, had been only the beginning. Dorothea had come out on Edouard's arm; and, with Mackintosh well in earshot, had called solicitously, 'Ought you to be doing that, Jocelyn? You're not used to work, remember.' Then Bea: 'You'll never get anywhere like that, Jocelyn. Here, let me show you.' She had put herself in charge. Jocelyn was not pleased. He wasn't pleased when he heard his father saying to Edouard, 'May's bringing some punch out. Fine woman, May.' He lowered his voice, but not quite enough. 'Sometimes I wonder how young Jocelyn would manage without her.' And he was far from pleased when Aunt Bea got him using the sledge to bring snow from an outlying drift. Talk about being at someone's beck and call! Aunt Bea was treating him like one of the slaves on the old plantation. ' "Tote dat barge, lift dat bale",' he was just muttering to himself bitterly, when he saw a sight that instantly restored his good humour: his wife May, looking absolutely radiant in a suède coat and fur-lined hood, carrying a large tray. And on the tray a great steaming bowl, and a supply of glasses, and a plate of mince pies. And on her face the smile whose serenity and friendliness embraced them all. He thought: eight years. Eight years I've been married, and my heart can still leap at the sight of my own wife.

Nor was Jocelyn's the only heart to leap at the sight of May. Edouard's did, as it always did at sight of a pretty woman. Grandpa's did, as it always did at sight of a bowl of punch. Schultz's did, as it always did at sight of another playmate.

The dog bounded joyfully forward to meet her. He just couldn't wait to go into his window-cleaner routine.

'Jocelyn!' screamed May. 'Quick! Get the dog! He'll knock the tray for six.'

'Eh? What's that old girl?' asked Jocelyn, whose excellent brain could cope with only one thing at a time, and was at the moment wholly engaged in thinking how little he deserved such a splendid wife.

'The dog!' cried May. The bowl of punch was beginning to slide across the tray.

'Down, Schultz!' yelled Jocelyn, cottoning on at last. 'Down I say.'

But 'Down' was not one of Schultz's few key words. In fact it was doubtful whether he had yet learnt that he was Schultz. He continued to bound.

'Get that damn dog off,' roared John Pentecost to all and sundry. The sight of a bowl of punch in jeopardy was something too dreadful to contemplate.

Jocelyn became the man of action. He grabbed the tray from his wife, and carried it safely to a wrought-iron table. He turned to receive May's plaudits, only to find her lying in the snow with Schultz standing on her ecstatically licking her face.

He sprang forward, but he was too late. Mr Mackintosh and the Frenchman were already succouring his wife in their very different ways. Mackintosh by dragging off the hound, Edouard by helping May to her feet, dusting off the snow, patting her hand, holding her arm, and uttering Gallic cries of concern and solicitude.

'May, are you hurt? What happened?' cried Jocelyn.

Mackintosh said, 'The dog tripped her just as you'd upset her balance by taking that heavy tray.'

'Formidable!' Edouard was sighing.

There was clearly something about Mackintosh that got under the easy going Jocelyn's skin. 'Are you suggesting that it was my fault?' he asked angrily.

The Scotsman shrugged. 'You certainly didn't help.'

Jocelyn tried to get near his wife; but Edouard was protecting her like a mother hen her chick. 'You must lie down,' he was insisting, 'in a darkened room. And perhaps a smelling bottle, or some sal volatile – '

'I'm hanged if I will,' laughed May. Though she had to admit her laughter rang a bit hollow. In the fall, her head had struck something hard with a force that surprised her. Her teeth had jarred. She was still seeing quite a firework display.

Jocelyn pushed his way in. 'Are you hurt?'

May seemed to become aware of him for the first time. She was one who hated fuss (though being pampered by an expert really was rather delightful). 'Of course not, darling,' she said. Then, with what seemed to Jocelyn a slight chill in her voice, 'Thank you for saving the punch, dear.'

Oh, Lord, he thought: the doghouse. And he'd been so pleased with himself. After all, it hadn't taken him long to assess the situation; and the moment he had, he had acted. Frankly, he'd expected a medal. Instead of which the general impression seemed to be that he'd done his best to clobber his wife.

May ignored the fireworks. 'Now then, everyone,' she cried. 'Let's have the punch before it's cold.' They gathered round the table, laughing, chattering, stamping their feet in the cold, lifting up their faces to the cold sun, staring with wonder at the blue and white emptiness that surrounded them. It was one of those rare moments when time and the world seem to stand still, and love and happiness are caught like flowers in a glass paperweight; one of those moments when it is as though a spirit of harmony touches the world with its wings – and passes on.

And passes on... May, having served the hot punch, said, 'Now Gaylord, see what your little friends would like.'

'What would you like, Julia?' he asked. 'Lemonade?'

'Yes, please, Gaylord.'

'Och, we don't want to chill your inside wi' that cauld stuff,' cried Miss Mackintosh. 'A wee glass of hot milk is what you want, child.'

Gaylord thought he had never seen anyone look as sad as his young friend. He said stoutly, 'I'll fetch you some lemonade, Julia.'

'She'll have milk or nothing,' said Miss Mackintosh.

There really must have been something very abrasive about the Mackintoshes; for now Gaylord did something that shocked and astonished him as much as it shocked and astonished his parents. He put out his tongue at Miss Mackintosh.

Miss Mackintosh very deliberately smacked his head.

Gaylord, pink as a lobster, stomped with tremendous dignity into the house.

May strode furiously up to Elspeth Mackintosh. 'How dare you?' Then she marched into the house, dragged out Gaylord, flung him towards Miss Mackintosh and told him in an awful voice to apologize.

Gaylord stood mute. 'Gaylord, will you apologize!'

'No,' said Gaylord.

Miss Mackintosh said, 'Duncan! If the wean has not apologized by midday, I'm awa' w' ma bags.'

'I think it would be as well if you did leave,' said May. 'Since you have so little self-control.'

Duncan Mackintosh was looking rather less like Aberdeen granite than usual. He took John Pentecost on one side and, with what was almost a smile, said, 'My sister is not one to make idle threats, Mr Pentecost. If the laddie doesn't apologize, we may find ourselves in a difficult situation.'

'We may, Mr Mackintosh? We may?'

The smile faded. 'I may, Mr Pentecost.'

'That's better. Oh, come and have a glass of punch, man. This is women's work. They'll sort it out.'

May said, 'Gaylord, you've been a very rude little boy, and I'm ashamed of you. Now will you apologize?'

'No.' He looked up at her piteously. His face was determined but apologetic, 'I'm sorry, Momma.'

Well, she certainly didn't blame him. 'Come into the house, Miss Mackintosh,' she said grimly.

Elspeth followed her in. May turned and faced her. 'Now, Miss Mackintosh. I apologize for my little boy's rudeness.'

Elspeth looked at her coolly. 'Aye. Since ye obviously haven't enough control over the boy to make him apologize, I'll accept that.'

May was silent. Then she said, 'But if ever you touch either of my children again, you'll leave immediately.'

'Och, ye canna dismiss me, Mrs Pentecost. And if ye're talking of dismissing my brother – ye'll have the old man to reckon with.'

The two women stared at each other – hard, defiant, relentless. Then May said, 'That will be all, Miss Mackintosh.' The Scotswoman stared at her insolently; then turned and went.

May sat down. She was trembling. She hated giving way to anger, feeling it was a dreadful waste of nervous energy. But there were times – Her head was aching. Most unusual. She really musn't let Miss Mackintosh work her up in this way. After all, Miss Mackintosh looked like being part of her life for a long time.

Edouard St Michèle Bouverie was desolated when May went into the house. On the feminine side it left only his fiancée; the lovely Becky, whose husband was sticking very close; the pale little Miss; and Bea, whom he was inclined to lump with the men. And, of course, an exquisite little girl of eight or so.

Edouard liked little girls; and not only because they grew up into big girls. He liked them because they were beautiful and graceful and sweet, and possessed an innocence that seared the heart. He took his drink and wandered over to the pale English Miss; he thought talking to men a waste of time when ladies were present.

Wendy Thompson looked at him gratefully. She had been having such a splendid morning. This leisurely, comfortable, amused world was something new to her. And talking to a famous author like Mr Pentecost had been a wonderful experience. But then, suddenly, she had found herself alone. Mr Pentecost had seemed to go away inside himself. So she had stood, self-consciously sipping her punch, and feeling her determinedly happy smile congeal on her features.

Gaylord, Henry Bartlett and Julia were toiling away at the snowman. the Frenchman smiled at Wendy and gave her a little bow. 'She is beautiful, the little one.'

'Yes, indeed,' said Wendy, trying hard not to gush. 'A lovely little girl.' She almost giggled. She wasn't used to punch. 'She's my favourite pupil, even though I know one shouldn't have favourites.'

'So? You are her teacher?'

She nodded. 'Actually,' she said confidentially, 'she wants to be a ballet dancer. But her father won't hear of it.'

'No! And what does this Monsieur her father want her to be?'

'Oh, I don't know. Something useful. A shorthand typist, I think.'

'Mon Dieu! But she is exquisite. Introduce me, please.'

Wendy called Julia. The girl came running. She looked up at them shyly. Wendy said, 'This is Julia. Julia, this is Monsieur Bouverie.'

He said, 'Give me your hand, child.'

Wondering, and a little afraid, she held out her hand. He stooped, kissed it. 'I salute,' he said smiling, 'the future Assoluta.'

It was absurd, but Miss Thompson felt the tears in her eyes. It was the rum punch, of course. She said, 'Julia must dance for you.' Again a stifled giggle. 'But not in her wellingtons.'

'No,' he said gravely. 'Not in her wellingtons.' He looked at Miss Thompson's small but determined face. 'You have spoken to the father?'

'Yes. Twice.'

'And what did he say?'

'He – was rather rude.'

'So.' He turned to the girl. 'And you really want to dance? All day, every day, until your legs are like lead, and it is an agony to lift your arms, and your back is breaking?'

'Oh, yes, sir.' Her face was radiant. But suddenly his face looked old, and helpless. 'Oh, damn.' He turned back to Wendy. 'What can we do? The man is her father. And – who knows – she might lose interest after a week.'

'I don't think so. I know her. She's a determined young woman for all her sweetness.'

He stared at her, long and hard. 'Which makes two of you,' he said cryptically. Then he shook his head. 'It's no good, Miss Thompson. We cannot play God.'

'We could have a jolly good try,' she said.

Another long stare. Then, gravely, he stooped and kissed her hand; and went to talk to Becky.

Grandpa buttonholed Jocelyn. 'I suppose you've not forgotten Becky wants us to have a word with Peter about this redhead?'

Jocelyn said, 'My dear father, we can't. We should make things a hundred times worse.'

'Nonsense! It's all a question of approach. Of course, if you go at it like a bull at a gate – But a bit of finesse can work wonders.' Nevertheless, he had to admit it wasn't the sort of thing anybody could do. It did need tact and understanding. Perhaps he ought to handle it himself. He went up to Peter and Becky, gave Becky a warning scowl which she rightly interpreted as, 'Leave him to me, girl, while I do a bit of Dutch uncle-ing,' slipped his arm into Peter's, and said, 'Now, my dear fellow, come and let me get you another glass of punch.'

'Thank you,' said Peter uneasily.

The old man pushed a full glass into his hand. They both sipped, while Grandpa decided on the most tactful approach, and Peter braced himself for what he felt was going to be a difficult ten minutes.

Grandpa said musingly, 'A sweet girl, Becky.'

'Very, sir.'

'Not – regretted your choice, I hope?'

'Good heavens, no, sir.'

'Then why the hell,' demanded Grandpa, 'are you making her so unhappy?'

'I'm – not, Father-in-law.'

''Course you are. Look at her. Moping.' Peter looked. Becky and the Frenchman were strolling in the sunshine, deep in conversation. Her hand rested lightly on his forearm. Edouard looked supremely happy, as indeed he was. Becky was smiling delightedly at what her uncle-to-be was telling her. It was a long time, thought Peter, since she'd smiled like that at him. He said bitterly, 'Moping? She's laughing her head off.'

'Rubbish! A wan little smile, perhaps. She looks to me like that girl in Shakespeare.'

'What girl in Shakespeare?' Peter asked sulkily.

'The "patience-on-a-monument-smiling-at-grief" one.'

'There's nothing of "patience-on-a-monument" about your daughter,' said Peter. ' "Impatience throwing saucepans at a chap" would be more like it.'

'Have some more punch,' said John Pentecost. 'How dare you criticize Becky?'

'She seems to have criticized me, right and left.'

'Well, dash it, she had good reason. Can't go playing fast and loose, my dear fellow. Not done.'

'I have not been playing fast and loose,' shouted the furious Peter.

'But you would if I gave you half a chance, darling,' called Becky sweetly.

'You keep out of this,' shouted Grandpa. He did wish people would mind their own business.

'This mistress of your husband's,' enquired Edouard with interest. 'She is beautiful, yes?'

Becky took her hand from his arm, the better to look him full in the face. 'I don't – who says she's his mistress?' she demanded in astonishment.

He shrugged. 'Naturally, I assumed – '

'Well, I'll thank you not to assume things like that about my husband,' Becky said, hoity-toity.

Edouard, not quite sure whose side who was on, decided to keep quiet. But it was all very puzzling. At last he said, 'But if she is not his mistress, then why all this brouhaha?' He gave her hand an avuncular little squeeze. 'May I give you a little advice, my dear?'

'Of course,' she said coldly.

He said, 'The great art of marriage is never to let the molehills grow into mountains. Keep them molehills, my dear Becky. Look what happened to Othello.'

She was laughing, now. 'I hadn't actually thought of smothering Peter with a pillow.'

'No. Now do you think your father would give us another glass of punch if we asked him?' They went across and joined a wary Peter and a John Pentecost who feared that all his tact and understanding were going to be wasted by this intrusion. Edouard addressed himself to Peter. 'My dear sir, may I speak from my heart?'

Peter looked even more wary. 'Yes?'

'Take back your wife, monsieur. She is so altogether charming, so beautiful, that I dare walk with her no longer. I am captivated, monsieur. And that is not good for an engaged man.' He took Becky's hand and put it on Peter's arm. 'Allez, mes enfants.' He shoved them away. Becky grinned up at her husband. 'Oh, Peter, you are a clot,' she said fondly. She reached up and kissed him. He looked embarrassed but pleased. They went off arm in arm. Becky said, 'Do you know, he asked me whether your mistress was beautiful.'

'Well, the cheeky devil,' said Peter.

John Pentecost watched them go. It was what he always said: tact and understanding. They worked wonders. He was glad he'd tackled it himself. Young Jocelyn would only have made a mess of it.

CHAPTER 10

It is a well-known fact that grown-ups can never concentrate on anything for very long, so Gaylord was not a bit surprised when, after the punch break, they rather forgot about the snowman, and drifted in twos and threes back into the house. Only Miss Thompson looked back wistfully at the two vast and trunkless legs of snow which were all they had achieved: wistfully, because he was a passing monument to a happy hour, a monument less enduring than memory, built of a stuff as transient as time itself.

Once, on holiday, when she was seventeen, Wendy Thompson had gone down to the seashore before breakfast.

Sea and sand had shed their long aeons. They gleamed as fresh as toys pulled from a Christmas stocking. Each little wave laid a cloth of lace on the wet sand. The wind whipped off the sea, slapping her cheeks to colour, laying salt on lips and tongue. On that sparkling morning, when she was seventeen, Wendy danced on a lonely shore, a dance of praise and exultation. On that brilliant morning, when she was seventeen, Wendy caught a glimpse of what life was, or could be, about. Ever since then, the dust of life with Mother had settled upon her, dulling the bright memory. The salt had been wiped from her lips. The wind still blew, the sea still ran; but the dancing, seventeen-year-old girl was gone for ever.

Strangely, her stay with the Pentecosts had reminded her of that faraway shore. There was a briskness about them, there was the tang of salt in their conversation. Being with them she again caught a glimpse of what life was, or could be, about.

But now it was time to go, to leave the salt wind and the spray, to go back to her genteel tomb of a house.

Jocelyn Pentecost saw her backward glance at the snowman. ' "My name is Ozymandias, King of Kings," ' he murmured. Grandpa gave him a funny look. No one else had heard him. Only Wendy Thompson laughed and said, 'I do love your quotations, Mr Pentecost.'

He smiled down at her. It really was rather refreshing to have someone around who not only recognized quotations when she heard them, but actually appreciated them. And Wendy thought how wonderful it must be to be friendly with someone whose mind, like Mr Pentecost's, was a veritable dictionary of quotations, and not to be just someone who had called to ask him about a lecture.

But now, it was time to go. She said, 'It's been so kind of you and Mrs Pentecost to put me up. But I must be finding my way home.'

'Stay for lunch,' he said. 'Then I'll drive you back. May,' he called, 'you can find Miss Thompson some lunch?'

'Of course,' said May, doing mental arithmetic with prime steaks and slices of Pavlova, and wishing her headache would go away. Her confrontation with Miss Mackintosh must have taken more out of her than she'd imagined.

'And can Henry Bartlett stay, Momma?'

She looked down at her son's eager face, at Henry's pink and anxious one. 'He can, dear. But I think he ought to go home. His mother will be worried,' she said, not very hopefully.

'She won't, Momma. She told him it was all right to stay if he was asked.'

Henry swallowed, blushed, and nodded in confirmation. All right for whom, wondered May, who had formed the opinion that Mrs Bartlett took her maternal duties with a little too much gay insouciance. 'Well, that's all right, then,' she said. Now if she could get it across to Jocelyn that he really much preferred biscuits and cheese to Pavlova – ? 'Say you don't want any Pavlova,' she hissed. 'It won't go round.'

'Eh? What's that, old girl?'

'Pavlova. Say you don't want any.'

'What's – ? Oh, I know. That meringue thing. No, that's all right, May. I'll have cheese and biscuits.'

'Right. Don't forget to say so.'

It was all very confusing. He had said so, hadn't he? Well, he'd just have to play it along and hope to recognize a clue. But he was worried. If, as he greatly feared, he was in the doghouse for saving the punch instead of May, he didn't want to make any more mistakes.

'Pavlova, Jocelyn?' May stood, cake-slice in hand, a noble Brunhild.

'Thanks, May,' he said. He looked up, met Brunhild's steely eye. CLUE! 'No thanks, old girl. Biscuits and cheese for me.' And then, with a piece of improvisation he thought brilliant, but which made no visible impression on his wife, 'Waistline and all that.'

'I'm sure you don't need to worry, Mr Pentecost,' said Miss Thompson. Jocelyn positively smirked.

You keep out of this, Wendy Thompson, May thought rudely. Aloud, 'Now, Henry?'

Henry swallowed, blushed and nodded. Gaylord said, 'Henry likes Pavlova better than anything in the world except baked beans on toast, don't you, Henry.'

Henry nodded. Grandpa, who had been staring at the silent child for some time could stand it no longer. 'Doesn't say much, does he?' he barked.

'He thinks a lot,' said Gaylord.

May said, 'After you with the cheese, Jocelyn.'

He looked at her in astonishment. 'Good Lord, you not having Pavlova?'

'There's none left, you fool,' said Grandpa.

'Oh dear,' said Miss Thompson. 'That comes of my staying for lunch. Mrs Pentecost, look, do share mine. There's far more here – '

Gaylord said, 'If you did Henry some baked beans, Momma, he'd give you his Pavlova. Wouldn't you, Henry?'

Henry swallowed anxiously, and nodded.

Great Aunt Bea shovelled in a large spoonful. 'Won't do your dental cavities any harm to miss a bit of this sweet goo, May,' she said briskly.

It was too much. 'Leave my dental cavities out of this,' snapped May.

'I say. Steady on, old girl,' murmured Jocelyn.

'I bet you'd rather have baked beans, wouldn't you, Henry?' said Gaylord.

If there was one thing Grandpa prided himself on even more than his old world courtesy, it was his tact. And if his efforts at conciliation could usually be likened unto those of a man who pours oil on troubled waters and then drops a lighted match on the oil, that just showed how prickly and unresponsive most people were. Now he said soothingly, 'Not often you underestimate things, May. Still, we can all make mistakes. Don't you worry about it, me dear.'

'I'll fetch the coffee,' said May.

Derek Bates was planning his revenge.

He sat with two of his mates in his bedroom. Each had a stocking over his head. (Derek had introduced them to this fashion, and they had accepted it with enthusiasm. It did something for them.)

Night and day Derek had brooded over his humiliation. His resentment, lovingly nurtured, had spread like a cancer through his whole being. It was a heavy weight, pressing him into the ground. His only pleasure now was in savouring his hatred. Revenge was his only hope of salvation. 'We could kidnap the boy,' he said. 'Dump him in the river.'

The other two, so far as one could tell through the stockings, did not seem very keen. One said doubtfully, 'That old chap – you know, the one who –' He could not bring himself to name the obscenity – 'did he take your number?'

'How the hell do I know?'

'He could trace you. I don't reckon we ought to let the kid drown.'

'Chicken!' snarled Derek.

Norman didn't like being called chicken. 'I only mean – it wasn't his fault.'

'What's that got to do with it?' asked Frank. He didn't think they ought to kill the kid, either. But he didn't believe in going soft on whose fault it was. Someone had chucked his friend Derek's bike in the river. Someone had got to suffer. It didn't matter who, surely?

'What about roughing up the old man himself?' suggested Norman.

Now it was Derek who didn't sound very keen. 'Wouldn't trust the old bastard,' he said doubtfully. 'He looks tough.'

'But he's old, isn't he?'

'He's still tough. I reckon the kid's best.'

Frank said, 'I seen a bloke carve another bloke up with a broken beer bottle. On telly.' He hugged himself at the memory. 'Didn't half make a mess.'

'I reckon you can't beat a broken bottle,' said Derek thoughtfully.

Frank was proud to have made a useful suggestion. Clearly, their plans had a long way to go yet. But they were getting something to work on. 'And we could smash the place up a bit,' said Derek. 'While we were waiting.' Much as he longed for his revenge, he didn't want it to be over too quickly.

It was time to go. Wendy Thompson walked sadly with Mr Pentecost to his car. She had said goodbye to Mrs Pentecost, thanking her warmly for her hospitality. Mrs Pentecost had replied charmingly; yet Wendy knew that to this busy woman she meant no more than did a fleeting guest to a hotel keeper. She had exchanged addresses and insurance companies with Great Aunt Bea, who had shaken hands, chortled hugely, and said, 'So long, young woman. And mind how you park next time, remember.' The old gentleman had looked up from his newspaper, struggled to his feet, and said earnestly, 'Now you get every penny you can out of Bea, Miss Thompson. She can afford it. Can't you, Bea?'

'Me? Bless my soul, John, you're not suggesting it was my fault, are you?'

Becky and Peter smiled politely, and bowed vaguely, not at all sure who the lady was, or why she was here, or where she was going. Aunt Dorothea said, 'Goodbye, Miss Crabtree, sorry you're called away.'

Only to the Frenchman did she seem more than thistledown blown on the wind. As he kissed her hand he looked at her admiringly and said, 'I wish you luck with your young pupil, Miss Thompson. Nowadays, when so many can only tear down, it is good to see someone trying – keep the torch of beauty burning.'

'Thank you,' she said, moved. 'It won't be easy.'

He put his card into her hand. 'All I can offer is money,' he said deprecatingly. 'But never be afraid – '

'Thank you,' she had said again. And now she was standing outside the garage while Jocelyn started his car. She looked back. The big gaunt house, the snowy lawns, the distant river, Ozymandias the Snowman. The bright morning had changed to a slightly shop-soiled afternoon. It was as though a curtain of wet muslin had been hung across the sun. And the happiness had gone with the sunshine. She wanted to cry. A voice at her elbow said, 'I'm sorry you're going, Miss Thompson. I wish you could stay here always.'

'Gaylord!' she cried. She'd been wishing so much that the boy could find a moment to say goodbye.

But Gaylord wanted to say more than goodbye. He said, 'I think you're even nicer than Miss Jones in the Co-op Butcher's, Miss Thompson.'

'Really?' she said delightedly.

'Ever so much nicer. Miss Thompson?'

'Yes, dear?'

'I wondered if you'd like to marry me when I grow up?'

'Darling, I'd love to. But I shall be too old by then.'

'I bet you won't be as old as Miss Jones in the Co-op Butcher's.'

She ruffled his hair. 'I shall be too old for you, my dear.'

He looked doubtful. 'Well don't marry anyone else, anyway.'

She was silent. 'There's no fear of that,' she said in a small voice.

Jocelyn backed out the car. 'Hop in, Miss Thompson.'

She hopped in, looked back at a forlornly waving Gaylord, at a melting snowman, at the house, some of its windows already glowing in the winter's afternoon. ' "I came like water, and like wind I go",' she murmured.

'Eh? What's that, Miss Thompson?'

'Nothing,' she said. 'I only gave a little cough.'

The winter's dusk crept into the lanes and fields, covering the good and the evil, the foolish and the wise, the creators and the destroyers. By the time Jocelyn reached Ingerby, the street lamps were lit, and Miss Thompson's bijou residence looked dark and cold. 'I'll just see you in,' he said, holding the front gate for her. She went ahead, unlocked the front door, switched on a dim hall light. He saw heavy, unwelcoming, Edwardian furniture. 'Do come in,' she said. 'Let me make you a cup of tea.'

'No, really, thank you. I must get back. The roads are still treacherous.' They both seemed shy, ill-at-ease, taking refuge in formalities.

'Well, if you're sure.' She held out a hand, smiled. 'Mr Pentecost, do forgive me for being such a nuisance. And thank you for being so patient and for – everything.'

'I'm awfully pleased to have met you,' he said. 'And I'll see you in April.' It had been a long hand shake. Now he turned and went, with that friendly smile. She waited while he started the car. Then she shut the door, and went into the front living room. It felt cold. She soon saw why. The window was smashed. A brick lay on the hearthrug. A piece of paper was fastened to it by an elastic band. On the paper was a crude drawing of a motor cycle.

CHAPTER 11

Night. In the river lands, the only lights were those from John Pentecost's farm, and from World's End Cottage.

Julia Mackintosh – curled up under the bedclothes with her most loved possession, her mother's coloured picture book of ballet – was reading it by the light of an electric torch (Aunt Elspeth disapproved of reading in bed). She gazed, fascinated, at pictures she had already devoured a hundred times. Every detail entranced her: the leotards, the tutus, the entrechats and pas de deux, the names: Pavlova, Diaghilev, Fonteyn; the whole glamorous, thrilling world of which she had heard so much, but would know only through the pages of an old book. She was like a poor prisoner gazing out, not at a prison yard, but at a bright garden where free men walked, and laughed, and played.

Yet, being a child, she dreamed. Someone – a prince, even Miss Fonteyn herself – would see her dancing in the meadows, and would spirit her away to Covent Garden where Nureyev would stride up to where she stood in the chorus and, with an imperious gesture, lead her to the front of the stage to dance the pas de deux. Yes. Being a child, she dreamed… But it was not Nureyev who came with imperious gesture. It was Aunt Elspeth who, stealing unheard into the bedroom, seeing the glow under the bedclothes, snatched the precious book and in her fury tore it in two, and then in two again.

Julia, in her fury, bit Aunt Elspeth's hand. A strange act, for so seemingly gentle a child; but just as Derek's motor bike was to Derek far, far more than a motor bike, so to Julia her book was far more than a book. It was her only window on to a life she could never know.

Aunt Elspeth screamed with rage and pain, and was beating Julia ferociously about the head with the remains of the book when Duncan burst into the room. He seized his sister, and grabbed the book. He saw her bleeding hand, 'Ye'd best put some Dettol on that,' he said quietly. 'Then pack your bags.'

'Aye. I will that,' she said bitterly; and marched from the room.

Julia, hanging her head, began slowly picking up the pieces of her precious book. Her father watched her. 'Did your aunt do that?'

The child nodded. There was no emotion in the big, dark eyes she turned on her father.

'And did you bite your aunt's hand?'

She hung her head. The light gleamed on her long hair. 'Aye.'

Wearily he sat down on the bed. 'Oh, lassie, lassie,' he said, drawing her to him. She held herself stiff. Then, slowly, she relaxed against him. 'Is Auntie Elspeth really going?'

He nodded. 'I'm glad,' she said.

He sat silent. 'But who will look after you, child?' It was a bleak prospect. But for perhaps the first time in his life Duncan Mackintosh realized that there were things that were too much for him.

At the farm, John Pentecost was doing his duty as a brother.

Jocelyn had started it. Jocelyn's mind, as he drove back from Ingerby, was working on many levels. Part of it was concentrating on the speed and direction of a lethal weapon on a treacherous road. Part of it was thinking that, only last night, little Miss Thompson had been in danger on this very road, and that this danger threatened them all, and that he ought to do something about it. Part of it was thinking of Miss Thompson, a woman who loved poetry and beauty, alone in that cheerless house in that dreary town. Another part, the creative part, was like a tangled skein, or a heavy, undigested lump with which no one – not May, not the cleverest in the land – could help him, for the road of creation is the loneliest of all roads. He thought of his favourite Aunt Dorothea, and of the happiness in her sweet face, and hoped this French chap was all right. He certainly seemed all right, knew his Shakespeare and all that, but he supposed that didn't really prove anything. So that when he found his father alone in the living room he said, 'Er, Father, this chap of Dorothea's. He's – all right, I suppose?'

'All right?' the old man glared. 'What do you mean, all right?'

'Well, I mean, what do we know about him?'

His father threshed about irritably in his chair. He never liked being asked questions he couldn't answer. 'Not suggesting the fellow's a crook, are you?' he demanded scornfully.

But at this moment Edouard came into the room. 'Ah, my dear Jocelyn, you have taken the little miss home? – She is a good woman,' he said. 'Trying to build up while, all over the world, men tear down and destroy.'

'Good Lord,' cried the impressed Jocelyn. 'Do you feel that? Actually,' he went on excitedly, 'I've started using this as a yardstick, for people and actions and policies. Are they creating? Or are they destroying? The world's future depends on this balance. And at the moment the balance is heavily with the destroyers.'

The Frenchman gave him a curiously intense smile. 'You are a wise and sensitive man, Jocelyn.'

'No!' said Jocelyn, almost angrily. 'Not sensitive, Monsieur.' He found he was trembling. 'I can watch children butchered, night after night, while I sip my Ovaltine.' He hurried from the room.

'Damned unpredictable, these writer chaps,' John Pentecost said half apologetically.

The Frenchman was silent. John went and poured two large brandies. 'Now come and sit down, my dear fellow.'

They sat, swirling the strong spirit round in their glasses, savouring the bouquet. John glanced sideways at his guest. What he saw confirmed his first impression. The fellow could be almost an Englishman. Nevertheless, he didn't want Jocelyn asking him any more awkward questions. So he settled himself very comfortably in his chair, and said casually, 'Dorothea tells me you work in a bank.'

There was a moment's silence. Then: 'I am a bank,' Edouard said with just a suspicion of hauteur. 'Bouverie et Cie, Paris.'

Good Lord! And there young Jocelyn had been suggesting the fellow might be a crook! 'My dear chap, I beg your pardon.'

Edouard shrugged, and smiled. 'And now I suppose I should ask your formal permission to marry your sister?'

'Nothing would give me greater pleasure. And I wish you both every happiness. When – had you thought?'

'April. If that would be convenient to yourself?'

'April. Dear Dorothea! If I may say so, Monsieur, you are a very lucky man.' He blew his nose loudly. He was greatly affected.

But it was not April yet. It was still a winter week-end, with the house still full of people, and May with a raging headache which was no better on Sunday morning than it had been on Saturday night. Of course, no one had realized that May had a headache. She was as cheerful as ever, her appearance was as elegant, she saw to every detail of the household. Only Gaylord, strangely, sensed that something was amiss. The All Seeing Eye was not quite as all-seeing as usual. He had actually managed to forget one or two of the things he always tried, and was never allowed, to forget, like washing his hands after playing with his printing set, or taking off his wellies to go up to the loo. Even the printer's ink on his counterpane and he muddy snow on the landing did not bring thunder and lighting about his head. He began to get worried. He hoped Momma wasn't sickening.

But May was counting the hours. Fortunately Bea and party, with a damaged car, wanted to leave straight after lunch, greatly to Gaylord's satisfaction. And Peter and Becky, gazing fondly at each other, were making vague remarks about being home before dark. Hearing which Gaylord said piteously, 'Don't go, Auntie Becky,' and got an agonized look from his mother which he promptly misinterpreted. 'Momma doesn't want you to go either, do you, Momma?'

'Of course not, dear. But the roads are very treacherous. I think perhaps you would be wise, Peter – '

So, thought May, one more meal. Two more hours of listening as through a blanket; and of hearing her own responses, courteous and seemingly intelligent, yet uttered without any apparent thought, as though she pressed a coin into her brain and the right response came out, nearly wrapped.

Two more hours. But here came Mr Mackintosh, just as she was about to serve lunch, in at the kitchen door, all grim granite, demanding to see her father-in-law. And, ten minutes later, here came her father-in-law, also granite-grim. 'May, are you busy?'

Since the joint, and the potatoes, and the greens, and the sauce, and the Yorkshire pudding had all reached one perfect moment of togetherness, since her cooking had arrived at the culinary equivalent of the finale of a Beethoven symphony, she could be said to be busy. But she asked, quietly, 'What is it, Father-in-law?'

'Mackintosh wants to give in his notice,' he said in an appalled voice.

'Oh, dear,' she said with some equanimity. It might mean the heavens were falling for her father-in-law. It didn't mean they were falling for her.

Oh, dear? Was that all she could say? 'It's damned serious,' he said. 'Best man I've ever had.'

'Mm. I'm sorry.' She began to wonder why he was telling her, and so evidently awaiting a response.

'It's that sister of his. She's leaving. She's catching the six o'clock train tomorrow morning.'

She understood. She was just lifting the heavy joint out of the cooking tin on to the carving dish. Fortunately she did not drop it back into the hot gravy, but it was a fraught moment. The old man said, 'He says he can't be fair to the girl and to me.' He waited hopefully.

'I see,' said May, putting the joint back in the oven. She began to stir the gravy.

'Poor little kid,' said Grandpa.

'Yes,' said May, still stirring.

135

'Can't see he'll be much better off anywhere else,' mused Grandpa.

'No,' said May.

'Unless, of course, they lived with the family.'

It wasn't just herself. It was Jocelyn's life, as well as hers. And Gaylord's. It wasn't fair to foist a constant companion on him. But here came Gaylord. 'Momma, I'm ever so hungry. Can we – ?'

May said, 'Your dear friend Miss Mackintosh is leaving, Gaylord.'

'You mean – really leaving?'

'Really leaving.'

'Whoopee!' cried Gaylord.

She did not give him long to rejoice. 'It means poor little Julia won't have anyone to look after her.'

He thought this over. 'She'll have her Poppa.'

'Poppas aren't very good at looking after children.'

No. He could see this. Much as he liked his own Poppa, he realized his limitations. He pondered. 'Couldn't you look after her, Momma?'

Grandpa tried to keep the gleam out of his eye. 'Your mother's got quite enough to do already, young man,' he said, somewhat half-heartedly.

May said, 'It would mean them living here. You wouldn't want a girl about the place, would you, Gaylord?'

No, he wouldn't. But if poor Julia hadn't anyone to look after her – ? He was a bit shocked that Momma even needed to weigh the matter. 'I wouldn't mind,' he said stoutly.

John Pentecost was looking astonished. 'You mean – you'd have them here, May? Well, that would be a solution. But – are you sure, my dear?'

She had just picked up a loaded tray. Now she put it down. She looked coolly at her father-in-law. 'Such an idea had never occurred to you, had it?'

'Good heavens, no. Still, now you have suggested it. It would be a help, May.'

Well, her headache wouldn't last for ever. And if she had been thinking, almost with tears in her eyes, of lying down once the visitors had gone – oh, she'd get over it. A good night's sleep, and she'd be as right as rain in the morning.

But she had reckoned without two men, those unpredictable creatures: Jocelyn, who always left the entire running of the house to her, but who now said flatly that he wasn't spending the rest of his life in the same house as Aberdeen Angus; the chap would be telling him how to write his novels in no time at all; and Duncan himself, who seemed to have put on a new personality with his Sunday suit, and said, 'Mrs Pentecost, this is most kind, and I can think of no one I would prefer to keep an eye on my lassie. But I'm a thrawn sort of man, myself, and would be ill at ease. So if I could stay at World's End, and Julia could stay here – I'd take her off your hands as much as I could.' He actually smiled. His smile was that of a man who has discovered gratitude in his heart.

Julia was also in her Sunday best – a blue coat, buttoned up to the throat, with a fur collar – very stiff, very formal and ladylike as, nowadays, it is only little girls who dare to be. 'Hello, my dear,' said May. 'Would you like me to show you where you will sleep when you are here?'

'Yes, please, Mrs Pentecost.'

As soon as the visitors had left, May had stripped the bed in Edouard's room, and remade it. Now she showed the room to Julia. 'Will you be all right, here? Gaylord's next door, and Mr Pentecost and I are just across the landing, and look – through the window you can see Daddy's cottage.'

Julia clasped her hands. 'It's beautiful, Mrs Pentecost.'

'Through the window – you can see Daddy's cottage,' said May.

The child looked at her with a touch of fear. May had a curious, set smile on her face. 'Through the window you can see – Daddy's cottage,' she told the now terrified child. And crumpled on to the floor.

Gaylord, in the next room, heard Julia's screams, and came running.

The sight of his mother lying helpless on the floor was curiously horrifying. It was a denial of nature. Momma was the life force, the binder up of wounds. It was she who raised up the fallen. And if she had now become one of the fallen, then the world had lost its prop. It was the end of all things. He put out a hand and seized Julia's, hurried her along to his father's study. He went in shyly, swallowing, moistening his lips. 'Poppa?'

'Hello, old man. Hello, Julia.' Jocelyn looked at his visitors. 'There's – nothing wrong, is there?' he asked.

Gaylord nodded. But there were some things you couldn't say, the words wouldn't come, like some swear words. 'It's Momma,' he said at last. 'I think – '

Jocelyn looked at the young, horrified faces. He rose slowly from his chair. 'Gaylord! What is it? Where is she?'

'In Julia's room. All still. I think she may be dead,' said Gaylord.

Jocelyn made a dreadful sound in his throat, and tore out of the room, heart pounding, legs like lead, his mind a mash of horror. May was still lying where she had fallen. She was very pale. Desperately he sought for her pulse. Nothing. But then he could never find a pulse, not even his own. Oh, what a helpless creature he was! Any sort of crisis he'd always left to May. And now? He managed to get a pillow under her head, and felt rather pleased with himself. He chafed her hands without visible effect. He ran out on to the landing. Gaylord and Julia were standing there. Julia looked frightened. Now that the first shock was over Gaylord looked torn between fear and his insatiable love of the dramatic. Jocelyn telephoned the doctor, then called his father who diagnosed delayed concussion. 'Must have caught her head on something when that damn dog knocked her over.' He was truly sorry. But he did wish his usually efficient daughter-in-law had developed her symptoms before the visitors had left. Then either Becky or one of his sisters might have felt morally bound to stay and look after him.

Jocelyn was in the ambulance, seeing his still unconscious wife into hospital, where she was to stay under observation. He watched her with desperate concern. Yet even with his whole future happiness depending on perhaps some tiny vein or nerve in that pale brow, he could not forget his other problems. Gaylord, Amanda; even Julia was suddenly his responsibility. And his father! The slightest change in the old man's routine, and the sparks would fly. He, Jocelyn, wasn't equipped for coping with this sort of thing. And just at a time when all his thought should be directed at his work! Wasn't it incredible, he thought, that the withdrawal of one woman's labour should create such mayhem.

Great Aunt Bea's Mini was skating cheerfully homeward along and across the treacherous roads. Becky and Peter were already home, looking with wonder at their pretty house, and at each other, and at the life that could be theirs provided they kept redheads and molehills in proportion.

At World's End Cottage, Duncan was in the parlour reading The Farmer and Stockbreeder. Elspeth was up in her room, packing. Both longed to unsay what had been said the night before. But the sticking plaster of their fierce Scottish pride was across both their mouths. Neither Elspeth's conscience nor Duncan's care for his child could make them utter an apology. What had been spoken was as strong as fate. And Duncan consoled himself with the thought that there was something about Mistress Pentecost that inspired confidence. A kind and capable woman. But it was hard, having to leave the lassie with a stranger. He sighed. Och, it had been cruel to take his Jeannie.

There were some (most of those who knew him, in fact) who felt that there were perhaps occasions when John Pentecost could be suspected of selfishness and even of opportunism. If so, this occasion was not one of them. Although the day was far spent, and he hadn't even seen The Observer yet, he determined to devote himself to his young charges. He put a hand about Gaylord's shoulders and said, 'Now there's no need to fret about your mother, boy. She's as strong as a brewer's dray horse, she'll be all right.'

'She looked funny,' said Gaylord, uncomforted. He remembered he was in the presence of an expert in these matters. He turned to Julia. 'Did your mother look like that when she – ?'

Julia looked unhappy. Grandpa said, 'I tell you what. I'll have a game of Monopoly with you if you'll promise not to worry about your mother.'

Gaylord didn't think it seemed quite right to play Monopoly when Momma was being taken off in that horrible ambulance. But he was an obliging child, and if Grandpa wanted to – He fetched the game, just making a little détour to make sure that Amanda was sleeping peacefully.

Nobody played very well: Gaylord, because he was following the ambulance along the Ingerby Road, and watching them slide that shrouded nightmare object that was unaccountably Momma out at the other end, just as they had slid it in so horribly at this; Julia, because her sweet nature lacked the dedicated ruthlessness the game demands; and Grandpa because he'd taken the precaution of propping The Observer leader between his stomach and the table.

But there was another reason why Grandpa played badly; he had a lot on his mind.

He didn't relish having Jocelyn getting his meals for him. So he was going through a muster of his female relatives. Becky? No. She wasn't likely to leave her Peter alone, not with that redhead lurking in the undergrowth. Rose, his elder daughter? No. Too besotted with that husband of hers. Dorothea? All steamed fish and yoghourt. Bea? Not that sadist, by George! That woman was quite capable of putting him on lemon juice and lettuce, with a glass of dry cider as a special treat on Sundays. He shuddered. There must b someone who'd look after an old man, he thought pathetically. But there wasn't. When it came to the push, human nature could be very selfish he decided, thwarted in his devious attempt to avoid landing on Mayfair by Gaylord, who had just erected some hotels there.

It was at this low ebb in John Pentecost's thoughts that the telephone rang.

Wendy Thompson had looked at the broken window, the jagged glass, the brick lying in the hearth, with a sense of fear and physical revulsion. She had run back to the door, hoping to catch Mr Pentecost, but his lights were already winking round the corner. So she had telephoned the police, who came and looked and seemed relatively unimpressed, even when she told them about the motor cyclist in the river lane.

She had boarded up the window with a piece of cardboard, and had then spent the evening in the kitchen at the back of the house, tense and taut, listening for every new sound, distressed and tormented by the thought that someone must dislike her sufficiently to do this to her, even if it was only an expression of hatred for all mankind. She slept badly, and spent Sunday wondering whether she ought to tell the Pentecosts. There might be no connection. Mr and Mrs Pentecost might well think it was just an excuse to continue an acquaintance. After all, in their position, they must get that sort of thing.

On the other hand, it might be important to them, to know that this menace still existed. Suppose she said nothing, and then they were attacked with their defences down? She would not forgive herself.

Decision-making was not easy. It was evening before she telephoned, hoping against hope that Mr Jocelyn Pentecost would answer, for she would not find it easy to explain to Mrs Pentecost.

It was the boy – breathless, tense. 'Hello. Who's that? Is that Poppa?'

She said, 'Is that Gaylord? Wendy Thompson. You remember me?'

' 'Course. I thought you were Poppa. He's taken Momma into hospital.'

'No!' She had delayed too long! 'What's the matter?'

'She's unconscious. It's like dead only it isn't.'

'But how – ?'

'When Schultz knocked her over. She must have banged her head.'

'I am sorry, Gaylord.'

'Thanks. Do you want to speak to Grandpa?'

'Yes, please.'

He went to see Grandpa. 'It's Miss Thompson.'

'Who's Miss Thompson? Oh, I remember.' A nice woman. Yes, it would be a pleasure to speak to Miss Thompson again. He went to the telephone. 'John Pentecost here, Miss Thompson.' No sucking dove ever cooed more sweetly.

She said, 'Oh, Mr Pentecost, I'm so sorry to hear your news. Is it serious, do you think?'

'Well, I'm afraid it will mean some time in hospital.'

'How difficult for you all! Is one of your visitors staying on?'

'No. They'd already left. And of course they all have commitments, anyway.' She heard a sigh. 'Oh, we shall manage well enough. It's only the children – especially the young baby. But – '

'Well, I am sorry. If there is anything I can do – ?'

He was deeply touched. 'My dear Miss Thompson! How very kind. But I wouldn't think of asking you, a stranger. No, we shall get by somehow. It won't hurt Jocelyn and me to rough it a bit.'

She couldn't bear to think of Jocelyn Pentecost roughing it a bit. He just wasn't the type to have to. Besides, his writing. She said, 'I'm not a very capable person. But it is half-term. I should be only too pleased if there was some little thing – '

The old man was even more deeply moved than before. But he said firmly, 'No, Miss Thompson. You are young. You have your own life to lead. Our problems are not insuperable – I hope and believe.'

'I do mean it, Mr Pentecost.'

'You do? You really do? I'll pick you up in half an hour then,' said John Pentecost. 'Where do you live?'

She told him. 'Pack your things,' he said and put down his receiver.

Wendy Thompson felt as some of the more irreligious among the Children of Israel must have felt when the walls of Jericho fell down flat. The capitulation had been both unexpected and sudden. Doubts began to trouble and even terrify her. When she had made the standard 'if there's anything I can do' response, she had made it sincerely. But she had been thinking in terms of a bit of shopping or baby sitting. Now, suddenly, she seemed to have a household on her hands, including two men and a baby. And what did she know of either men or babies? She would do it, and gladly. She would be very pleased to get away from her menaced and lonely house for a few days. It would be an honour to be able to help a man like Jocelyn Pentecost. It might be an opportunity to work on Julia's stubborn father. But it frightened the life out of her.

John Pentecost went and put on his shoes and his overcoat. He was well pleased with himself. A few minutes ago, the future had looked bleak and uncomfortable. Now, thanks to his decision and tact, the status quo was restored. He said, 'I have to go out the moment your father returns, Gaylord.'

'But we haven't finished the game,' said Gaylord, who now owned most of London. He listened. 'There's Poppa's car now.' He tore off, and out at the front door. 'Poppa! How's Momma?'

Jocelyn slipped an arm about his shoulders. 'She'll be all right. She's all tucked up, ever so comfortable.'

'Is she breathing?'

'Yes, of course.'

'Oh, good. Poppa, Grandpa pretended he'd thrown twelve when he'd only thrown nine, so that he wouldn't land on Mayfair.'

John Pentecost went and met his son. 'Ah, there you are. How's May?'

'Still unconscious,' said the forlorn Jocelyn. 'And they're not committing themselves.'

'I'm sorry, Jocelyn.'

'Thanks. How are things here? Has Amanda wakened?'

'No. And I've kept the others entertained,' he said virtuously.

Jocelyn looked wan. 'We're in a hell of a mess, Father. Amanda's the biggest worry. I just don't know how we're going to cope.'

The old man clapped his hand on his son's shoulder. 'Everything's arranged, boy. I'm just off to bring help: housekeeper, nursemaid, call her what you will.'

'Who?' Had a spangled, wand-waving fairy godmother appeared in the hall, Jocelyn could not have sounded more amazed, delighted and impressed. 'Who?' He'd been trying to think of someone all the way home. But there wasn't anyone.

'Wendy Thompson,' said Grandpa smugly.

'But – but you can't ask her!'

'Didn't need to. She volunteered. Look. I must go. She's sitting with her bags packed.'

Jocelyn said, 'Father, we can't have Wendy Thompson.'

'Why not?'

Jocelyn didn't know why not. But when you've been married eight years, the heart has its reasons that the reason knows not of. He simply knew that May would just as soon have a boa constrictor about the house during her absence as little, inoffensive, not-terribly-attractive Miss Thompson.

'Must go,' said John. And went.

145

Jocelyn had never felt so lonely in his life. It was more than loneliness. It was amputation. It was an amputation of his very being.

The doctor had been fairly reassuring. Just a case of keeping her under observation, my dear fellow. But doctors could be wrong, especially when it came to blows on the head. Jocelyn's writer's imagination supplied all the details he could want. Oh, how unbelievable that only yesterday morning she had stood, radiant and beautiful, in the snow, she who in his mind now smiled wanly up at him from a nest of pillows. A few hours ago, a few hours. And yet it was already a lifetime away.

Gaylord slipped his hand into Poppa's. He thought it very unlikely they would ever see Momma again. And suddenly he wanted to, very much. The thought of not seeing Momma again made him want to cry and cry and cry. But he didn't. He mustn't upset Poppa. 'Henry Bartlett's Auntie Pam was taken off in an ambulance,' he said.

Jocelyn was silent. 'Henry Bartlett says it's the last they ever saw of her,' said Gaylord.

They returned to the living room. Strange, thought Jocelyn. May hasn't been out of the house more than an hour or two. Yet already everything has changed. The fire is still as bright, the flowers are still as fresh, the curtains are drawn against the night. But it is as though the house has died.

This, however, was getting him nowhere. He had to think, to make plans. Suddenly he was in charge, responsible. He had to do the organizing. And he was simply no good at organizing. He just didn't know where to begin.

Gaylord said, 'Julia and I can bath Amanda, Poppa. Can't we, Julia? And isn't it a good thing Momma was weaning her. We can give her her bottle, and put ourselves to bed. So if you just get Grandpa's and your supper, that will be everything. Julia and I can wash the dishes tomorrow.'

Jocelyn looked at his son in astonishment. 'When did you think all this out?'

'I didn't, Poppa. It sort of came.'

Well, he supposed some were born organizers, and some weren't. He wandered into his study, slumped into his chair. His static novel mocked him from his desk. He thought of all the days he had sat here so industriously writing, happy in the knowledge that May was bustling about the kitchen. Oh, how little he had appreciated those days! How often had he let minor irritations, sheer unawareness, cloud the sunshine. If only those days would return, how he would revel in his wife's every smile, how his heart would leap whenever he heard her singing at her work! Never again, never, would he take such things for granted, if only – Come back, come back, oh days of long ago!

He heard his father's voice on the landing. 'Now you may as well have your old room, Miss Thompson. Here you are.' And then Miss Thompson: 'Thank you. Oh, dear, I do hope I shall be able to cope.'

'Of course you will.' He patted her hand. It was something he found he rather enjoyed doing. 'And you won't find me any trouble, I need hardly say.'

She sounded reassured. 'Of course, I already know some things.' She laughed. 'Mr Jocelyn Pentecost likes tea and toast for breakfast, and you have egg and bacon and sausage and toast and marmalade.'

'And coffee,' he reminded her.

'And coffee.'

Jocelyn erupted from his room. 'Father, can I – ? Oh, hello, Miss Thompson. Father, can I have a word?'

147

'Of course, dear boy. You just sort yourself out, Miss Thompson.' He followed Jocelyn into the study. He was in a strong position. By the time Jocelyn had said his say, Miss Thompson's nightie would be laid on her pillow, and her toothbrush perched in the tooth mug. And if all that didn't add up to a fait accompli, thought John Pentecost, he'd like to know what did.

Jocelyn shut the study door. 'Now look, Father, we can't do this.'

'My dear boy.' He put a hand on his son's arm. 'She's only too pleased to do it.' He looked very moved. 'Do you realize, Jocelyn, that that poor, lonely woman lost her mother only last month, and hasn't a soul in the world. Why, we're doing her a favour. It'll take her mind off her own troubles.'

'But – '

It was seldom that John Pentecost waxed poetic. But he waxed poetic now. 'I've been talking to her in the car. And do you know what she reminded me of?'

'The answer to a selfish old man's prayer?' Jocelyn said nastily.

His father ignored this. 'I felt she was like some spent swimmer, carried helplessly along by life's current, who suddenly finds that she has been thrown a lifebelt. Her gratitude was touching, most touching.' He groped for his handkerchief, blew his nose loudly.

Jocelyn was silent. He had another reason, one he had not really formulated to himself, one that his natural humility would not let him formulate: that, while he himself had no thoughts for anyone but May, Miss Thompson, ridiculous though it sounded, was emotionally attracted by an author whose work she greatly admired. But he couldn't say this to his father. So he said firmly, 'Well, I'll agree to her giving a hand with the children. But you and I can look after ourselves, Father.'

'Of course we can, dear boy. Now. What are you giving us for supper?'

Jocelyn went off miserably to take a look in the kitchen. To him, the cooking of anything more exotic than a boiled egg was shrouded in a mystique he had never attempted to pierce. So in spite of himself he was very relieved when the door was shyly opened and Miss Thompson came in, looking scared but helpful. 'Now, Mr Pentecost. Just let me ask about Mrs Pentecost. Then tell me what I can do.'

He was just telling her what little he knew when his father marched in. 'Ah, there you are, Miss Thompson. Now I think what we all need after a day like this is a pleasant, leisurely meal to pull us round. What do you say, Miss T?'

Jocelyn said coldly, 'I was going to suggest that Miss Thompson concentrates on Amanda.'

'Oh, no need for that yet. The kid'll soon yell when she's hungry.' It occurred to him that he might have sounded unfeeling. 'Poor, motherless babe,' he added, trying to make up. 'So. What about supper?'

There was no doubt about it. The thought of a hot meal was enticing. Jocelyn said, 'Well, if you insist on making a general servant out of Miss Thompson, Father – And if Miss Thompson really doesn't object – I'll show her where everything is.'

'Do that,' said John. He paused in the doorway, took his cigar out of his mouth. 'You will let me know if there's anything I can do?' he enquired anxiously.

Miss Thompson gave him a sweet smile. He went. As soon as they were alone, Jocelyn said severely, 'Look. Did my father bulldoze you into this?'

She actually laughed. 'Bulldoze me? I had the greatest difficulty in persuading him to let me come. I almost went down on my knees.'

'You mean it was actually your suggestion?'

Her eyes were grey, and clear, and honest. 'Of course. I'd love to do anything I can. If you'd like me to.' She hung on his answer.

He said, 'Quite frankly, I really don't know what I should do without some help. But that doesn't mean – '

'Then that's settled,' she said. She was curiously excited. A lonely spinster, suddenly finding herself at the hub of a family, suddenly finding herself in an inevitably close relationship with a man she greatly admired. Besides: 'You've got enough to worry about,' she said. 'But something rather unpleasant happened last night.' She told him about the smashed window. 'So it's really rather nice to be out of the house for a day or two.'

He felt very protective. 'Miss Thompson, how very nasty for you. And – you think it's all connected with that motor cyclist in the lane?'

She was silent. 'Since you ask,' she said at last. 'Yes. But – it's not your fault.'

She was wrong. He knew it was their fault. His father had answered violence with violence. His father had joined the destroyers. And from the old man's one act of violence the ripples were spreading out even as they had spread out from the submerged motor bike. He said, 'We're all to blame. The world is as we have made it.'

'No. Not you, Mr Pentecost. You're so – good.'

'Good? Me?' He was genuinely amused. 'Hamlet mirrors me, as he mirrors all men. "Oh what a rogue and peasant slave am I." Ah! Now this is the larder. Various tins: soups, salmon, baked beans.'

'Now I don't think you're being fair to yourself, Mr Pentecost. Hamlet hadn't your moral principles. Would some Minestrone be all right to start with?'

'It would if we can find the Parmesan. Otherwise all hell would be let loose. Yes, I agree you wouldn't expect middle class morality in an early Danish prince. Oh, there's the Parmesan. But what does middle class morality amount to?'

'Quite a lot, I would have thought. Would omelettes be acceptable?'

'With some ham in, they would. Father feels cheated if you give him a meal without some kind of meat. No. I think it's little more than a veneer. Look, you say I have it. But all over the world, people are starving to death. And do I care, really care, so long as they do it quietly, and don't trouble me? Oh, that's the cooker, May says it's a bit headstrong since we went Natural. And – saucepans and things/'

'But you can't take everybody's troubles on your shoulders. How many eggs do you think?'

'About a dozen. I don't see why not. Sometimes I remind myself that there are millions who would give everything they possess for one of the three meals I take for granted every day; millions who would give all they possess to walk, free and unaided, down the meanest street of the meanest town. Do I care, so long as my ears are not affronted by the cries of the prisoners, my nostrils by the stench of the sick room?'

She looked at him with awe. 'How wonderfully you express yourself, Mr Pentecost.'

She was a nice girl! It would have been very pleasant to have slipped a casual arm about her waist as he showed her the kitchen. But at the moment she was looking at him as though finding the light from his halo a little dazzling. He couldn't bear to risk spoiling that. Besides, he thought of poor May who, despite all this chat about morals and cooking, was uppermost in his mind. He said, 'But there's no feeling there, any more. Thanks to the telly, we've all supped too full with horrors. Oh, here's Amanda's tipple. In this tin. Thank goodness she's taken to the bottle like a duck to water.'

Miss Thompson said, 'Believe me, Mr Pentecost, there are not many people doing more for humanity than writers like you –'

John Pentecost put his head round the door. 'Look, I'll get the children to put the things on the table, Miss Thompson. No need for you to do everything, you know.' He looked round the kitchen, said rather dubiously, 'Tell them we're about ready, shall I?'

Jocelyn, the heel, said nothing. Miss Thompson said, 'I'm afraid we're not quite, Mr Pentecost.' So happy and excited was she that she gave a little chuckle. 'We've been discussing middle class morality instead of getting on with things, haven't we, Mr Pentecost.'

'Good God,' said Grandpa, and disappeared back into the living room. 'Don't know what the world's coming to,' he muttered, angrily squirting soda into his whisky.

He was shaken. A married man, discussing morals with a young woman, alone with her in the kitchen – when they were supposed to be getting his supper!

A child, running across an April meadow, arms outstretched to catch the end of a rainbow: that, wise men say, is a picture of mankind pursuing happiness. Happiness, they say, is no more than a by-product of some activity: of work, of love, of achievement, even of destruction.

So it was with Miss Wendy Thompson. She had not sought happiness. But happiness had come to her, in her thirty first year, in another woman's kitchen, listening to the disjointed thoughts of another woman's husband. Happiness, such as she had seldom known, had come to her, not in the long dances, not in an aura of silken gowns and silver shoes, but in her apron, and among the pots and pans.

She felt wanted! She had felt wanted when Mother was alive. But, looking back, it had been an arid, inward-turning life, she and Mother revolving round each other for ever, like those waltzing manikins on a gramophone turntable. The world was wide, and free, and terrible, and she and Mother had crouched together in a corner; seeing, hearing, feeling, knowing – nothing.

Yet now – a famous author needed her; his sturdy young son, his baby daughter, his old father, all needed her. It seemed that strength flowed into her. She said, 'Do you think, if I went on with supper, you could see to Amanda, Mr Pentecost?'

He said, 'Please call me Jocelyn. Mr Pentecost sounds so unfriendly.'

She looked doubtful. 'I shall feel awfully cheeky.' But she said the name to herself: Jocelyn : a musical, gentle name, befitting the man. 'Thank you, Jocelyn.'

They smiled at each other. She was brimming over with happiness, knowing in her heart it was a happiness that could only accentuate her eventual loneliness and heartache; yet prepared for once to enjoy the moment while it lasted.

It didn't last long. Jocelyn said nervously, 'Now that I've shown you where things are, would you mind if I just go and telephone the hospital?' He loped off. When he came back he looked between tears and laughter. 'She's conscious. They say I can see her for a few minutes. So – ' he stood on one leg. 'Would you mind awfully if I left you to – ?'

'Of course not,' she said, smiling but afraid. If the old man refused to settle for tinned soup and omelettes and Amanda for her tipple, it was now she, and not Jocelyn, who would have to weather the storm.

'Oh, good. Right.' He looked round rather helplessly. 'I'll get over there.'

He went, without a backward glance, returned and put his head round the door. 'Er, goodbye, Miss Thompson,' he said vaguely.

'Goodbye, Mr Pentecost. I do hope you'll find every – thing – '

He was gone. She was infinitely lonely.

CHAPTER 12

It was awful. Bed after bed, each containing a lady. Jocelyn didn't like to stare at ladies in bed; but somewhere among this stricken throng lay his beloved, and he had to find her. Somewhere inside this assortment of Marks and Sparks nighties was his May. He had to find her.

'Hey! Jocelyn!' called a voice. He looked in the direction of the voice. Yes, there she was. But how different she looked, in these drear surroundings. He hurried across.

'Jocelyn, you ass, that's not me,' came the voice again. He checked, stared. The lady for whom he had been heading grinned, shook her head. 'There's a pity. Been raising my hopes nicely, hadn't you, boyo.'

He said, 'I do beg your pardon,' smiled, and veered a few points. And there at last was May, pale but beautiful. 'You can talk to her if you'd rather,' she said. The two women grinned cheerfully at each other. This was one of those feminine strongholds in which even the nicest and most loving of wives cannot resist ganging up against the lone male chauvinist.

He went and kissed her. Love and tenderness flowed out of him, he was enfolding her with them, but somehow May didn't seem to be on the receiving end. She was still listening to the Welsh girl, who was saying, 'Have to keep an eye on them, don't you, love.' 'You do indeed,' said May. And now from across the ward someone else was joining in. It looked as though Jocelyn's little mistake would keep the dorm happy till lights out.

He sat down, took her hand. 'Darling, how are you? I've been so worried,' he said anxiously.

'Oh, I'm fine. I just don't know what all the fuss is about. How are the children? And' – suddenly, for a moment, he was no longer a male chauvinist pig – 'and how are you, my darling?'

He smiled his anxious smile. 'Don't you worry about us. We're managing splendidly. But – are the doctors really satisfied with you?'

'Of course. Don't worry so.' She gave him a too brilliant smile. She squeezed his hand. He could feel the nervous tension in her grip. 'Now listen carefully, I've got everything organized.'

He looked alarmed. May said proudly: 'I bullied them into bringing me the telephone trolley, and I rang up Elspeth Mackintosh.'

'Elspeth Mackintosh?'

She misinterpreted the horror in his voice. 'Oh, it wasn't easy. I had to abase myself, she made sure of that. But when she'd rubbed my nose in the dust long enough, she agreed to unpack, and she and her brother will move in tomorrow.'

'But – ?' he said.

'Oh, I know it's not ideal. But she deserves some credit. And you will all be looked after.' She lay back, and waited for the applause.

It didn't come. She looked at him sharply. He said, 'As a matter of fact, May, it sounds an ideal arrangement, and it is wonderful of you, lying on your bed of pain, to have done all this. I really do appreciate it.'

'But –?' she said. He heard the tinkle of ice.

'Well, Father's gone ahead – you know Father – '

'I do indeed. That rather portly old gentleman who lives with us.'

'No. I mean you know what he's like.'

She said, exasperated, 'Jocelyn, when they quibbled over letting me have the telephone trolley, I threatened a relapse. And if you don't tell me what you've all been up to I shall have another.'

'We haven't been up to anything. It's Father.' Jocelyn wouldn't normally sell anyone down the river. But he knew when the storm cones were being hoisted.

'What's he done, for heaven's sake?'

'Well, he's brought Miss Thompson in to housekeep. Sort of,' he finished lamely.

'What do you mean, "sort of"?'

'Well, housekeep.'

'And she's actually installed?' He nodded.

There was a long silence. 'How very obliging of Miss Thompson,' May said at last.

'Yes,' he said warily.

Another silence. May said, in a rather tight voice, 'The fact that I happen to have a jealous nature doesn't make it an any the less satisfactory arrangement.'

'My dear May, you're not jealous of little Miss T?'

'Of course I'm jealous.'

He said, 'But May! A splendid woman like you, jealous of that fragile little creature?'

'That's what I'm afraid of, her fragility. Haven't you noticed? Every man in the house has been just yearning to comfort and protect her, ever since she arrived. Even Gaylord. Still' – to his astonishment her eyes filled with tears. Reaction, he decided. She must still be very weak – 'so long as she sees my children fed, and looks after you, my darling – '

'May, don't torment yourself. You trust me?' he said hopefully.

'As much as I'd trust Amanda with the bleach,' she said coolly. She sat up, looking troubled. She reached out and took his hand, clung to it rather desperately. Then she shook herself, and said, 'I can rely on you to telephone Miss Mackintosh and tell her she won't be needed after all?'

'Of course, darling.'

'Frankly, I will admit, I'm not sorry. I think she'd have established a dictatorship. But you will thank her? And humbly apologize?'

'I will.'

'Good. Now. The joint's in the fridge and there should be enough for you to have it cold for lunch tomorrow, unless Miss T's a shepherd's pie expert. And there's an apple tart – ' She gave him a complete résumé of the household situation. Then she said, 'But, darling, you will – help with Amanda?'

'Of course.'

She said, 'You know, I think I envy her Amanda almost as much as I envy her you.' She looked bleak.

They stared at each other gravely. 'Poor old May,' he said.

'Why? Because I've got to give up for a few days something she has never had and may never have?'

It was his turn to be silent. Then he said, 'Bless you, May.'

A nurse appeared at the end of the ward, and rang a surly, sullen bell. And for good measure, she gave Jocelyn a surly, sullen look. Well, he didn't blame her. If nursing was left to him, the sick and dying would litter the streets.

It was time to go. And that nurse had scared him. Hurriedly he kissed his wife, turned away. 'And watch it,' she called with a sudden grin.

He grinned back. A woman who could look her own feminine nature straight in the eye, and tell it where to get off! A woman who could feel compassion for a fragile creature whose very fragility was a weapon! 'Sweet rois of vertew and of gentilness,' he murmured, for he could be very sentimental on occasion. 'What you say, bach?' asked the Welsh girl, whose bed he happened to be passing. He felt foolish, smiled apologetically, and passed on.

Gaylord and Miss Thompson had done a splendid job. Amanda – clean, warm, full of babyfood and bonhomie, wrapped in a warm, sweet-smelling nightie, was on top of the world. To begin with she had been a little put out that May, who was quite literally her world, had disappeared. But the present incumbent seemed eager to please, and Gaylord was there to lend continuity, so she took the sensible view that so long as the service was satisfactory, she wouldn't enquire too closely about the staff.

She stared about her with grave, wondering eyes. She looked at Miss Thompson, shouted an unintelligible remark, slapped down a tiny palm to give it emphasis, then suddenly chortled at the recollection of her own wit. Then she snuggled back against Miss Thompson's arm, crowing and gurgling in drowsy well-being.

The gas fire hissed, filling the room with warmth. Outside the window, the earth lay silent under its snow. Miss Thompson was in very heaven. To hold this warm, happy little creature in her arms; to hear its infant murmurs of content; to know that it was she who had, by her ministrations, created this rare perfection of human happiness – it was her moment of paradise. She looked across at Gaylord, sturdy and grave. She tried to imagine what it must be like to be May Pentecost, mother of these two, wife to Jocelyn; yet reminding herself, sensibly, that babies can be screaming devils, small boys intractable, husbands unbearable.

It occurred to Gaylord that if Miss Thompson was supposed to be doing all the things Momma usually did, and if Momma telephoned from the hospital to ask whether Gaylord was in bed, and he wasn't, Miss Thompson would be in dead trouble. So, much as it went against his principles, he said, 'I think perhaps you ought to tell me to go to bed, Miss Thompson.' To go to bed without being told was, of course, unthinkable.

'Do you, Gaylord? Right, off you go. We'll just put Amanda down, shall we?'

They put Amanda down. She looked aggrieved at first, but soon accepted the situation. 'Now, Gaylord, can you bath yourself?'

' 'Course.' It was his turn to feel aggrieved, though he was too kind to show it. But there he'd been protecting Miss Thompson all day, a knight in shining armour if ever there was one, and she suddenly turns round and asks the knight whether he can bath himself!

'Right. I'll bring you some supper. What do you have?'

'Hot milk and honey sandwiches. Please, Miss Thompson.'

She put a caressing hand on his head, went down to the kitchen. When she came back with his supper he was perched up in bed in his red pyjamas, sleek of hair and scrubbed of face. Don't children come up clean, she thought. Any woman would give a fortune for a complexion like that. He said, 'Is Poppa home?'

'Not yet, dear.'

He sounded forlorn. 'I hope Momma's all right.'

'She will be.' She longed to comfort him. 'Now, have I brought you enough sandwiches?'

'Super. Momma only brings me half those.'

'Night, night, darling.'

'Night, night.' He held up his face to be kissed. It was already sweet with honey. But it had a sweetness of its own, she thought. She peeped into the nursery. Her other babe was sleeping peacefully. With a full heart, she tiptoed downstairs.

Jocelyn came home.

When one visits a hospital expecting to find a loved one lying pale and wan and silent; and instead finds her perched up and apparently bursting with nervous energy and female bossiness; then, however thankful one is, one cannot help feeling slightly cheated. So with Jocelyn. He had gone filled with love and tenderness and sympathy. And May didn't seem to want any of them.

He went in at the back door, and into the kitchen. Miss Thompson was sitting at the table. She rose, smiling. 'There you are. I do hope you don't mind. I waited to have my supper with you.'

'You shouldn't – '

'Frankly, I was a bit scared of eating with your father. I knew I shouldn't be able to think of anything to say.' She was already at the cooker. 'Ham omelettes? How is Mrs Pentecost?'

'Doing very well.'

'I'm so glad. That is good news.'

'Yes,' said Jocelyn, who still couldn't quite get over the feeling that May had rather overdone the girlish excitement.

'Let me get you a sherry.'

'Thank you. That would be wonderful,' he said. Goodness, he was tired. 'Do get yourself something. I'll just go and have a word with Gaylord.'

The omelettes had been delicious. So had the crusty bread and the Stilton. They had said little, she sensing his weariness, and his absorption in his problems. But now, over the coffee, she said, 'It was wonderful for me, finding Julia here. Is her father living here, too?'

'No, I think he's staying on at the cottage.'

'Oh, well, he'll be around. I want to get that gentleman in a corner and talk to him.'

The idea of anyone getting Duncan Mackintosh in a corner – especially anyone as diminutive as Miss Thompson, filled Jocelyn with amazement. Wendy said, 'Did you know his wife was a ballet dancer? And he won't let Julia follow in mother's footsteps. It'll break the child's heart. Still – I haven't worked on him properly yet.'

He looked at her small, resolute jaw, and marvelled. The idea of Wendy working on Duncan Mackintosh was like the idea of working on granite with a fretsaw. Still, he had seen granite pebbles smoothed and rounded by the sea. It took the sea a few hundred million years, of course. But he was never one to underrate the power of women. She said, 'What are you smiling at?'

He said, 'I was just feeling a little male sympathy for Duncan Mackintosh. But seriously, Miss Thompson, I wish you luck.'

'Thanks.' Then she asked the question she had been longing to ask ever since his return. 'Did you tell Mrs Pentecost I was here?'

'Yes. She's so grateful to you.'

Wendy was silent. She didn't somehow think that gratitude would be Mrs Pentecost's prime emotion. 'I'm glad she's so much better,' she said.

And so they finished their first meal. A man and a woman, at meat, their conversation drifting and dying like summer breezes. Yet this will go onward the same, Though Dynasties pass...

Only Miss Thompson heard the sound of the motor cycles in the lane. And snuggled deliciously in her bed. For almost the first time in her life, there were men in the house in which she slept. Danger was no longer her responsibility. Besides, there were plenty of motor cycles around nowadays. No reason to assume it was her tormentor. She lay and thought about Mr Pentecost, and quickly drifted back into sleep.

Only Schultz heard the footsteps in the stackyard. Playmates! He began to bark joyously, for he was always bored at night. He just didn't know where everyone went to.

The footsteps were coming nearer. Now the latch on the door of Schultz's outhouse was being lifted. Schultz was in very heaven. He bounced forward eagerly to meet his new playmates...

No one heard the silence when Schultz's barking ceased. Not even Gaylord. Gaylord slept peacefully, knowing that Momma had stopped being unconscious and would soon be home again; and that until that happy day came his dear Miss Thompson would be looking after him; and that the dreaded Elspeth Mackintosh was catching the early train to Scotland.

Wendy Thompson was preparing breakfast when Miss Elspeth Mackintosh marched in at the back door, dumped a suitcase on the kitchen floor, looked Wendy up and down aggressively, and said, 'Aren't you the schoolteacher who's always blethering about Julia and ballet school?'

Wendy said bravely, 'I am Julia's teacher. And I do think it will be a very great shame if she is not allowed to follow her bent.'

'You do? And what are you doing with that frying pan, may I ask?'

'Mr John Pentecost asked me to lend a hand – '

'Aye? Well, Mrs Pentecost asked me to take over while she's in hospital. So ye can awa' hame.'

'I'm hanged if I'll awa' hame.'

Elspeth's rage was cold as ice. Mrs Pentecost's cry for help had been music in her ears. It had meant she could stay on without losing face. It had meant she could be condescending and patronizing to that Pentecost woman. It had meant she could knock a bit of discipline into the wee boy, and give the dreamy Jocelyn Pentecost the dusting around he so sorely needed. Power was in Elspeth's grasp. She wasn't having any pale schoolteacher taking it from her. She said, 'Don't you adopt that line with me, Miss Thompson. Everything's arranged.'

Wendy felt quite capable of hitting Miss Mackintosh over the head with the frying pan. She was delivered from this temptation by the entry of Gaylord, who could not have looked more taken aback had he found the White Nun of Shepherd's Warning in the middle of the kitchen. But before he could gather his wits Elspeth said, 'Now laddie, I suppose that with your mother in hospital you thought you needn't wash your neck this morning?'

' 'Course not,' said Gaylord, who had thought just that. He stuck his lower lip out. 'I thought you'd gone,' he said in a disappointed voice.

'No. Your mother asked me stay and look after you all.'

'But Miss Thompson's looking after us.' He went and stood beside Wendy, who put an arm about his shoulders. He was beginning to feel insecure. Momma, do a thing like that? Never! Momma had her faults, he'd be the first to agree. But she'd never put him and Poppa in this woman's charge.

Gaylord had left the door open. Julia came dancing through it on her toes, smiling, crooning happily. Aunt Elspeth should be well on her way to Scotland by now, leaving her with Daddy and nice Miss Thompson and Gaylord. Oh, she had a lovely day before her. She –

She went down on her heels. The smile faded. The crooning stopped. 'Aunt – I thought – ?'

'Aye. You thought I'd go and leave you uncared for. Not me, lassie. I've got a heart in my body,' she said virtuously.

Gaylord looked as though he doubted it. Miss Thompson, seeing the fear in Julia's face, said, 'Don't worry, Julia. Your aunt may not be staying. Nothing has been decided.'

'Havers!' said Elspeth rudely. 'Everything has been decided.'

It was at this fraught moment that Jocelyn Pentecost came warily into the kitchen.

There had been only one thought in Jocelyn's head when he awoke: to telephone the hospital.

He put on his dressing gown, went into his study, telephoned. Mrs Pentecost was satisfactory.

Satisfactory. A grudging word. But picking up the telephone had stirred something in his mind, awakened some still-unidentified memory. Telephone. He had to telephone. Someone – could it be May? – had asked him – ?

The awful truth flooded in on him. He ought to have telephoned Miss Mackintosh last night! He looked at his watch. The train from Shepherd's Warning had gone an hour ago. Miss Mackintosh would not be on it, simply because he had forgotten to ring her. Far worse, she'd probably be lording it in the Pentecost kitchen. The inferiority complex that always bedevilled him where the Mackintoshes were concerned, swelled like a balloon. He had two choices: to bath, shave, and dress, and hope that while he bathed, shaved and dressed someone – his father, or fate – would have resolved the crisis; or to go down and face what promised to be some very Wagnerian music.

As so often happened, the Bard advised him. ' "Be bloody, bold and resolute",' Jocelyn murmured, and marched downstairs, a very unwarlike Macbeth.

The dreaded Elspeth viewed the dressing-gowned and unshaven Jocelyn with a disapproval that amounted to contempt. 'Lord save us, Mr Pentecost, and is that the way to appear before two spinster ladies?'

Spinster lady yourself, thought Wendy rudely. She said, 'Mr Pentecost, will you tell Miss Mackintosh that your father asked me – '

Jocelyn said, 'Miss Mackintosh, I'm most terribly sorry. I should have telephoned you yesterday evening, but – I believe the 10.40 from Ingerby does connect with the London to Glasgow express.'

As an explanation, it could be said to be lacking in the clarity one expects from an author. Miss Mackintosh said, 'I am catching no train, Mr Pentecost. Whatever gave you that idea? Mrs Pentecost asked me to stay and stay I will. No one can say that Elspeth Mackintosh hasn't a heart in her body.'

Wendy said, 'If you really wish Miss Mackintosh to stay, Jocelyn, then there is no point in my staying. Goodbye.'

'Oh, please, Miss Thompson,' wailed a stricken Gaylord.

'Don't go, Miss Thompson,' cried a tearful Julia.

'There is no question of your going,' said Jocelyn. He turned to Elspeth. 'As I explained, it was all a mistake. But for me, you'd have been on that train now.'

'I wish she was,' said Gaylord frankly.

Duncan Mackintosh came in, stamping the snow from his boots. 'Och, it was cold before sunrise. I've been inspecting the drainage in ten-acre.' He looked at the dishevelled Jocelyn. 'And you've no objection to my moving in here, as Mrs Pentecost suggested?'

'Well, as a matter of fact – ' began Jocelyn.

But Duncan wasn't listening. He seemed in an unusually good humour this morning. He hugged Julia to him, and said, 'Miss Thompson, and what are you doing here, wielding a frying pan instead of a primer?'

Jocelyn said, 'There's been a mix-up, for which I am afraid I'm responsible.'

Duncan looked as though that didn't surprise him. Jocelyn said, 'My father – '

'What about your father?' asked a voice. 'Morning, Miss Thompson. My breakfast ready yet?'

Wendy said, 'It would have been. Only Miss Mackintosh seems to think she's in charge.'

Jocelyn explained once more, stressing his own part in the affair. Like Duncan, Grandpa looked as though that didn't surprise him. Like Duncan also, he seemed in a good mood. 'Well, that's soon settled. Miss Mackintosh can look after the children, and Miss Thompson after the cooking.'

'I don't want Miss Mackintosh to look after me. I want Miss Thompson.' That was Gaylord.

Grandpa sympathized. He wouldn't have minded having Miss Thompson look after him. But he hardened his heart. He didn't relish having Elspeth in charge of his cooking. He wanted something better than oatmeal, herrings, and haggis. 'So that's settled,' he said.

'It is nothing of the kind,' said Elspeth. 'Mrs Pentecost put me in charge, and in charge I will be.'

Grandpa said, 'I put Miss Thompson in charge. And in charge she will be. And it's my house,' he finished, bristling.

Wendy said, 'If Miss Mackintosh really wishes to do all the work, I shall be very happy to look after the children.'

'I want you cooking,' said John Pentecost.

Jocelyn said, 'Father, you are dealing with volunteers, remember.'

'Oh, very well.' He turned and stabbed a finger at Elspeth. 'But I will not eat haggis, mind.'

She said contemptuously, 'Och, I ken fine what the English eat. Dinna fash yerself, man.'

So taken aback was John Pentecost by this curt dismissal that Jocelyn thought: Good Lord! Can it be that the old man has met his match? And this feeling was reinforced when his father muttered: 'I'll be in the living room. Just give me a call when the meal's ready.' John Pentecost went off. He was a little put out to find that the fire had not yet been lit. But he didn't complain. One couldn't expect everything to go like clockwork immediately. Give them a day to play themselves in. After all, he reflected with some satisfaction, it wasn't every man in this sort of situation who would have two women fighting for the honour of looking after him. It couldn't all be his tact and courtesy. It must also, he decided, have something to do with his personal magnetism.

But on the lower deck there was near mutiny. As soon as breakfast was over, Julia, Gaylord and the faithful Henry began digging an Aunt Elspeth trap. It was master-minded by Gaylord, and was to consist of a deep hole covered cunningly with cardboard and the bottoms of seed boxes.

But it was Julia who began to sow doubts. 'What do we do when she falls in, Gaylord?'

It hadn't occurred to Gaylord that they did anything. The ball, it had seemed to him, would then be strictly in Aunt Elspeth's court. But now that the matter had been raised, he began to wonder whether they did not toil in vain.

'We could put big spikes in the bottom of the pit,' said the amiable Henry.

Julia shuddered.

Gaylord had to admit it: catching Aunt Elspeth in an Aunt Elspeth trap, with or without spikes, would get them nowhere. It would take far more than that to deal with the lady. But they couldn't waste the hole. 'I vote we dig down to Australia instead,' he said.

Henry was always pleased to do anything his friend Gaylord suggested. And the kind-hearted Julia was very relieved not to be digging a pit for her aunt. So they all worked with a will, driven on by the thought of the astonishment on those upside-down faces when finally Gaylord, Julia, and Henry Bartlett, earthy but triumphant, stepped forth on to antipodean soil.

But they were still quite a long way from Australia when it occurred to Gaylord that he hadn't seen his friend Schultz this morning.

'And what have you been doing, Gaylord?' asked Miss Thompson.

'Well, we started digging an Aunt Elspeth trap for Aunt Elspeth. But then we decided not to.'

Wendy stifled the question 'why?' and just smiled understandingly.

Gaylord said, 'So we went to Australia instead.'

'Did you really? What was the weather like?'

'Bit misty. Miss Thompson, where's Poppa?'

'In his study. I don't think you ought to disturb him, do you?'

'Can I disturb you, instead?'

'Of course.'

'I've lost Schultz. His front door was open, and he's gone.'

'You don't think you left him in Australia?'

'No. He didn't come.'

'Well, he can't be far away, can he? Shall we go and look for him?'

'Oh, yes, Miss Thompson.'

They set off briskly through the snow, in the morning sunshine. Her right hand held Julia's tight; her left hand, Gaylord's. Henry Bartlett tagged along behind, silent, self-contained. They kicked up the snow with their wellies, they laughed, they chattered. 'One man went to mow,' they sang. 'Went to mow a meadow.' Their hearts, even Wendy's, were light and gay as the hearts of children.

But they didn't find Schultz.

The food at lunchtime was copious, nourishing and enjoyable.

Elspeth, having served everyone, went and sat herself down in May's chair. This irritated and distressed Jocelyn; though, fair-minded as always, he had to admit there was nowhere else she could sit.

Gaylord was less fair-minded. He said hotly, 'That's Momma's chair.'

'And Momma's in hospital,' Elspeth said coolly.

Gaylord was nearly in tears. He wouldn't have minded Miss Thompson sitting there. But not Aunt Elspeth.

Jocelyn said, 'It doesn't matter, Gaylord. Please!'

'But it's Momma's chair.' Now he was really crying.

This wasn't like Gaylord at all. He was never one to fuss about inessentials. Jocelyn, secretly sympathizing, said sternly, 'Stop being silly, Gaylord.'

'Excellent shepherd's pie, this,' said Grandpa.

To everyone's astonishment Duncan Mackintosh rose, went and nudged his sister out of her seat. 'Change places, lass.'

'I will do no such thing,' said Elspeth.

'Oh yes you will,' said Duncan.

Everyone except Grandpa watched with bated breath.

Elspeth sat tight. Then, slowly, she picked up her plate and went and sat in Duncan's place. 'Pandering to a neurotic child,' she muttered.

'What's neurotic?' asked Gaylord, interested in spite of his tears.

'You are,' said Elspeth.

'Oh no he's not,' said Wendy. 'His mother's illness must have been a traumatic experience. And his dog's wandered off this morning. I think he's been very brave.'

More than ever did Gaylord want to marry Miss Thompson. He smiled tearfully. Duncan sat down. 'Is that better, laddie?' he asked.

'Yes, thank you,' said Gaylord.

Jocelyn gave Duncan a quick smile. 'Thanks,' he said quietly. He remembered something. 'You say Schultz has wandered off again?'

'Yes. We've been looking for his spoors. But we can't find them anywhere, can we, Miss Thompson.'

Duncan addressed himself to the old man. 'Mr Pentecost, I wanted to store some potatoes in the small outhouse, but there's a Mini in the way. Do you know anything about it?'

'Oh, dear,' said Wendy. 'It's mine. The garage people are supposed to be collecting it today. But you know what they're like, these days.'

'Aye. Well, if they've not been by this evening, I'll have a look at it for ye.'

'That's awfully kind of you,' said Wendy.

As, on a cloudy day, a thin gleam of sunshine will flit for a moment across the high corries of the mountains, so now something that could almost be called a smile flickered over Duncan's features. 'I'm thinking of my potatoes, Miss Thompson,' he said quietly.

CHAPTER 13

That Monday passed, as even Mondays do.

The group of comparative strangers who now inhabited the farmhouse already began to take on a certain cohesion, to find points of contact, to decide that, since for a time they had to live together, they might as well look for each other's good points, if any.

Gaylord, really worried now that Schultz had not appeared at feeding time, formed himself into a search party, complete with rope, electric torch, and dog biscuits. Jocelyn set off to visit his wife. John Pentecost went and snoozed in his easy chair before the now bright fire. He was still congratulating himself. Today, without his initiative, he and Jocelyn might well have been facing each other miserably across a plate of cold mutton. Instead, no sooner had he finished a splendid breakfast, it seemed, than Elspeth had bustled in with what she called a 'fly cuppie': a pot of tea, fortified with an assortment of baps, scones and pancakes. And now, after that excellent lunch, here came Elspeth with another fly cuppie, baps, scones and all, to keep him going until high tea. Like all her race, Miss Mackintosh believed that the human frame cannot survive unless it is nourished copiously and well at two hourly intervals. He said appreciatively, 'Miss Mackintosh! You're spoiling me.'

'Och! It'll do you good to get some decent food in your vitals.'

John tried to imagine May's reaction to this remark, but soon gave up. He was too comfortable: warm, replete, lazily munching scones while he drifted between sleep and waking.

May was less buoyant today. 'Darling,' she greeted him. 'You look pinched and hungry. Has that woman not fed you?'

'Actually,' he said, 'I had egg and bacon for breakfast, then a – '

'You never have my egg and bacon,' she said suspiciously.

'Then a fairly substantial meal at eleven; brought, mark you, to my study. And an excellent lunch at one.'

There was a long silence. 'Are you asking me to give in my notice?' she said at last.

'No.' He laughed. 'You have other qualities which the dreaded Elspeth lacks, my love.'

'Elspeth? But she's in Scotland.'

It was his turn to be silent. 'I forget to tell her,' he said at last.

'Jocelyn. You idiot. So you had to get rid of Miss Thompson instead?'

'No. They're both there.'

Silences, it seemed, were the order of the day. At last she said, 'And which of my duties has little Wendy taken over?'

'The comfort and solace of your children.'

'Not the comfort and solace of my husband?'

'No.'

'Honestly,' she said. 'I'm out of the way for five minutes, and you get two of them running after you. I really wouldn't have believed – How are the children?'

'Fine. Gaylord's worried. Schultz has gone off again. Oh, and Gaylord took considerable umbrage when Elspeth sat in your chair.'

'Bless him. Quite right too.'

'And something very surprising happened. Mackintosh made her move. I don't think he's a bad chap at all.' He remembered something. 'How are you feeling, May?'

'Frustrated. Bloody-minded. Jealous.' Suddenly she drummed her fists on the bedclothes. 'I want to get out of here.'

'Have they given you any idea?'

'No. Look! There's Sister. Go and ask her.'

There were several classes of citizen who terrified Jocelyn. Hospital sisters were high on the list. 'Er, Sister, can you tell me how long – my wife – ?'

'It'll depend on the results of the tests, won't it, Mr Pentecost?'

'And – you haven't any results yet?'

'We haven't done any tests yet.'

'But – my wife's been here since Saturday.'

She gave him a long, cool stare. 'I take it you have a five day week, Mr Pentecost?'

'No, I jolly well don't,' he said angrily. 'As an author I work seven days a week.'

If you can call it work, was implicit in her glance, though she didn't actually say it. He came away fuming. 'I gather they all knock off for the weekend,' he said. 'Your chaps aren't back from the country yet.'

'Oh, Lord,' she said. 'Do you think it would help if you saw Matron?'

'I don't think so,' he said. 'I'm just not the type.'

She laughed; her old, gay laugh. 'Oh, darling, you are sweet.' But then they sat silent. They did not feel like laughter. This parting was very hard for them. They had grown accustomed to being together.

'Tell me about your mother,' said Wendy.

Julia, sitting at her feet, her arm across Wendy's knee, stared at the carpet. 'She was ever so pretty,' she said.

'Did you ever see her dance?'

'No. But – one night – she used to let me read in bed – one night she came in when I was reading, and – ' Now the dark eyes were looking up solemnly at Wendy.

'And – ?' said Wendy.

'She's put on her ballet dress – bodice, tutu, shoes, everything. And painted her face, and combed back her hair. Oh, she – ' the child's hand gripped Wendy's knee. 'She was more beautiful than a fairy. She was the most beautiful thing I shall ever see.'

'What did she do?'

'She just stood there, smiling down at me. And she had diamonds in her hair. They sparkled in the candlelight.'

Wendy, strangely moved, could see it all: the homely bedroom; the wonder and love in the child's eyes; the woman, moved by who knows what hunger or frustration to try to recreate a beauty that was past. 'And that was in the Mearns?' she said.

'Yes.'

'What happened?'

'She said, "One day, Julia, you will look like this. Only more beautiful." Oh, I wanted to jump out of bed and hug and kiss her. But she was so – strange. I was shy, and afraid.'

'So you didn't?'

'No. Then Aunt Elspeth came in and made her cry.'

'No!' Wendy said in a horrified voice. 'Why, how, did she make her cry?'

Julia looked blank. 'I don't know. But I always wish I'd kissed her.' She was thoughtful. Then: 'She died soon after,' she said in a matter of fact voice.

'Schultz!' cried Gaylord. 'Schultz! Where are you, boy?'

The afternoon stayed silent and still. Melting snow, black trees, a brooding sky. A heron flew lazily into the still reeds. Nothing else moved in the whole wide world.

Gaylord had a cold, empty feeling that his life was built not, as he had always assumed, on rock, but on shifting sands. If Momma was not invulnerable, what possible hope was there for lesser mortals? If Momma could be hurt, the whole fabric of life was threatened. So was the comforting assumption that lost dogs always came home, that everything must, in the nature of things, end happily. He trudged on through the darkening afternoon, anxious and cold at heart.

He came to the river. The water ran black and chill. 'Schultz,' he called. 'Schultz!' The river moaned, and sighed. That, and the cold dripping of the snow, were the only sounds. Gaylord remembered, from a lifetime that was forty-eight hours away but that seemed like some dream world, the merry barking of Schultz, the laughter of his mother. He peered down into the swirling waters. There was a piece of weed, drifting and curling, brown, in shape almost like an ear.

To any small boy, any water weed has only one purpose: to be prodded. Gaylord found a stick and prodded the piece of weed shaped like an ear. He prodded again. For water weed, it had a curiously heavy texture. And when he looked closer, it seemed to be attached to something, large and brown, that heaved very slightly with the current.

Gaylord walked home, gravely and thoughtfully. 'Poppa,' he said, 'I think – '

'What, boy?' his father said gently.

'I think Schultz is in the river,' said Gaylord. And just managed to reach the bathroom before he vomited his heart up.

Derek Bates and his friends had done a good job. They hugged themselves as they gloated over their revenge, as they wondered who'd make the discovery, the kid or the old bastard, as they tried to picture their victims' faces when they learned that it didn't pay to cross someone of the calibre of Derek Bates.

And this revenge was not only sweet. It also encouraged them for the future. The old bastard needn't think he'd paid the full price for his wickedness yet. Or his family. Oh, no. Derek and his friends had quite a few more, equally humorous, tricks up their sleeves. They could hardly wait to put them into practice.

That Monday passed, as even Mondays do.

Jocelyn, heavy-hearted, telephoned the police. They said they would deal with poor Schultz, consider the possibility of foul play, and look into it. They were unimpressed by suggestions that the affair could be connected with their other enquiries.

Gaylord wanted to go and watch. 'No,' said Jocelyn. 'Oh, please, Poppa,' said Gaylord.

'Very well,' said Jocelyn. The child would grow up in an increasingly brutal and bitter world, he thought sadly. So he might as well see the results of violence early. This time it was only a dog. Next time it might be – ? 'I'll come with you,' said Jocelyn.

The police worked by the light of the car headlamps. The water looked black and oily, the snow starkly white. Water birds, disturbed, fidgeted crossly. Outside the brilliant light the world was a black, infinitely menacing void.

Gaylord held Poppa's hand very tight. 'Don't look, son,' called the sergeant as they prepared to pull the dog out. 'Don't look,' said Jocelyn, putting a hand over Gaylord's eyes. Gaylord pulled the hand away angrily. And stared. And stared, his horror only slightly anaesthetized by his love of the dramatic. Up came Schultz, limp and lifeless, water pouring from him and out of him. Gaylord made a little noise in his throat, but remained silent. 'Bleeding throat cut,' muttered someone. 'Shut up,' said an angry voice. They covered Schultz with a blanket, put him in a van, drove him away. The river ran in darkness now, the blood spreading thinly towards the sea.

'Coming, old chap?' Jocelyn said quietly.

But Gaylord went on staring. He'd seen dead things before: rabbits, mice, a cat, even Great Aunt Marigold; and he'd found them very interesting. But this was the first time he'd seen a dead friend. Though he would never have admitted it to a soul, he rather wished he hadn't come. For he knew that the dead Schultz would be with him all his days.

Later that evening, May said, 'By the way, has Schultz turned up?'

'Oh, yes,' said Jocelyn cheerfully.

She gave him a quick look. 'Unhurt?'

'Yes, of course.'

'Why "of course"?' The quick look had hardened. 'Now look, Jocelyn, you know it's not the slightest use trying to keep anything from me. What's happened?'

He said, 'I didn't want to worry you.'

'You'll worry me a lot more if you don't tell me.'

It was no use. He said, 'Someone killed him. And threw him in the river.'

She gave a little gasp, took his hand. 'Horrible! Poor Schultz. Poor Gaylord. How's he taken it?'

'A bit quiet. I left him with Miss Thompson. He wanted

to watch the police at work, so I let him.'

'Jocelyn! Was that wise?'

'I think so. They learn all about conception and birth, these days. Shouldn't they also learn about death? It's all part of the same process.'

'I don't know.' She sat staring at the bedclothes. 'I must say I'm surprised. I would have expected you to want to shield him.'

'I should have done, until recently. Now, I think – one cannot be shielded for very long. The momentum is frightening.'

'Into violence?'

He laughed. 'Here am I, worrying and depressing you. But – I wasn't going to tell you, May.'

'Poor Gaylord,' she said again. 'Me – and Schultz. We shall be confused in his mind. Bring him tomorrow, Jocelyn, so that he can see I'm in better shape than his friend.'

Gaylord was inclined to cling. Wendy Thompson's heart bled for him. She was also troubled in her conscience. Suppose, in the night, when she heard those motor cycles, she had risked looking foolish and wakened Mr Pentecost? Might this horrible and frightening thing have been avoided? She would never know. She would always wonder.

Gaylord said, 'I bet Schultz is in Heaven now.' He had a beatific vision of Schultz doing his window cleaner act against St Peter, while the Pearly Gates rattled to the thumping of his tail.

Julia said, 'Aunt Elspeth says animals don't go to Heaven.' She caught Wendy's eye. 'But I think she's wrong.'

Gaylord thought it was just the mean sort of thing Miss Mackintosh would say. Nevertheless, it depressed him. 'Well, I bet Schultz will, anyway,' he said loyally.

'Of course he will, Gaylord,' said Wendy; thinking wryly that if he did he might frighten the life out of her late mother's little horror. 'Now would you like a game of Monopoly?'

But at that moment Duncan Mackintosh came in. 'I see your car's still there, Miss Thompson,' he said without preamble, but gazing down at Julia, who had come running into his arms.

'Yes. I rang the garage again, and they promised. But they still haven't been. Is it really in your way?'

'It will be tomorrow,' he said gruffly.

'I really am sorry.'

'I'll take a look at it for you.'

'Oh, thank you, Mr Mackintosh. Can I come and hold things?'

'Ye might as well.' Gently he released himself from his daughter, though letting his hands linger as long as possible on her shoulders, and went out of the room.

She ought to help. But she couldn't leave Gaylord to his nightmare thoughts. She said, 'Come on. Let's all go. But wrap up well.'

Scarved and coated, they ran hand in hand to the outhouse. Inside, an inspection lamp cast black shadows about a beamed roof, lit brilliantly the earth floor. Duncan had got the bonnet up, his finger was touching wires and points with the gentle precision and concentration of a doctor.

Wendy went and stood beside him, peered. 'Get in and turn her over,' he said, not looking up. There was no doubt about it. The good mood of breakfast time had fled with the sunlight.

She fished her key out of her bag, went and turned the starter. It made the flat, grinding noise one would expect from an unoiled rack.

To Wendy it sounded as though the car were in its death agony. But Duncan seemed unperturbed. In fact he gave a satisfied 'Aye.'

'Is it serious?' Wendy asked.

'No. You wouldn't understand, so I may as well save my breath to cool my porridge. But it'll take about an hour. Then I'll straighten that wing for you.'

'Thank you, Mr Mackintosh.'

'Och, it's nothing. Now if you can hold the lamp so – ?'

In the flickering light of the inspection lamp, Julia looked wonderingly round the barn. 'What shall we play at?' she said.

Gaylord didn't think he wanted to play at anything. He said, 'They wrapped him in a blanket. Like they did Momma.'

Julia said, 'Don't worry, Gaylord. I bet they're giving him all sorts of nice things in Heaven.'

But he won't have me to play with in Heaven, thought Gaylord. It seemed, however, a rather conceited thing to say, so he didn't say it.

Julia misinterpreted his silence. She thought he was moping. 'I know,' she said, leaping to her feet with a very creditable entrechat, considering she was wearing wellingtons. 'Let's do a pas de deux.'

'What's a pahdidah?' asked Gaylord glumly.

'Dancing. See.' She took his hands. 'I stand so, and you – '

Gaylord was affronted. Boys didn't dance. He stood, feet firmly planted on the English earth, arms grimly folded. Nothing would have made him shift a leg, or move even a finger. Yet it was at this defiant moment that he had an idea so exciting that it drove out his nightmare memories;

made him forget his stricken Momma and even Schultz. And what gave him this brilliant idea was the sight of Miss Thompson and Mr Mackintosh standing with their heads close together under the bonnet of the car.

Miss Thompson was saying, 'Did you see that entrechat of Julia's? She's a born ballet dancer.'

'Screwdriver,' said Duncan, like an impatient surgeon. 'Small spanner. What entrechat?'

'Just then. She did an entrechat where most children would have done a hop skip and jump. It's in her blood, Mr Mackintosh.'

He straightened up. 'Give the engine another turn, will you?'

She climbed into the driving seat, turned the key. Things sounded a little livelier. 'That all?' she said.

'Yes, thanks.' She came back to the front of the car; and said, 'She's got the right figure. Long legs, sturdy body; and that proud, wonderful set of her head on her shoulders.'

'See if you can find a washer. I dropped it down there somewhere.'

She found it. 'And the right temperament. Oh, she seems shy, even timid. But she'll hold her own. And that's what matters in ballet.'

He said, 'Miss Thompson, I think you are the most irritating woman I have ever met.'

'I know I can be,' she said. 'But it's only when I get a bee in my bonnet.'

'Well, I wish you'd get this bee out of your bonnet.'

'I can't,' she said. She took a deep breath. 'I know I shouldn't say this, Mr Mackintosh. But – it's what your wife wanted.'

He straightened up, stared at her. In the stark light from the lamp, his eyes glinted out of deep shadows. 'I'll thank you to keep Jeannie's name out – ' he began furiously; broke off; and said quietly, 'How do you know?'

'The child told me.' She repeated Julia's story bravely, yet hating herself for twisting the knife in who knew what wounds.

He was silent. She said quietly, 'I think it is really your sister, not you, who is so opposed – '

'How dare you?' It was a growl, almost a snarl.

She said, 'I know I've said a lot of things I shouldn't. But it's only for Julia's sake.'

'My daughter,' he reminded her bitterly. 'Just try the engine again.'

She turned the starter. The engine ran sweetly now. 'I'll just straighten this wing,' he said, 'so that you can drive the car. The garage will have to do the respraying, of course.'

'Of course.'

He began hammering, tapping. The noise precluded conversation. At last he said coldly, 'That'll do. If you wouldn't mind finding somewhere else for the car, first thing tomorrow.'

'Thank you,' she said. 'It's been very kind of you.'

He pulled on his jacket. They would both be thankful to go their separate ways: she because she knew she had said quite enough – probably far too much – for one evening; he because, ridiculous though he knew it to be, this woman shook the hitherto unshakeable convictions by which he lived.

But: 'Where are the children?' she said.

'Probably slipped out while I was hammering. You go and open the door. Then I'll unplug the lamp.'

She crossed to the door, lifted the latch. The door would not open.

No one liked asking Duncan Mackintosh for help. She pushed, pulled, rattled. The door would not budge. 'Hurry up!' he called.

'I can't get it open,' she said.

'Oh, let me do it.' He strode across, pushed. Pushed again. 'It's locked,' he said, surprised.

'Perhaps they did it for a joke,' said Wendy. 'Gaylord,' she shouted. 'Come and unlock this door. At once, do you hear!' She was beginning to feel panicky, shut in with this man she had so angered.

'Joke!' he muttered with a whole world of contempt. He went and fetched the lamp, shone it into the keyhole. 'Is the key there?' said Wendy.

'No.'

A terrifying thought struck Wendy: I might have to spend the night here with him. In an agony of embarrassment she said, 'There must be some way.' She heard the high, nervous pitch of her own voice.

'Of course there's a way, woman. Smash the door down. Simple. But I don't want to damage property if that boy's just playing a joke. Come on. We'll go and sit in the car for ten minutes. He'll have tired of it by then.'

'I'd rather wait here,' she said.

'You'd be quite safe,' he said contemptuously.

She supposed, miserably, that she'd given him the right to speak to her like that. She said humbly, 'I meant – I could call from here.' She bent down to the keyhole. 'Gaylord. Come and open this door.'

The country night stayed silent. She walked across to her car, lowered herself into the driving seat. He came and joined her in the car. He said, staring hard in front of him, 'I'm sorry – my last remark. It was very rude.'

'And cheap,' she said.

He was silent. Then he said, 'Yes, I suppose it was.' Another silence. 'I'd never thought of myself doing or saying anything cheap,' he said, surprised.

'I wouldn't have expected it, knowing you,' she said generously.

They sat on. It was cold. And silent. A dank chill rose from the earth floor.

And there was nothing left to say.

The idea that had flooded like a spring tide into Gaylord's mind was this: if nice Miss Thompson married Mr Mackintosh, she would become Julia's mother, and Aunt Elspeth could then go jump in the lake.

He pondered. It would call for a considerable sacrifice on Gaylord's part. If Miss Thompson didn't wait for him, he just didn't know whom he'd marry. There simply wouldn't be anyone left.

But for Julia's sake he was prepared to sacrifice all. And it wasn't, frankly, just for Julia. No one would be happier than he to see Miss Mackintosh on the train for Scotland. He said, 'I've been thinking, Julia.'

'Yes, Gaylord?' She had been pirouetting before him. Now she stopped, one hand on his shoulder, and gave him her attention.

'If Miss Thompson married your Poppa, she'd be your mother.'

'She wouldn't, Gaylord. She'd be my stepmother.'

He waved aside this quibble. 'Aunt Elspeth could go back to Scotland.'

She looked at him with sudden, dawning hope. It faded. 'She might not want to marry Daddy. Or he might not want to marry her.'

Gaylord couldn't see why not. She was ever so nice.

Nevertheless, it was a good point. He gave his not inconsiderable intelligence to it. He came up with the answer. He said, 'I think, if a lady and a gentleman spend a night alone together, they have to get married.'

'They do? Why?'

'Dunno. I suppose it's a Law of Nature,' said Gaylord.

Julia, gazing thoughtfully at Miss Thompson and Daddy, remained unconvinced. 'How do you know?'

'Poppa told me,' said Gaylord who, while usually taking his father's pronouncements with a pinch of salt, was always prepared to accept them as ex cathedra when it suited his purpose.

Julia mulled this over. 'But they don't spend the night together,' she pointed out.

'They would if we locked 'em in,' Gaylord said triumphantly.

John Pentecost, having today had three major meals, and three supporting ones to see him through the intervals, was almost in the seventh heaven.

The reason that he was not quite in the seventh heaven was that Elspeth had replaced eight o'clock dinner with a splendid six o'clock high tea; which meant that by nine o'clock he was feeling decidedly peckish. He began to worry, knowing that for a man of his age to go to bed hungry was to put a great strain on the system.

He need not have worried. The Scots do not take that kind of risk. Prompt at nine o'clock Elspeth marched in with a tea pot and a dish of cakes and scones. John Pentecost fairly purred. 'Miss Mackintosh. Another meal?'

'Aye, well, a man needs to sustain himself. Now are you accustomed to take a tray up in case ye need something in the wee small hours?'

'Well – ' began John. He caught his son's eye. 'No. No thank you, Miss Mackintosh.'

'I'll wish ye goodnight, then. Goodnight, Mr Jocelyn Pentecost.'

'Goodnight.' The two men half rose. 'Goodnight, Miss Mackintosh.'

But before she could leave the room, Duncan marched in, followed by Miss Thompson. He went and stood before the old man, and said formally, 'Mr Pentecost, I have to report breaking down the door of one of your outhouses.'

'Well don't stand there, man, like a bally army sergeant. Sit down and have a cup of tea. Miss Mackintosh, another cup, please.' He spotted Wendy. 'Two more cups.'

Mackintosh sat down. John said amiably, 'Now then. Been smashing my property, have you?'

'I have reason to believe your grandson – and my daughter – locked Miss Thompson and me in.'

'Gaylord wouldn't do a thing like that,' Jocelyn said without total conviction. 'And I'm sure Julia wouldn't.'

'I thought it was mebbe an English joke,' Duncan said drily.

Jocelyn went to the door, called. 'Gaylord! Come here!'

Gaylord and Julia came in. Gaylord looked chagrined to see his plan so obviously in ruins. Julia just looked scared. Jocelyn said, 'Gaylord, did you lock Mr Mackintosh and Miss Thompson in an outhouse?'

'Yes,' said Gaylord. 'Sort of,' he qualified, not liking the look in his father's eye.

'Why?' said Jocelyn coldly.

It wasn't an easy question. 'It's a bit complicated actually,' said Gaylord.

'Take your time.'

Gaylord had never seen his Poppa so magisterial before.

He supposed it was because he was having to stand in for Momma. He said, 'If a lady and a gentleman spend a night alone together they have to get married.'

'You surprise me,' said John Pentecost.

'They do, Grandpa,' Gaylord said earnestly. 'It's a Law of Nature,' he explained.

'So – ?' said Jocelyn.

'So I thought if we locked Mr Mackintosh and Miss Thompson in the outhouse all night they'd have to get married and then Miss Thompson would be Julia's mother and Miss Mackintosh could go back to Scotland. I thought Julia would like Miss Thompson to be her mother.'

Miss Thompson was scarlet. Jocelyn said, 'I'm sorry, Mr Mackintosh.' But he was hanged if he was going to abase himself too much. He said, 'I'll admit Gaylord often does the wrong thing. But it's always from the highest possible motives.'

'I know fine how I'd deal with him,' Elspeth said grimly. She spun round on Julia. 'And with you, ma lassie.'

Jocelyn said quietly, 'But it isn't for you to deal with him, Miss Mackintosh.' He remembered Gaylord's face as he watched Schultz being pulled from the river. He saw the embarrassment on Wendy's. He saw Julia, shrinking away from her aunt. He said, 'I think it was agreed that Miss Thompson should be in charge of the children. Miss Thompson, would you like to take Gaylord and Julia, and deal with them as you think fit?'

'Come along, children,' said Wendy. She looked at Duncan Mackintosh. After what they'd been through together she thought he might have wished her goodnight. But he remained staring at one of his employer's hunting prints. She said tartly, 'Goodnight, Mr Mackintosh. It seems we can both congratulate ourselves on a lucky escape.'

He turned slowly and looked at her. 'Aye,' he said.

As soon as they were out of the room, Wendy said, 'I am absolutely furious with you both.' She seized Gaylord's head with both hands, held it so that he must stare up at her. 'Have you any idea how you've humiliated me?'

'I don't see why,' said Gaylord sturdily. 'I thought you'd have liked to be Julia's mother.'

'That's not the point,' cried Wendy, exasperated.

Gaylord thought it was the point, the whole point, and nothing but the point. But he'd long since given up trying to reason with grown-ups, even with nice sensible ones like Miss Thompson. He stuck his lower lip out. 'Well I think it was a good idea,' he said.

Later, coming out of the bathroom, he met Mr Mackintosh. He was still put out. But he said politely, 'Goodnight, Mr Mackintosh.'

'Goodnight, laddie.'

The greeting was friendlier than he had expected. He said, 'Julia would like to have Miss Thompson for a mother, Mr Mackintosh.'

'I've no doubt about that,' said the Scotsman.

'Well then,' said Gaylord reasonably.

'There's just one wee snag, laddie.'

'What's that, Mr Mackintosh?'

'I should have to have her for a wife.'

Well, Gaylord couldn't see anything wrong in that. But he knew it was no use arguing. Grown-ups lived in a world of their own. You could never tell them.

CHAPTER 14

Wendy couldn't sleep, for a number of reasons: her humiliation over that dreadful Mackintosh; her anger with the children; but most of all because she wanted to take a cold, clear look at her feelings for Jocelyn Pentecost before it was too late.

Jocelyn Pentecost! Even to whisper his name to herself gave her tremendous pleasure. He was grave and wise and kind and very vulnerable. His usual expression was a mixture of concern and amusement. He was a man to whom she could devote her life with complete happiness. But – he was a married man, and if she did not want to destroy her own happiness for ever, the sooner she took to her heels the better.

But she couldn't take to her heels. She must stay, living in the same house as this gentle person, this man who was so far above anything she had thought possible. She couldn't avoid seeing and talking to him. But she must not, must not, fall any further in love with him. Or she would receive a wound from which she would never, quite, recover.

There was a noise in the still night. Her door was creaking open. She froze, not daring to analyse what hopes and doubts and fears she had in that moment. Footsteps padded across the carpet. 'Can I come in?' said Gaylord.

'Of course, dear.' He slid into the crook of her arm. 'What's the matter?' she asked.

'It's Schultz,' he said. He swallowed. 'I wish he wasn't dead.'

'There, dear,' she said tenderly. 'There!' yearning to comfort.

More footsteps padded across the carpet. 'Miss Thompson?'

'Hello, Julia. Are you coming in, too?'

'Yes, please, Miss Thompson.'

'Come round here. Gaylord's on that side. What's the matter?'

'I don't know. Mother, and ballet school, and everything. And you being cross.'

She lay, murmuring endearments, one child in the crook of each arm, telling herself severely that her own misery was in her hands, to intensify or to cure; but that these children were victims of the world's evil, and the world's stupidity.

Gaylord and Julia wept, and were soon asleep. But Wendy Thompson lay for a long time, staring up dry-eyed into the darkness.

Tuesday. Jocelyn took Gaylord to see his mother.

Gaylord knew all about hospitals. He'd been in one, hadn't he. Nevertheless, he approached his mother's bed with some trepidation, even when he saw her sitting there, smiling away and holding out her arms to him.

He stood and stared. May had been right. In his mind she and the dog were strangely mixed. He could not believe now that Momma was alive and dry and smiling, while Schultz was dead; sodden and dead, wrapped in a dripping grey blanket.

'Oh, darling,' she said, her voice breaking, for she knew the gropings of his perplexed mind.

It did the trick. He ran into her arms. 'Momma, we have baps and scones with our elevenses. Aunt Elspeth says a man needs a wee bittie something in his inside about mid morning.'

'Does she, my pet?' She grinned up at Jocelyn, who asked every visiting relative's 64,000 dollar question. 'How are you?'

'Fine. Fine. Coming out tomorrow. You can pick me up about eleven. If you've nothing else on, that is.'

'No!' He heard the unsteadiness of his voice, felt his features crumpling. 'You mean – everything's all right?'

'Perfectly. The doctor says he'd pass me for jet fighters.'

They smiled at each other. 'I'd rather you came home and looked after the kids and me,' he said unsteadily. He began to discuss her homecoming in unnecessary detail. But it was so wonderful a subject that he could not leave it alone. Only later did he say, 'Oh, I almost forgot.' He fished in his coat pocket. 'This came for you this morning.' He gave her a small parcel.

'For me?' Unknown, neat handwriting. She tore off the outside wrappings. Inside, an inner parcel; and a note. She read it, said: 'A thank-you letter from Edouard Bouverie. And will I give the parcel to the little schoolteacher whose address he does not know.'

'Intriguing.'

'Most.' She felt the parcel. 'Could be anything.' She handed it to Jocelyn. 'If you give it her without finding out what's in it, I'll never forgive you, never.'

'I can hardly stand over her while she opens it.'

'I don't care how you find out. But I'm fascinated. That little creature's got all you men eating out of her hand. Even Gaylord.'

Gaylord actually blushed. Jocelyn, putting a hand on his son's shoulder said, 'Gaylord has plans for Miss Thompson. Haven't you, old chap?'

May looked enquiringly at her son, who said: 'I thought it would be nice if she could be Julia's mother. But it means her marrying Mr Mackintosh, and I don't think she wants to much. I think – ' He fell silent.

'You think what, dear?'

'Oh, nothing,' he said, trying to sound casual, but knowing desperately that being in a hospital bed wouldn't stop Momma getting her teeth in.

Jocelyn was always slightly on edge when Miss Thompson was under discussion. So he was relieved when he saw the nurse with the bell appear grim and purposeful in the doorway. 'Well, better be off – ' he began briskly.

'You think what, Gaylord?' said Momma.

'I think she'd rather marry Poppa,' said Gaylord.

'CLANG,' went the bell. 'But she couldn't, could she,' said Gaylord reasonably, 'because he's married already. So that's all right, isn't it.'

'That bell woman's giving me a look,' Jocelyn said nervously.

'She's not the only one,' said May. 'Gaylord, why do you think Miss Thompson wants to marry Poppa?'

Jocelyn ruffled his son's hair. 'Oh, come along, you old matchmaker.'

'Why?' said Momma remorselessly.

'She sort of looks at him,' said Gaylord.

'I see,' said May. She kissed them both rather absently. The temptation to defy Sister, Matron, and if need be the entire Health Service, and insist on going home now, was almost overwhelming, and she was quite capable of carrying it out.

But she overcame the temptation. She thought it might give her husband the impression she was jealous.

'I've some splendid news,' said Jocelyn. 'May's coming home tomorrow. They can find nothing wrong.'

'Mr Pentecoost, I am glad.' Wendy beamed all over her friendly little face. She was glad. For him. But not for herself. Tomorrow. Tomorrow it would all end: the company, the sweet responsibility for the children, the gentle presence of this man who now smiled at her with such simple happiness from across the supper table. Tomorrow his wife would walk back into his life; and she, Wendy, would walk out of it, and out of his heart and mind, for ever. He would scarcely notice her passing. And that was how it had to be. There was no other answer. This way to the tomb. This way to the empty, sunless years. Farewell, farewell, my love.

He said, 'I can't tell you how grateful we all are to you. It really was incredibly kind.'

She said, speaking slowly to keep her voice steady, staring down very hard at the tablecloth, 'You could never understand what a privilege and a pleasure it's been for me; what a wonderful experience to spend a few days among your family.'

'It's we who are grateful, Wendy.' The sudden use of her Christian name brought the tears to her eyes. He remembered something. 'Oh, I've got a parcel for you. It's from Dorothea's Frenchman. He didn't know your address, so he sent it to May.'

She took the parcel, turned it over in astonishment. 'But – are you sure it's for me? We scarcely spoke to each other.'

'Certain.'

'How very strange. Do you mind if I open it?'

'Please do.' He'd be in dead trouble if she didn't.

She unfastened the paper, and found inside a battered shoe box. She opened the box. Inside was a pair of ballet shoes. They were well worn, and rather shabby. There was also a clean, crisp card, on which was written: 'For you, or for your pupil, as you think best. They belonged to a girl who danced at the Bolshoi, long ago. Fight the good fight. E. St M. B.'

It was too much, too sudden, too overwhelming. Wendy was already in a suppressed, emotional state. This kindness, this discovery that she had an ally in what she had assumed must be her private war, simply opened the floodgates. 'Excuse me,' she said, rising, 'I – '

'What is it?' Jocelyn was on his feet, yearning to comfort and protect. But she groped her way, blinded and choked by tears, to the door. And when he tried to seize her shoulder, to turn her to him in his distress for her, she shook him off almost roughly. 'Wendy,' he cried, 'what is it? Tell me, so that I can help.'

'You – can't – help,' she sobbed. 'No one – can.' And she went through the door and up to her room, clutching the crumpled paper, and the card, and the shoes of the dancer.

That night, Gaylord ran with Schultz in the summer meadows, laughing until his sides ached at the antics of his amiable friend. But then, suddenly, his friend was no longer there, and there was only something wrapped in a grey, sodden blanket, and when Gaylord pulled aside the blanket he saw the dead eyes of Momma staring at him out of a marble face. Wendy, hearing his screams, leaped out of bed and went to her door, only to see Jocelyn disappearing into his son's room. She made herself turn, and go back to bed, thinking: tomorrow night I shall say to myself, bitterly, 'Last night, you could have helped him comfort his son. What more innocent? Yet you didn't. Why? Because of your folly, or your integrity? Or your fear? Whatever the reason, whether noble or base, you will not have the choice again tonight, or tomorrow night, or ever.'

John Pentecost, wakened by he knew not what, sat up and eyed the thermos of tea, and the plate of scones which Elspeth had this time (in the absence of Jocelyn) persuaded him it would be prudent to bring up with him. He poured a cup of tea. He munched a scone. Thus fortified, he settled down to sleep until breakfast time.

Derek Bates and his friends prowled about the farm. A petrol bomb, the product of their combined intelligences, lay in Derek's pocket. They weren't out to do damage this time. They'd had a few jars at the Prince of Wales, and were strangely relaxed. Peace on earth, goodwill towards men, just about summed up their feelings tonight. All they wanted was a giggle.

The most humorous thing, it seemed to them, would be to set fire to the hen roost. But while they were looking for the hen roost Derek suddenly threw up all over his gear, after which he began to lose interest in the proceedings, so they chucked the petrol bomb into an outhouse, where, disappointingly, it failed to explode, and made for home so that Derek's mother could clean him up, Derek being of a somewhat fastidious nature.

May had once read that a man, taken into captivity, sees his former life of freedom as something too wonderful and beautiful for belief. She felt much the same about being in hospital. All night she lay awake thinking: tomorrow I shall be at home, keeping an eye on my dear Jocelyn, battling endlessly with Gaylord, being the whole world once more to Amanda, in charge of my own kitchen, head of my own table, mistress of my own house; with the admirable Miss Thompson, to whom I am of course extremely grateful, safe back in Ingerby.

And so it was. Jocelyn fetched May out of hospital. And by mid-day Miss Thompson was driving sadly along the river road in her little Mini, with the charmingly expressed thanks of Mrs Pentecost still in her ears, and the memory of Jocelyn saying goodbye while just a little too obviously eager to get back to his wife; and trying hard to be sensible and adult about the fact that Gaylord had not shown up to say goodbye.

This was the spot where that horrible motor cyclist had appeared – so long ago, it seemed. And now a small figure was running towards her flagging her down. She stopped, ridiculously pleased. 'Gaylord! How nice. I thought –' She reached over, opened the passenger door. He climbed in, panting.

He said, 'I wish you wouldn't go, Miss Thompson. First Schultz, and then you.'

'But you've got your mother back. That's all that matters, isn't it?'

' 'Course.' But he was looking doubtful. 'Momma and I sometimes fail to see eye to eye.' He pointed to the river. 'That's where I found Schultz. It's still a bit bloody, in places.'

She said, 'You know, darling, I don't think you ought to come down to this bit of the river. It's – not very nice.'

He was silent. Then he said, 'I wish you would marry Mr Mackintosh. Then you could be Julia's mother, and live at World's End Cottage, and Miss Mackintosh could go back to Scotland, and I could come and have tea sometimes.'

'Perfect. There's only one snag,' she said.

'I know. You don't want to marry Mr Mackintosh. That's what I told Momma and Poppa.'

'Gaylord! You haven't discussed this with your mother?'

'Sort of. But I said you'd rather marry Poppa.' He wriggled down more comfortably in his seat. 'But you couldn't, could you.'

At the back of her mind had been a foolish hope that one day she might met this family again; perhaps, who could say, even be accepted as a friend. Now she knew it was impossible. It was as though her most shameful longings had been revealed to the wife of the man she so wrongly, yet so honourably, loved. She had been going home with heartbreak and loneliness. Now she would take shame as well. 'What did your mother say?' she asked. Her voice was harsh.

'She said, "I see".'

'Just "I see"?'

'Yes. But in the voice she uses when we're failing to see eye to eye.'

'I'm not surprised,' she said. Then she suddenly turned and kissed him. 'Oh, Gaylord, you little chump!'

Well, he didn't understand. How often did he understand grown-ups? But he thought Miss Thompson sounded a bit upset. So he said, comfortingly, 'Never mind, Miss Thompson. You can always marry me. Any time,' he added generously.

'Thank you, Gaylord,' she said gratefully. She opened the passenger door.

He got out. 'Goodbye, Miss Thompson.' He walked back along the lane, kicking moodily at the grass that lined the road. He was melancholy. It was strange how two friends, lost in so short a space, could empty the world.

He came home, and went poking about the stackyard, looking for buried treasure.

Now he was too young to be called a conservationist. But he was an ardent protector of milk bottles. Grandpa had told him how scarce they had become. Besides, their shining glass, the perfection of their form, the exquisitely embossed 'Ingerby Co-op', or 'Northern Dairies' on their flanks – to Gaylord all this made them things of great price. So that when he found one filled with what smelt like petrol, and stuffed with bits of dirty rag, he was incensed. He put the rags in the dustbin, emptied the petrol down the drain, washed the bottle carefully under the stackyard tap, and took it to Momma. 'Momma, look what someone left lying about. All full of petrol and stuffed with rags.'

'Petrol?' said May. It was the key word.

'Smelt like it.'

She had come home, to husband and children and freedom. She had known an intensity of happiness that only deprivation can bring. She had known it could not last, that it must burn down like a too-bright flame. But she had hoped it would linger. Now it was extinguished – by a milk bottle, and a single word. 'What did you do with the rags?' she asked.

'Put them in the dustbin.'

'And the petrol?'

'Poured it down the drain.'

'And you washed the bottle?'

He nodded. She said, 'When it comes to destroying evidence, Gaylord, you are in the premier class.'

'Is that good?' he asked hopefully.

'It depends on the circumstances,' she said.

Later she told Jocelyn. 'It must have been a petrol bomb,' she said. 'But thanks to Gaylord the only evidence is a bright and shining milk bottle.'

'Which wouldn't particularly impress the police,' he said.

'Impress them? They think we've all got bees in our bonnets already.'

They sat staring into the fire. She said, 'They've frightened Miss Thompson twice. They've killed Schultz. And now – a petrol bomb in a stackyard. I tell you, Jocelyn, they've frightened me.'

He was silent. 'Fire,' she said. 'In the night perhaps. Or – the children. I shan't dare to let them out of my sight.'

'It's damnable,' he said.

He found to his surprise that the controlled May was quietly weeping. He took her in his arms. 'It was so – marvellous, coming home,' she said. 'And now? They've spoilt everything.'

'They always do,' he said.

'Who?'

'The destroyers.'

'Oh, yes. Your theory.' She managed a smile. 'But why? Why do they want to destroy?'

'Because of the darkness in our souls,' he said.

CHAPTER 15

It was the April meeting of the Ingerby Writers' Club.

Miss Thompson sat on the back row in a state of considerable ferment. She hadn't wanted to come. After Gaylord's revelations she felt that she could never look either Mr or Mrs Pentecost in the eye again. But come she had, telling herself it was her job as Speaker-Finder to be present, yet knowing in her heart that nothing could stop her taking this last look at Jocelyn Pentecost. But she would keep in the background. With any luck he would have forgotten her connection with the Club, and wouldn't even notice her.

He came into the room, looking slightly nervous. Wendy knew it was really her job to meet him, to introduce him to Madam Chairman. But she sat tight. Madam Chairman could cope. And so she did. She led Jocelyn to his seat, and opened the meeting, while Jocelyn pulled his notes out of his briefcase and then sat looking rather hard at the members. As though he were searching for someone? She hoped so, even though she did try very hard to keep herself hidden by Mrs Carter on the row in front.

Jocelyn stood up to speak, and she could no longer hide behind Mrs Carter. Nor did she want to, anymore; for he had spotted her immediately, and was giving her his gentle, friendly smile. And as soon as the coffee break began he excused himself to Madam Chairman and came and sat beside Wendy. 'Miss Thompson, I so much hoped you would be here.'

'I wouldn't have missed it for anything,' she said. 'It was a splendid talk.'

'Thank you. And how are you?'

'Very well. How's Mrs Pentecost?'

'Fine. No repercussions at all.'

'And the children? Has Gaylord got over that horrible business of his dog?'

'He still has nightmares. But you know Gaylord. He only tells you as much as he thinks is good for you to know.'

Then, suddenly, they were silent; she feeling warm seas of love flooding deliciously over her; yet knowing that she had torn the covering from the wound, which would throb and burn and stab again in the long nights. She looked at him hard, trying to fix this last picture of him in her memory for ever. She said, 'It was so kind of you and Mrs Pentecost to send me those flowers. And, did you know? Your father sent me a large box of chocolates.'

'It was the least we could do. Er – Miss Thompson?'

'Yes?'

'My Aunt Dorothea's marrying her Frenchman on the twentieth. We would like very much to send you an invitation, if – you would care to come.'

She was in a sudden panic. 'No, I don't think – I was wondering – a little holiday about then.'

He said, 'We should all like you to come.' Was there a slight emphasis on the 'all'? 'May feels she has never had a chance to thank you properly.'

'But I couldn't possibly. Weddings are family affairs. I'm not even a friend of the family.'

'You're very much a friend of the family, Miss Thompson. Now look. We shall send you an invitation. And if you don't come we shall all be very sorry and very disappointed.' He rose, gave her a quick smile, and went back to the chair.

Spring! Such a turmoil, such a turmoil of birth and begetting, of cleaning and furbishing, of painting the April skies and the semi-detacheds, of hanging leaves on the black woodlands, and changing the gun-metal Trent to cloth of silver, of burnishing pale faces with a touch of sunburn and a splash of fresh air, what a turmoil! And to what end? thought Jocelyn, who had never been world-weary before, and didn't like it. To the overworked birds and the bustling bees, to the travailing sheep and cows, it was just routine. Only man, foolish man, saw and understood the whole scene; and hailed absurdly the re-awakening of an earth he seemed all too eager to turn into a hell.

Derek Bates and his pals came out of their semi-hibernation. They polished and tuned and gloated over their machines. They bought new gear, new gadgets, they assembled at street corners revving their engines, chatting above the uproar, occasionally taking off in ones and twos for a quick pirouette or a hurried pas de deux. But Derek's machine gleamed in the spring sunshine a little less brightly than the others. There were patches of rust. His bike had become an ever-present reminder of his humiliation. And his dad, failing to realize the psychological damage he was doing to his son, flatly refused to buy him a new one. Derek's resentment spread into every fibre of his being.

Spring. Miss Thompson, after much careful thought, said, 'Julia, that French gentleman who came to Mr Pentecost's has sent you a present.' She gave her the ballet shoes.

The child looked at them with delight. Wendy said, 'They're not to wear, of course. But he thought you might like to have them. Long ago, before you were born, a lady wore them to dance at the Bolshoi. I think,' she said, putting two and two together and making goodness knows how many, 'I think perhaps he was in love with her.'

But the child was still staring entranced at the shoes. Wendy didn't think she'd heard a word. 'Can I write and thank him?'

'Of course. I have his address.'

The next day, Mackintosh was waiting for her in one of the corridors when she finished school. 'Miss Thompson, my lassie doesn't wear anyone's cast-offs.'

'They're not cast-offs, you silly man,' said Wendy, laughing angrily. 'They're just a souvenir from someone who is very sad, as I am, that you won't let Julia dance.'

That 'you silly man' seemed to have hurt. He said stiffly, 'I'm sorry. And I'm sorry if I seem silly to you. But I want what's best for Julia.'

'And you think being a woman policeman or a typist will be best for her?'

'I didn't say that.' He looked round rather helplessly. 'Look. Is there somewhere we could talk, Miss Thompson?'

'Of course.' She took him into her empty classroom; sat him down on the edge of a dais, sat beside him.

He was silent so long that she said, 'How's Miss Mackintosh?'

He sat, elbows on knees, watching his hands clasp and unclasp. 'It's – not been a great success, Miss Thompson.'

That didn't surprise her. 'But she's still with you?'

'Aye.' He pondered. 'I want what's best for the lassie,' he said again.

She waited. He said, 'I thought I knew what was best for everything and everybody.' He slammed his fist into his palm and turned and faced her. 'Aye. And I do, in my job. But these last months – without Jeannie –'

Again she waited. He said, helplessly, 'It's in what ye might call personal relationships.'

'Yes.'

The silence lasted nearly a minute. Then she said, very hesitantly, 'If you did ever feel you'd like some information about ballet as a career – I imagine Mr Bouverie might be very helpful. In fact, I think he'd be only too happy to help financially. But of course,' she said hurriedly, 'you're the last man to want that.'

'Aye. If Julia did go in for ballet, she'd do it the way I could afford.' He looked at her sideways. 'I'm not a pauper, Miss Thompson.'

'Good heavens, no.' She rose. 'Well, you must think about it, Mr Mackintosh. No doubt you'll want to talk it over with your sister.'

He too had risen. 'I doubt that'll not be necessary.' Then, with a touch of the old arrogance, 'I can make my own decisions, Miss Thompson.'

Her glance was full of admiration. 'You don't need to tell me that, Mr Mackintosh.' She held out her hand. 'But I was about to say: if you do feel you'd like to take this a step further, let me know. I might be able to be of some help. Goodbye.'

'Aye. Thanks. Goodbye.' He let himself be steered to the door, vaguely surprised that the interview should be ending here. He hoped her teacher wasn't losing interest in Julia. Wendy shut the door behind him. Then she pirouetted solemnly round the classroom. But this time she did not fall weeping into a chair.

CHAPTER 16

John Pentecost looked at himself in the glass with some complacency. There was no doubt about it. A certain portliness did something for a morning coat, gave it something to work on. He turned sideways. Yes. He had the figure of one of those well-groomed blackbirds who so obviously take such a pride in their appearance. He picked up his white carnation, held it against the black lapel. He examined carefully his white moustache. Every hair in place. He picked up his gloves and black topper, and went majestically downstairs.

May, dressing, and with a hundred things on her mind, thought: we're leaving the house empty for hours. We're going to be seen leaving it empty. How awful if this happy day were spoilt by some wanton aggression. Still, she consoled herself, it was weeks now since Gaylord found the petrol bomb. Perhaps their tormentor had found something else to occupy his mind. But she wasn't very hopeful. What her dear Jocelyn called the darkness in our souls was a hardy plant, she thought fearfully.

At World's End Cottage, Aunt Elspeth poised a hat pin against her skull, and drove it home. The sight of her brother in his grey morning suit and carnation seemed to enrage her. 'All this blether about an auld woman who ought to be thinking about hell fire instead of marriage.'

He said, adjusting his tie, 'You're a hard and intolerant woman, Elspeth.'

'Aye. Well, there's one thing I'll tell you, Duncan. Ye've soon let the English corrupt you. Look at you. If Aberdeen Cattle Market could see you now!' She laughed, harsh and taunting.

'But I'm not going to Aberdeen Cattle Market,' he said mildly. 'I'm going to my employer's sister's wedding. And part of my job is to be correctly dressed.'

'But ye like it. Ye like it fine, getting yourself up like a tattie-bogle. And my lady here.' Julia had come in, grave and exquisite. Her aunt shrank away, holding up her hands in mock primness. 'Och, dinna touch me, fellows.'

Duncan said coldly, 'Are you ready, Elspeth?' He looked at his daughter. He said, 'Take no notice of your aunt, child. You're very beautiful, and I'm proud of you.'

'Man, that's no way to talk to a child. There'll be no living with her.'

'I shall talk to my own daughter as I wish, Elspeth. And, since we are in good time, I shall ask you to go and wait in the car.'

'Who? Me?'

'You, Elspeth. I've something to say to Julia.'

'That ye can't say in front of me?'

'That I'd prefer not to say in front of you, Elspeth.'

She went off muttering. All these months, looking after them both, washing his socks and his underpants, nothing but trouble from the girl, ingratitude –

Julia looked up at him, scared. He said, awkwardly, 'I just wanted to say, lassie. If you're really set on ballet school – I'll give it a wee trial.'

She couldn't believe it. She went on looking scared. Then she flung her arms round his neck, pressed her face against his. 'Daddy! Daddy!' It was all she could manage.

Gently he unwound her arms, straightened his rumpled carnation. He stared at her, said sorrowfully, 'Julia, does it mean so much to you?'

'Oh, Daddy! Everything!'

'I'll tell your aunt,' he said. 'Later.'

Miss Thompson sat, a church mouse, on the back pew of St Saviour's, Shepherd's Warning.

She had come early, so that she could tuck herself away out of sight of the main guests; and also, since she was only human, and a woman, so that she could see them arrive.

M. Bouverie, of course, was already in position with his best man. But now the others were beginning to arrive: the radiant Becky and her Peter; Great Aunt Bea, striding up the nave as though following up a splendid wood shot from the west door; a cluster of elegants who, since they chattered like starlings all the way up the nave, genuflected profoundly and then seated themselves with an immense fuss and palaver on the decanal, or starboard, side, were clearly friends of the groom.

Then Miss Thompson's heart gave a great leap. For here came Jocelyn, looking unbelievably splendid in his grey morning suit; and on his arm the lovely, smiling May; and, a little way behind, and achieving a dignified solemnity all his own, Gaylord.

Miss Thompson expected to cry at weddings. But not quite so early in the proceedings. And before she could compose herself a small figure slipped into the pew beside her and whispered, 'Miss Thompson, Miss Thompson, Daddy says I can go to ballet school.'

Wendy's delighted 'No?' was heard all over the church. Julia's hand was flat on the pew seat. Wendy pressed it fervently. 'Darling, I'm so pleased. So pleased.' But here came Elspeth, clucking Julia out of the pew like a bad-tempered hen. Elspeth had seen enough already: candles, altar cloths, it was a far cry from the wee kirk in Kittybrewster. But just what you'd expect in England.

Then, at last, the organ piped up a familiar note. The congregation rose. Dorothea entered on the arm of her brother: Dorothea, vague and fluttering, as though racking her brains as to what she'd come for. John, solid as a rock. They advanced. Edouard St Michèle Bouverie stepped out of his pew, turned and smiled at his bride. Dorothea looked delighted. 'Hello, dear, now isn't this nice,' she said in a pleased voice. John Pentecost stood back. 'Dearly beloved, we are gathered together – ' began the priest, speaking the words that have brought more tears to more female eyes than any other words in the language. And not only female. John Pentecost was deeply moved. Little Dorothea! Why, it seemed only yesterday he'd let her share his first cigar. And now, here she was marrying a bally Frog, bless her.

There was no escape. There simply was no escape. The whole thing, it seemed to Gaylord, had been arranged with devilish ingenuity. Just inside the doorway were Uncle Edouard and Great Aunts Dorothea and Bea, and Momma and Grandpa. Out here in the hall was everybody else, waiting to go in one or two at a time. And the moment they got in Aunts Dorothea and Bea fell on them and kissed them. Insatiable! He remembered a traumatic experience he had had one Christmas, when they'd made him play a similar game. He looked up at Miss Thompson. 'Is it Postman's Knock?' he enquired anxiously.

'No. It's the Reception. We all go in to be welcomed by the bride and groom.'

'Do I have to?'

She laughed. 'Of course. Look, you come in with me. I'll show you what to do.'

Well, there seemed no help for it. But he did think grown-ups were childish. He went in, scowling madly. A man in the doorway looked enquiringly at Miss Thompson, who whispered to him. The man cried in a loud voice, 'Miss Wendy Thompson. Mr Gaylord Pentecost.'

Gaylord cheered up. He could just imagine the awe on Henry Bartlett's features when he told him he'd been called Mr Gaylord Pentecost. And now Uncle Edouard was shaking him gravely by the hand and saying, 'Ah, my delightful new nephew,' and Aunts Dorothea and Bea were most restrained and civilized, eschewing the usual bear hugs and simply brushing his cheek with their lips. And when Grandpa and Momma both gravely shook hands with him, Momma murmuring, 'Dr Livingstone, I presume,' and when a waiter offered him a glass of sherry, and he took one, and Momma just grinned at him, he began to wish more than ever that Miss Thompson would marry Mr Mackintosh, so that he could repeat this gratifying experience.

Edouard St Michèle Bouverie bowed low over Wendy's hand. 'My dear Miss Thompson.'

'Mes félicitations les plus profondes, Monsieur,' she said. Then, sotto voce but with what was almost a delighted little skip: 'Julia's going to ballet school.'

He looked at her radiant face. 'A thousand thanks.' He too lowered his voice. 'This is wonderful news.'

'Yes. And the ballet shoes were what you might call the catalyst.' She passed on.

Mr Gaylord Pentecost, strolling elegantly round the room, sipping his sherry, met Julia. 'Why haven't they given you some sherry?' he asked indignantly.

'Aunt Elspeth won't let me have any.'

He looked round the room. Aunt Elspeth's grim back was to them. 'Have some of mine. I can always get some more,' he said loftily.

She sipped. 'Do you like it as much as Coke?' he asked.

'Mm. Lovely.'

Gaylord wasn't so sure. Frankly, he'd had cough mixture that tasted better. Julia shocked him by saying, 'Would you like to kiss me?'

'What for?' he asked suspiciously.

Her face was absolutely radiant. She could hardly keep still. 'Because I'm going to ballet school, and I just want to kiss everybody.'

Gaylord thought this sounded potty. 'Have you tried my Aunt Bea?' he suggested hopefully.

'I want you to kiss me.'

'Oh, all right,' he said grudgingly. He kissed her, wiped his lips. But now, something was happening. People were moving to the big, horseshoe table; laughing, chattering, as they searched for and found their places. But there wasn't much laughter and chatter when Gaylord found his place. They'd stuck him next to the dreaded Elspeth!

Surprisingly, however, they eventually found a bond. For Gaylord, sipping his first glass of champagne ever, knew one of the disappointments of his young life. It was horrible!

Yet not to drink it was unthinkable. At his age, to be allowed champagne was an event. He'd have drunk it if it choked him.

In this dilemma, it was Elspeth who came to his rescue. She too sipped her champagne, pursed her thin lips, gave every appearance of having been poisoned. 'Sour, thin stuff,' she muttered, and reached for the sugar basin. 'Ye want some?' she said to Gaylord.

'Yes, please,' said Gaylord.

She gave him two heaped teaspoonfuls, and stirred. It was an improvement. Aunt Elspeth looked round at the sipping company. 'Aye. There'll be a few uneasy stomachs after that acid stuff,' she announced with satisfaction.

Gaylord was so grateful that he decided to chat. 'Isn't it nice, Julia going to learn dancing.'

'What's that?' demanded Aunt Elspeth sharply.

'Julia, going to ballet school.'

'Who says she's away to ballet school?' Miss Mackintosh, quite impervious to the humanizing effects of champagne, put down her knife and fork, and glanced at her young neighbour.

'She does.'

'We'll see about that,' snorted Elspeth. She speared an anchovy with venom.

After the meal, everyone circulated most delightfully. Edouard Bouverie, smiling and relaxed, thought: it's true. After a few drinks the English can be almost human. He caught the passing Gaylord to him. 'Well, my nephew. Did you enjoy the champagne?'

'Not much,' said Gaylord frankly. Then, doing his usual balancing act between being truthful and not hurting people's feelings, he said, 'It was all right with some sugar in, though.'

Edouard shuddered. He appeared to wrestle within himself. Then he said kindly, 'Gaylord, now that I am your uncle, will you let me speak freely?'

Gaylord nodded.

213

Edouard said gravely, 'There is a special hell reserved for those who put sugar in good champagne.'

Gaylord was impressed. Momma came up. 'Now, Uncle Edouard, you're very serious. Nothing wrong?'

'No. I was just telling Gaylord about the dreadful fate that awaits those who put sugar in their champagne.'

Gaylord didn't relish the thought of spending eternity with Aunt Elspeth, however special the hell. So he was rather relieved when Momma chuckled and said, 'Well, I hope he'll never do anything worse than that.'

Edouard looked for a moment as though he thought there couldn't be anything worse than that. But he wasn't going to waste a chance of talking to a beautiful woman. So he said, 'My dear May, I have not yet had the chance to tell you how lovely you look.'

She said, 'I haven't told you how delighted I am to have such a distinguished uncle.'

'Oh!' He purred. He drew her to him. They kissed fondly. Gaylord did his disappearing act. If there was going to be another outbreak of kissing, he decided, he was better out of the way.

But when he saw Aunt Elspeth having what looked like a very interesting conversation with her brother, he hove to. He didn't listen, of course. He just stood where he couldn't help overhearing.

And Elspeth was saying, 'So ye've decided to put the wean to dancing?'

'Yes.'

'And ye didn't think to tell your ain sister?'

'Not at this stage,' he said coolly.

'Ye leave it to an English bairn to tell her?'

He said, 'I should have told you in good time, Elspeth.'

'Aye. And ye ken fine what I should have said. Well, I'll not give ye another chance to affront me, Duncan. I'm awa' the morn.'

He said wearily, 'I'm grateful for everything you've done for us, Elspeth. But I'll not stand in your way.'

Gaylord turned into an intrepid explorer and hacked his way briskly through a jungle of light grey trousers. 'Miss Thompson. Miss Thompson. Aunt Elspeth says she's awa' the morn. Does that mean she's leaving?'

'It sounds like it.'

'Whoopee,' said Gaylord. 'Now you'll have to marry Mr Mackintosh and look after Julia.'

Miss Thompson said, 'Dear child, I wouldn't marry Mr Mackintosh for all the tea in China.'

But before Gaylord could pursue this fascinating subject further, there was a surge towards the door, and Miss Thompson grabbed his little fist and said excitedly, 'Come on, the bride's leaving.' They went out into the forecourt of the hotel where, it seemed to Gaylord, everybody was behaving very childishly, laughing and chattering and throwing confetti. Momma gave Gaylord some to throw, but he preferred to lurk in the background, rightly fearing another bout of kissing. And his prudence was rewarded. Aunt Dorothea was halfway to the airport before she remembered she hadn't said goodbye to her little pickle.

But Miss Thompson knew, sadly, that it would soon be time for her to go, too. As a non-family guest she must not out-stay her welcome. But just as she was thinking of the loneliness of her house after this bright and happy day, an arm was slipped into hers, and May's voice said, 'Come back to the house with us, Miss Thompson. I'm sure you're dying for a cup of tea. And I've never really had a chance to thank you for all you did for us.'

'Mrs Pentecost, I really couldn't. It will be a family occasion.'

'Considering that you're Gaylord's intended, I think you could be regarded as family, don't you?' said May. 'Now have you got your car, or can we take you?'

CHAPTER 17

On that calm and perfect April evening, Edouard and Dorothea sat, hands clasped, flying out of the sunset and over a tranquil sea, to his great house in a wooded valley.

Jocelyn Pentecost, back in slacks and a pullover, sat in the garden with his wife and his father and watched the sun go down, and sipped his wine. May was back with him, it had been a good day, a happy day. He was as content as he could ever hope to be, now that words, his stock in trade, had changed from bright jewels to heavy stones.

May thought: all through the wedding, all through the reception, I had a sense of disaster, poisoning my happiness. And see, nothing has happened. We have come home to a house of safety and peace, to a gentle evening.

John Pentecost sipped his brandy. He was feeling rather pleased with himself. It wasn't everyone, he reflected, who'd have been broad-minded enough to let his sister marry a foreigner. But thank God he'd never been one to have any silly prejudices. If it was what Dorothea wanted, it was good enough for him.

'O Caledonia, stern and wild!' murmured Elspeth Mackintosh, as the Midland plain was left behind and the northern hills began to cluster round the train in preparation for the grandeur that was Scotland. Yet, despite these noble sentiments, she was put out. She'd never expected Duncan

217

to let her go. But he had, without a murmur. And her unsuccessful brinkmanship had left her with a conscience.

Derek Bates was not content, this April evening. (No one had ever told him about contentment, so the poor little devil just didn't know what it was.) He mooned around. His mood was vicious and idle. His pals had found a couple of birds, so Derek could go hang. Listlessly, he took the Shepherd's Warning road; accelerated noisily and dangerously through the village; then ambled along the river road, drawn to the farm like an ignoble Ahab to his leviathan.

He parked his bike in a ditch, began wandering about the outbuildings, ripe for mischief...

Wendy Thompson was content. She loved children: their darting minds, their gravity, their logical reasoning; she loved their young faces, fresher than newly-laundered linen, their hopes and fears. And this evening she was with two of the nicest of them, she thought. She was having a picnic with Gaylord and Julia; with Gaylord, who wanted to marry her; with Julia, who was going to ballet school.

'Momma,' Gaylord had said. 'Can Julia and I have a picnic?'

'I'd rather you didn't, dear. Not on your own.' Not after Schultz. Not with that sense of disaster flaring again at the core of her being.

Wendy said, 'If I went with them, Mrs Pentecost? Would you – ?'

'Oh, please, Miss Thompson,' cried Gaylord and Julia. But Momma had said, 'Miss Thompson's just been to a wedding, dear. She's not dressed for picnics.'

'It doesn't matter, really, Mrs Pentecost.'

So Momma had agreed. And here they were. May and Wendy had cut sandwiches and cake, and found lemonade and glasses, and a thermos of tea for Miss Thompson. And Gaylord had found an old travelling rug to sit on, so that Miss Thompson's navy blue wedding suit would stay as good as new, and he had carried it into the paddock and spread it on the spring grass. And Wendy's eyes were gladdened by the sight of two young and eager faces; and beyond them, a chequer board of fields glowing in horizontal sunlight, the patchwork counterpane of an April sky, and all the peace of England. She put out an arm, drew the girl to her so that the dark head rested on her shoulder. 'I am glad your father's relented.'

Julia was silent; but sat, rolling her cheek happily and fondly against Wendy's arm.

Gaylord said stoutly, 'It's all Miss Thompson's doing. I bet she bullied him into it.'

Wendy laughed gaily. 'Can you imagine me, bullying anybody?' she asked. Nevertheless, it was pleasant to think that, without her, it wouldn't have happened. That she had tilted the world just a tiny fraction towards happiness.

Derek Bates had discovered that farm outbuildings gave very little opportunity for mischief. Great, heavy pieces of machinery were far beyond his capabilities to damage. And having hurt his toe by kicking savagely at a pile of beet in an outlying barn, he gave up. Even revenge called for thought and effort. And thought and effort were both things Derek instinctively eschewed.

So he flung himself down on a pile of hay, smoked a fag, and resigned himself to the thought that, now that his pals had deserted him, revenge wasn't going to be easy, since being out-numbered was something else Derek eschewed.

Unless he met one of those kids on its own, of course. But that seemed too much to hope for.

Or was it? For now a small figure was coming stealthily into the barn. Alone? Yes, for she shut the door carefully behind her.

It seemed to Derek that things were being handed to him on a plate.

Julia knew exactly where she was going to hide. She remembered noticing a pile of hay in a dark corner of the great barn. And no one had said that the game of hide and seek was confined to the out of doors. So, while Gaylord and Miss Thompson sat in the paddock, covering their eyes and counting up to fifty, she tip-toed out of the paddock and then ran across the fields, on those dancing feet of hers, towards the barn, into the barn, into the dark corner.

It was then that reality became nightmare; and the happy game of hide and seek became reality.

For Derek could scarcely believe his good fortune. Had he been a praying man, he would have regarded this little victim, walking straight towards him, as a direct answer to prayer. His listlessness disappeared. He chucked his cigarette down in the hay, pulled his mother's stocking over his face, and waited till Julia was within reach. Then he stood up, and grabbed at her.

The sight of this faceless creature, coming at her out of the shadows, almost robbed Julia of her reason. She screamed; but her throat muscles were so constricted with fear that the only sound was a dry, despairing croak. Yet her dancer's body served her well. She twisted herself out of the man's grasp, and ran. But where? She had shut the door behind her. Now, in the half-dark, and blinded by her terror, she did not know where to find it. She ran, as a hare runs, this way and that, trying to scream, but producing only piteous whimpers. And always, behind her, close at hand, the heavy breathing and the footsteps.

One thing she saw: a ladder, leading up through an open trap door. The hayloft. She'd been up there. It was, she knew, a cul-de-sac, a trap. Yet she went, stamping desperately up the ladder. Once, for one dreadful moment, his fingers reached up and closed about her left ankle. She kicked him off, and went on, and into the hayloft.

If only she could slam the trap door on him! She seized the edge of the heavy wooden square, heaved. It did not budge. She thought, despairingly, that it was too heavy for her. But then she saw that it was held back by a metal hasp. Her fingers were almost nerveless with fear. Nevertheless, she got the hasp undone. Now she found that by exerting all her strength she could just lift the trap door. Thirty degrees, sixty, it was vertical. Another half second, and she could have let it fall. Its weight would have dealt savagely with the emerging Derek.

But she was half a second too late. Derek was out, and grabbing the trap door to stop it slicing him. He let it fall into the closed position. Then he straightened up, and stared at his victim. Behind the nylon mask his features twisted into a triumphant grin.

'Please,' she begged. 'Oh, please!' He made a sudden grab, missed. She began again her pitiful, hare-like running from this faceless creature – man, beast, ghoul, she had no idea which. Fingers caught at her, missed, caught again. Nails tore her flesh. The only sounds in the hayloft were the stamping and scampering of feet, the heavy breathing of the pursuer; the terrified whimperings, the despairing little cries, of the pursued.

In the hayloft was a doorway, fitted with a windlass, for loading and unloading the hay. The door was usually left open. It was open now. It was open to the clean, free air of the world outside this place of torment.

The brilliant, evening sunlight streamed through this doorway. It drew the terrified girl as the candle draws the frenetically circling moth. She ran towards it, sobbing, knowing that this was no ordinary door, that it opened on to – nothing; on to a twenty foot drop to the field below.

She paused in the doorway, looked down, recoiled with a choking sob, turned.

Now, at last, she could see him. The level beams of the setting sun brilliantly lit every detail as he stood there, blinking in its light: the leather clad body, the hands hanging, gorilla-like, at his sides; the head, made bald and top-knotted by its stocking, like some shoddy Samurai; the face which, behind its smooth veil, appeared mindless, emotionless, de-humanized.

For a long moment they stared at each other, frozen. Then he lifted one heavy, booted foot, and set it forward, a few inches nearer his victim. He began to lift the other. Julia put up her hands before her face, and stepped backwards. Too late, she tried to steady herself. With a great cry she fell into the field. Derek grasped the lintel and looked down. She lay there, very still, very graceful. 'Christ!' said Derek. 'Oh, Christ!' The sooner he got out of here the better. He was trembling in every limb, in every finger. He ran back to the trap door. All he'd got to do, he told himself, was keep calm. Just go down the ladder, slip out of the door, walk quickly but quietly to the old bike – and away. The thought of that powerful steed gripped between his thighs was heartening him already. Once in the saddle, he'd run anyone down who tried to stop him. He would that.

He bent down, and grasped the trap door. He lifted. It came up slowly, for Derek was not one of the strongest. But then something rather strange happened. A blast of hot air struck him in the face. He was suddenly frightened. He wrenched the trap door further open, and peered down. And discovered that his cigarette, so lightly tossed aside, had set the barn on fire. Flames crept across its floor like an incoming tide. The ladder, his only way of retreat, was already enveloped in them. And, even as he watched, the flames burst through the newly opened trap door like water through a broken dam. 'Help!' cried Derek. 'Help! Help!' But no one came running. And Derek was furious, as well as terrified. He shouldn't be exposed to this sort of situation! Someone must come to his rescue.

But nobody did.

Chapter 18

Jocelyn said, 'There's something painful, almost unbearable, about an evening as beautiful as this.'

'I know what you mean,' said May, smiling.

John Pentecost never agreed with his son's more effete remarks, on principle. But, to himself, he had to admit there was some truth in this one. His own store cupboard of summer evenings was growing empty. One day soon, inevitably, he would open it and find it – bare! He tipped a spot more brandy into his glass.

'Listen,' said May. 'Someone's calling.'

They listened, idly. What did it matter, on this calm and peaceful evening? A man, calling his dog in the lane? A woman, gathering her hens?

The silence was complete. It stretched, beyond the sunset, it stretched into the far blue depths of sky. 'I heard nothing,' said Jocelyn.

'Listen,' said May. 'I thought – a man's voice.'

Again they listened. Nothing. Normally, May would have had to find out. But the evening was so calm, and the day had been so perfect, all she wanted was to rest in this blue peace of evening, like a bather drifting in a green pool.

They sat on. The sun edged a little further down the sky. Jocelyn refilled his wife's glass, then his own. They toasted each other, smiling, without words. A little breeze came and rustled the leaves of the garden, a breeze of evening. They shivered. Soon they would go in, now, to supper, and the lighting of the lamps. A perfect end to a long, perfect day.

'Forty-nine. Fifty,' said Gaylord. He opened his eyes. 'Coming!' he called.

He and Miss Thompson set off. They searched the drive, various outhouses. They went into the garden. 'Momma, we're having a lovely game, hide and seek, only if you've seen Julia you mustn't tell us, it wouldn't be fair.'

May was relieved to see Gaylord and Miss Thompson, so happy and carefree. There had been something just slightly disturbing about that heard or imagined voice – like the eerie, distant sounds that haunt a Chekov play. She said, 'Now you mustn't tire Miss Thompson. She's a wedding guest, remember.'

'Oh, I'm loving it,' said Wendy, laughing. They passed on. They searched. They did not find her. 'Perhaps she'll be like that girl they couldn't find and years later her mother went to the chest to get a tablecloth and found her skeleton,' Gaylord said hopefully.

'I shouldn't think so,' said Wendy, but with a touch of fear. 'Julia,' she called loudly. 'Come out, now. You win.'

Silence. Stillness. Then: 'Look!' cried Gaylord.

They had come in sight of the distant barn. Smoke was pouring out of the hayloft door, eddying and billowing out of holes and crannies. And, as they watched, a great tongue of flame licked out of the high doorway. 'Quick! Tell your parents to dial 999. And wait – tell them we still haven't found Julia. Then come to me at the barn.'

He tore off. She ran towards the barn. 'Julia!' she yelled. 'Julia!' her voice dry and harsh. Even to herself she sounded a mad woman.

There was a new sound on the still evening, a yo-yo wail, coming rapidly nearer, filling the whole air, banishing thought. She looked round as she ran. The great red fire engine towered behind her. Madly she stabbed her finger at the barn. 'That way, that way,' as though the firemen might not recognize the fire. 'There's a child missing,' she called. 'She might –' They did not hear a word. They swept on. By the time she reached the barn they had run their hoses out. The flames spat and hissed, angry as serpents, as the water struck them.

For a few moments she stood, wringing her hands, screaming the child's name. She ran up to one of the firemen. He ignored her. She tugged at his sleeve. 'There could be a child in there,' she sobbed.

'We're getting topside. Leave it to us, miss,' he said calmly.

Sanity returned. Like a blow in the chest. She was a grown woman, a teacher, the child had been left in her care. Her first duty was to warn the father. She ran to World's End Cottage, arrived breathless. She hammered on the door. Duncan came out. 'It's yourself,' he said curtly. 'Go and stay with Julia while I help with the fire.'

'Why? Where is she?'

'In her room, of course.' He hurried off. 'The doctor's on his way,' he called after her.

In her anger she ran after him, seized his shoulder. 'What happened?'

He spun round, stared at her. 'She must have been in the loft when the fire started.' Wendy caught her breath. 'Then she must have panicked, and jumped from the hayloft door.' He went to see to the fire.

Miss Thompson went into the cottage, ran two at a time up the cramped stairs. A door on the landing was open. She went in. Julia lay there, pale, her eyes closed. Wendy sat down, took her hand. The child did not stir.

It was, without doubt, one of the most exciting moments in Gaylord's life. And by Jove he made the most of it. He burst into the garden. 'Momma! Poppa! Grandpa! Quick. Dial 999. The great barn's on fire.'

They sprang to their feet. May led the way to the house. But at that moment they heard the approaching wail of the fire engine. Gaylord was bitterly disappointed. Someone must have beaten him to it. And he had wanted to dial 999.

Grandpa said, 'Mackintosh must have alerted them. Good man that.' He began to head towards the barn. 'But what would start a fire, Jocelyn? It's not as though everything's dry.'

May remembered something. 'Gaylord!' Her voice was sharp. 'Did you find Julia?'

'Not yet, Momma. When we saw the fire we stopped the game, and Miss Thompson said, "Gaylord, run as fast as you can and tell them to ring 999. Then come back here." ' He was rather surprised that Momma should think them so lacking in public spirit that they would go on playing hide and seek while Rome burned.

'I – see,' said May. 'But – where is Miss Thompson?'

'Well, there's Mackintosh, anyway,' said Grandpa. For now they had arrived at the fire. And there were the firemen, doing absolutely fascinating things with hoses and axes and ladders. Gaylord looked hungrily at the gushing hosepipes. 'Do you think they'd let me help, Momma?' he asked, but without much hope. Grown-ups, he realized, were never very keen on sharing their toys.

Grandpa put a hand on his manager's shoulder. 'Good man, Mackintosh. You soon got the brigade here.'

But May brushed him to one side. 'Where's Julia?'

'At the cottage. Miss Thompson's with her.'

May had a cold feeling in her stomach. 'She's – not hurt?'

'Aye, she is that.' But now he strode forward to speak to the firemen. 'If you need another hydrant, there's one – '

May said, 'Jocelyn, I'm going to the cottage.'

Jocelyn nodded absently; but never took his eyes from the blazing barn. The leaping flames, the spurting smoke, the age-old struggle between water and fire absorbed him. Coming on this calm and lovely evening, it seemed to him a symbol of everything that nowadays so haunted his thoughts: the mindless violence of the flames was one with the mindless violence that threatened his world.

So he stood, until he was aware of an urgent voice: 'That will be the doctor's car, Mr Pentecost. Tell your father I'm away, will you.'

'Of course,' said Jocelyn. 'And I do hope – '

Duncan ran and joined the doctor. They went up into Julia's room. May and Wendy rose. 'We'll leave you,' May said.

'Aye,' Duncan said ungraciously.

Wendy said coldly, 'Do you mind if we wait downstairs?'

He was looking at his daughter. He shrugged. They went down into the little parlour. May said, 'She may be all right, Miss Thompson. It was a long fall. But she's young.'

Wendy looked grateful. But said 'Yes,' rather heavily.

May said, watching the schoolteacher closely: 'And you think it's your fault.'

Wendy nodded.

'Of course it's nothing of the kind. You mustn't think that, Miss Thompson.'

'But I do. Of course I do.'

May was silent. Then she put a hand on Wendy's and said, 'I'm going to leave you now. This is your concern. But' – a sudden, understanding smile – 'come and tell me when you know something.'

Wendy smiled gratefully, and sat on in the fusty little parlour with its smells of geraniums and upholstery and dried bulrushes and honesty. She waited a long time. And even when at last she heard the heavy footsteps of men coming down the stairs, her vigil was not over. There was a long, muffled conversation before finally she heard the door close behind the doctor, and Duncan's footsteps begin to ascend the stairs once more.

She ran into the hall. 'Mr Mackintosh, what does he say?'

He checked on the second step; turned and stared. He smelt of smoke and charred wood. His eyes were bloodshot, there was soot on his cheek. He looked tired, and gaunt. 'She'll be all right,' he said.

'She will?' Her voice soared with joy. But – what was 'all right'? She said, breathless: 'You mean – she'll be able to dance still?'

He stood staring grimly down at her. A long stare. Then he said brutally, 'She will not.'

Wendy said furiously, 'How can you know? How can anyone know at her age?'

He said, 'All her weight went on her right leg.' He turned, took another step up the stairs. 'If I had a beast with a leg like that, I'd shoot it.' He paused again, looked at her bitterly. 'As far as ballet school goes, you could have saved your breath to cool your porridge, Miss Thompson.'

Once again he set off up the stairs. Hating him at that moment, she yet said, 'Has she to go to hospital?'

'Yes. The doctor's arranging it straight away.'

'Will you let me help to – get her ready?'

'Thank you. Yes.' He actually came down a step. 'That would be kind, Miss Thompson.'

'I'll go with her if you like.'

'Thanks. I'm not so good at that kind of thing.' He gave his fleeting, thin smile. 'Poor lassie! It'll be good for her to have a womanly body with her. And I'll come and run you back, when I've had another look at the fire.'

On the way back from the hospital she said, 'Isn't it awful, the poor little soul left alone in that great place.'

'Aye.' He sighed; and said formally, 'Miss Thompson, I wouldn't want you to think I don't appreciate all you've done for the lassie.'

'Thank you,' she said.

They drove on in silence. She was still frozen with the horror of it – one bent and twisted limb destroying all the ecstasy of movement. And on this was piled another horror. She said, with a dry mouth, 'Julia was in my charge when this terrible thing happened, Mr Mackintosh.'

His hands clenched on the wheel of the Land Rover. He turned on her sharply. 'You're never to think such a thing. Julia is my responsibility.'

'Thank you,' she said in a tight voice.

Later she said, 'Afterwards, when she comes out, it won't be easy for you, will it?'

'No.'

'I did wonder – of course you'd need to think it over – I wondered whether you'd let her come and stay with me. She and I could go to school together in my car.'

He was silent. 'You could come and see her any time you wanted.' She added pleadingly, 'You know, I'm very, very fond of her, Mr Mackintosh.'

'I know you are, lassie,' he said. 'Aye. You'd make her a bonny mother,' he muttered; he seemed to be speaking to himself.

It was Wendy's turn to be silent. He said, humbly for him, 'But I doubt ye'd want me for a husband.'

She was taken completely off guard. She gave a nervous laugh; 'I don't think you'd want me for a wife, Mr Mackintosh.'

He sat, staring ahead; thoughtful, unsmiling. 'It could be quite a satisfactory arrangement,' he said.

She said, scornfully, 'When I marry, Mr Mackintosh, it will have to be much more than "quite a satisfactory arrangement". There'll have to be love, for one thing.'

'Och, ye've been reading too many story books,' he said. 'But I'll not press ye. Just remember we've one thing in common.'

'What's that?'

'Julia,' he said quietly.

Wendy Thompson went back to the farm. She found May Pentecost in the kitchen. 'Well?' asked May anxiously.

'They think she'll be all right. Except that – '

'Except that – what?' May asked.

'She'll never dance,' said Wendy.

'They can't know,' May said.

'Her father seems sure, after what the doctor said. And Mr Mackintosh has a way of being right.'

'I'm sorry.' She looked up from her work, gazed at Wendy with a great sadness. 'I really am, Miss Thompson.'

Wendy knew what she had long suspected: that her beautiful and elegant hostess was also a warm and understanding human being. She sighed again. 'It is a tragedy.'

May said quietly, 'Yes. But a small tragedy, Miss Thompson. In a world filled with vast tragedies.'
Wendy was silent. May said, 'Don't think I'm belittling it, my dear. Just trying, rather callously, to put it in proportion for you.'
'I know,' Wendy said, miserably but gratefully.
'And I'm so sorry for him,' said May. 'He's so helpless.'
'Who?' Wendy asked in astonishment. 'Not Mr Mackintosh?'
'Yes.'
'But – he's terribly capable.'
May put down the carving knife, smiled. 'Which would you say was the more helpless? Duncan Mackintosh, or my husband?' She laughed. 'You needn't be polite.'
'Well. Of course, I admire Mr Pentecost's books enormously. But – I would have thought – '
'Don't you believe it,' said May. 'Oh, I know Jocelyn relies a great deal on me. But he's got tremendous reserves. He knows what things are about. Whereas Mackintosh – outside farming, he's lost.' She grinned at her disciple. 'He needs a woman to guide him through the labyrinth of human relations, Miss Thompson.'
Wendy felt herself blushing. But so taken was she with her understanding hostess that she said, 'Between ourselves, Mrs Pentecost, he did make a sort of proposal. But – I couldn't – '
'You'd be doing him a great service if you did,' May said briskly. 'And as for the girl – '
The two women smiled at each other. Wendy shook her head. 'Thank you for being so understanding, Mrs Pentecost. And now I really must be going.'

It was already dusk as she returned home. But no one rose up to waylay her in the river lands. And her house was snug and safe at her homecoming.

The barn smouldered and stank and hissed. But the danger was past. 'I wish I knew what started it,' muttered John Pentecost. He glared at his son and daughter-in-law. 'Could be arson, I suppose. That youth – '

But Duncan Mackintosh had come into the room. 'Mr Pentecost, I've found something rather strange. A motor cycle. It was parked in a ditch, not far from the barn.'

'A motor cycle?'

'I did wonder – whether it might be the one you – '

'I'll come with you,' said John Pentecost.

The machine was half hidden by the spring leaves. It glinted and gleamed in the light of Mackintosh's torch. It looked powerful; and, in the darkness, evil.

'Somewhere,' said John, 'I have a note of the number.' He pulled a handful of envelopes from his breastpocket, began to peer at them by the light of Mackintosh's torch. 'Here we are,' he said. He looked at a number pencilled on the back of an envelope. He looked at the bike. 'It's him,' he said.

'Revenge.' said Mackintosh. 'Well, we'll give him revenge. If his bike's here, he's here. I'll just wait till he comes for it. Then nab him.'

'Then nab him,' said Grandpa.

But Derek Bates never came for his motor bike. And in the end John Pentecost said, 'Good Lord I suppose he didn't – ?'

'What?' said Jocelyn.

'Oh, nothing,' said John. That line of thought was too horrible.

Yet he did think: if it were that! What did I start, when I answered violence with violence? A boy's pet, a girl condemned to walk instead of fly, a youth dying most horribly before he started to live. He said, 'That bike's still there, Mackintosh. Give the police a ring, will you.' And to himself he added: 'I've got to know.'

The passing of Derek Bates caused singularly few ripples. 'Death by Misadventure' was the headline in the Ingerby Advertiser, which reported Inquest on Local Youth next to Octogenarian to Wed, and published a smudged photograph which could have been any one of a thousand local youths. His mates weren't a bit surprised. Derek, they had always sensed, was born to trouble as the sparks fly upward. This was just the sort of thing the silly devil would do. His teachers felt horror, but again no surprise.

His dad blamed Society, full stop. Even the maternal breast was too busy apportioning blame to be too lacerated by grief. Mrs Bates blamed everyone: his friends, his teachers, his dad, the police, the old man for his carelessness in not locking a barn with all that dry hay in it; everyone, in fact, except Derek and herself.

So poor Derek – who should have been borne to Valhalla by Valkyries on 100 cc motor bikes with wide open throttles – poor Derek, or what was left of him, went to Ingerby Cem. in a decrepit hearse at 15 mph, and was laid to rest with Granddad Bates, who had never been able to stand the sight of him, or he of Granddad.

But – if I hadn't, all those months ago, made him chuck his bike in the river; he'd be alive now, thought John Pentecost. Alive to harass and terrify more children, more old people; anyone, in fact, weaker than himself. But no one appointed me his executioner.

May said briskly, 'This is absolute nonsense, Father-in-law. It's a terrible and horrible business, I know. But it's Death by Misadventure. It didn't begin with you and the motor cycle. It began with his tormenting Julia in the river meadows. And that began – when? In his childhood, in his conception, somewhere in the ages-long procession of men and women whose genes gave him form.'

'You'll be quoting Freud at me next,' muttered Grandpa, who believed that half-baked amateur psychology was responsible for most of our current ills.

'Oh, no, she won't,' said Jocelyn. 'You know May better than that.' But later, alone in his study, he thought: the old man could be right. Should violence ever be the answer to violence? Did not a creator, once he resorted to violence, however righteously, join the destroyers? For he saw even more clearly now, that all mankind was divided into two: the builders up, and the destroyers; that the world's future rested on the creators retaining the balance; yet every time he saw a smashed telephone kiosk, a trampled flower bed, the loud mouths proclaiming their triumphs, the tanks grinding into a once-peaceful town, his heart failed him; for he knew that the destroyers, an army no man could number, were on the march. And, if they could not be opposed by violence, since he who uses violence automatically joins them, then where in God's name lay the answer for a threatened world? He didn't know. All he knew was that, if there was an answer (which he very much doubted), he could find it only by letting it come out in his writing. In sadness, and near despair, yet with a creative excitement he thought had deserted him for ever, he turned to a blank page, and took up his pen...

Summer came early that year. Not thunderous and wayward; but gentle, sweet, the mornings proudly seeming to say, 'Look, O man, what another brilliant day we have created for your delight and happiness.' The noontides saying, 'Here is warmth, and shade, for your rest; and the sound of the river to lull you to your sleep.' The evenings saying, 'See how the daylight lingers; now you may sip your wine, and talk, and dance the long, long dances.'

Amanda took full advantage, sleeping under the boughs, or holding out her hands with delight to the leaf-dappled sky. And one day May and Jocelyn put Gaylord in the car, refusing to answer any of his questions, and took him to a nearby farm where, in an outhouse, a sheepdog fussed over a litter of puppies. And Gaylord was told he could choose one of the puppies. He took one, crooning over it tenderly, vowing to love and cherish as besottedly as any bridegroom at the altar. And though he wept a little at the memory of his dear friend Schultz, he really thought this was the happiest moment of all his young life.

Miss Thompson was often at World's End Cottage, loving and caring for Julia like a mother, and remaining placid when Duncan pointed out where she went wrong with her cooking or her washing up; and, the highlights of her life, occasionally dropping in for a chat with her friends May and Jocelyn Pentecost, or taking Gaylord for a walk or a picnic, and feeling her unacknowledged and unrequited love for Jocelyn grow mellow and tender like an October sun. Duncan had not mentioned marriage again; but her woman's instinct told her that one day he would. And, when he did, she thought she might say yes. There were worse things than honesty and plain speaking and dourness. There were worse materials than granite. And May had been right. He did need her, perhaps even more than Julia needed her.

And the little girl danced, alone, in the water meadows.
She was beautiful, and grave, and eight years old.

She danced alone. No one, not even her dear Miss Thompson, was allowed to see her dance.

For she danced as a broken grass dances in the wind, or as a lame bird flutters to reach the treetops.

Eric Malpass

The Lamplight and the Stars

Nathan Cranswick's third child comes into the world on the day of Queen Victoria's Diamond Jubilee. Whilst the Empire celebrates, Nathan's concerns are about his family's future. A gentle and wise preacher, he gratefully accepts the chance to move from the dingy, cramped house in Ingerby to the village of Moreland when he is offered a job on the splendid Heron estate. Anticipating peace and tranquillity for his wife and young family, his hopes are cruelly dashed when their new life is beset by problems from the beginning. A family scandal and the Boer War menace their whole future, but finally it is the agonising choice facing his gentle daughter which threatens to tear the family apart...

Morning's at Seven

Three generations of the Pentecost family live in a state of permanent disarray in a huge, sprawling farmhouse. Seven-year-old Gaylord Pentecost is the innocent hero who observes the lives of the adults – Grandpa, Momma and Poppa and two aunties – with amusement and incredulity.

Through Gaylord's eyes, we witness the heartache suffered by Auntie Rose as the exquisite Auntie Becky makes a play for her gentleman friend, while Gaylord unwittingly makes the situation far worse.

Mayhem and madness reign in this zestful account of the lives and loves of the outrageous Pentecosts.

Eric Malpass

Of Human Frailty
A biographical novel of Thomas Cranmer

Thomas Cranmer is a gentle, unassuming scholar when a chance meeting sweeps him away from the security and tranquillity of Cambridge to the harsh magnificence of Henry VIII's court. As a supporter of Henry he soon rises to prominence as Archbishop of Canterbury.

Eric Malpass paints a fascinating picture of Reformation England and its prominent figures: the brilliant, charismatic but utterly ruthless Henry VIII, the exquisite but scheming Anne Boleyn and the fanatical Mary Tudor.

But it is the paradoxical Thomas Cranmer who dominates the story. A tormented man, he is torn between valour and cowardice; a man with a loving heart who finds himself hated by many; and a man of God who makes the terrifying discovery that he must suffer and die for his beliefs. Thomas Cranmer is a man of simple virtue, whose only fault is his all too human frailty.

ERIC MALPASS

THE RAISING OF LAZARUS PIKE

Lazarus Pike (1820–1899), author of *Lady Emily's Decision*, lies buried in the churchyard of Ill Boding. And there he would have remained, in obscurity and undisturbed, had it not been for a series of remarkable coincidences. A discovery sets in motion a campaign to republish his works and to reinstate Lazarus Pike as a giant of Victorian literature. This is a cause of bitter wrangling between the two factions that emerge. For some, Lazarus is a simple schoolmaster, devoted to his beautiful wife, Corinda. For others, who think his reputation needs a sexy, contemporary twist, he is a wife murderer with a deeply flawed character. What follows is a knowing and wry look at the world of literary make-overs and the heritage industry in a hilarious story that brings fame and tragedy to an unsuspecting moorland village.

SWEET WILL

William Shakespeare is just eighteen when he marries Anne Hathaway, eight years his senior. Anne, who bears a son soon after the marriage, is plain and not particularly bright – but her love for Will is undeniable. Talented and fiercely ambitious, Will's scintillating genius soon makes him the toast of Elizabethan London. While he basks in the flattery his great reputation affords him, Anne lives a lonely life in Stratford, far away from the glittering world of her husband.

This highly evocative account of the life of the young William Shakespeare begins the trilogy which continues with *The Cleopatra Boy* and concludes with *A House of Women*.

ERIC MALPASS

THE WIND BRINGS UP THE RAIN

It is a perfect summer's day in August 1914. Yet even as Nell and her friends enjoy a blissful picnic by the river, the storm clouds of war are gathering over Europe. Very soon this idyll is to be swept away by the conflict that will take millions of men to their deaths.

After the war, the widowed Nell leads a wretched existence, caring for her husband's elderly, ungrateful parents, with only her son, Benbow, for companionship and support. But Nell is a passionate woman and wants to share her life with a man who will return her love. Meanwhile, Benbow falls in love with a German girl, Ulrike – until she is enticed home by the resurgent Germany.

This moving story of a Midlands family in the interwar years is a compelling tale of personal triumph and disappointment, set against the background of the hideous destruction of war.

Made in the USA
Middletown, DE
16 December 2023

45704414R00139